THE DOCKPORTER

A Mackinac Island Novel

Dave McVeigh
Jim Bolone

PREFACE

Although Mackinac Island is a real place, and many of the locations mentioned do exist, *The Dockporter* is wholly a work of fiction. Any resemblance between the real people of the island and the characters in the book is coincidental and unintended. In reality, there are three major ferry boat docks and many hotels. We simplified to serve the story. That said, those who know the place will feel the echoes, and hopefully it will take you back when you need a winter fix. If you've never been there, you should go. There's nothing quite like it. And remember to tip your dockporter. Also, there's some salty language. It's a story about young guys shlepping suitcases on a dock all day, not the Vienna Boys Choir. That said, we're confident you can handle it. Think PG-13. Enjoy!

Look for more in the **Mackinac Island Series** soon.

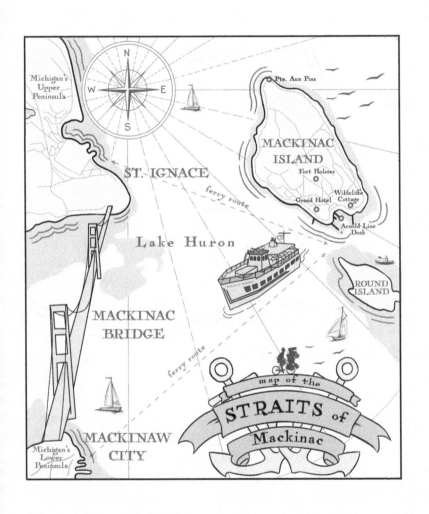

CHAPTER ONE

Great Lakes State of Mind
August 12, 1999

*pin class? What the hell am I doing in a spin class? It's
Friday night. I'm a single, thirty-one-year-old man with a
job in a hipster field in a city that worships precisely my
demographic.*

That's what Jack was thinking.

He'd been spinning a lot lately. He should have been
trolling a local Venice Beach watering hole with one of
his actor/writer/*whatever* friends, looking for meaningful
conversations with smart women that might lead to
something less meaningful later. He should not have
been concerned with things like *spinning*. He should have
been basking in the glory of having it all: a flourishing
career as a fashion photographer in the fastest-moving
city in the Western world.

Yet here he was, sweating buckets all over the worn cement floor of a perfectly designed, perfectly weathered "studio," pedaling a fake bike in a fake room, listening to fake music with fake people. The harder he pedaled, the more depressed he felt. Earlier in the day he had likely sunk his career. So, there was that.

It was a photo shoot for General Motors. The highly paid commercial agency had brought in a stylist from New York who had dressed up the two models like Sid and Nancy. That might have been fine. He could do the whole "retro late-seventies punk garbage" look as well as anyone in the business. In fact, he was known for it. But the thing is, the car was an SUV, and the SUV had a brand-new kayak on the roof. It made no sense. This was not a stylish retro mash-up. It was just stupid.

Jack thought back to the shoot as he pedaled his fake bike. He could see himself, playing the part of a Big-Shot Photographer: black T-shirt and black jeans, clicking away with rock and roll blasting from the PA system. But it was evident to everyone on the set that his heart wasn't into it. Jack snapped the two beautifully made-up-to-look-not-that-beautiful models, and he felt utterly dead.

"Lose the sneer." *Click-click.* "Smile. Come on now, Corey. It's Corey, right?" *Click-click.* "It's a good thing. You're getting out of the city. Yeah, you're going kayaking." *Click-click.* "Yeah, and shit—forget it." Jack lowered his camera and looked toward the rafters, shaking his head. The music died, and there was a low groan from the suits. Jack rubbed his eyes. "Take five, everyone."

A slick, young manager-type—who looked that way because he was, in fact, Jack's slick, young manager— moved in. His name was Adam Taylor, but he went by

Babyface due to his soft, boyish features. A female assistant, also in the requisite black T-shirt and black jeans, trailed with a clipboard.

"Is everything cool, bro?" asked Babyface.

Jack pulled Babyface aside as they walked from the worried suits grouped tightly together like a pile of hungry newborn puppies, whispering to each other.

"It's not a good moment," Jack said.

"*Not a good moment*," Babyface responded. "That's your standard line. And what do I always say? Take your fancy camera and *make* it a good moment. That's why you're Jack McGuinn!" He kicked out a fake laugh and slapped Jack on the back.

Jack shook his head. "No, listen. That model looks like Sid Vicious's pretty-boy brother. See him?"

Babyface looked over at Pretty Sid as if he hadn't been watching him all day.

"I see him. He's standing right there."

"We're supposed to believe that guy is going *kayaking?* Dressed like that? He'd ruin his leather jacket. His mascara would run."

Babyface watched Pretty Sid while calculating his next statement. The assistant, sensing a lull, broke in, glancing down at her clipboard. "Annie left three messages. The last one said ... I can't read my own writing ... oh: 'It's over.'" She caught herself and gasped. "I mean. Oh no! I'm so sorry. That was super untactful of me." She faded back.

Jack still focused on Babyface. "Guys who look like that don't *kayak*. They stroll up and down catwalks looking bored. And SUVs in cityscapes always look phony. I told you this when I saw the concept drawings.

We need a desert." He turned to the assistant. "Wait. The message said 'It's over'?"

She stepped forward, overflowing with sympathy. "Yeah. I'm *so* sorry."

Babyface put a gentle hand on Jack's shoulder, like a horse trainer dealing with a jumpy gelding. His voice was calm, but not without a slight hiss.

"Listen, buddy. The client likes it. Maybe you've heard of 'em? Big outfit. They're called *General-fucking-Motors.* I think they're from your neck of the woods. Michigan or some shit? Anyway, *I love it.* It's extreme."

"You're right. It is extreme. Extremely *ridiculous.*"

Babyface suddenly lost his baby face and leaned in close to Jack, transforming into a full-fledged grown-up, the kind of person who gets paid not to put up with nonsense. "Walk with me," he said.

When they were far enough from the lights and crew, he turned and faced Jack, eyes now blazing.

"I'm going to be honest with you because nobody else will," he said. "I've been watching you spiral down the toilet like a turd for a month. I don't know what's eating you up, but you've lost your mojo. Now, you better get it back, or you'll never work again."

He indicated the suits with an angry flick of his eyes. "Those people over there? They know people who know people. One phone call from anyone in that little club, and you're blackballed at all agencies. No Grey, no McCann, no *nada.* You'll be setting up lights at weddings. There's an entire *campaign* riding on this shoot. They're *evaluating.* So do us both a favor. Dial down the useless opinions, amp up the cool artist attitude, and *get the damn shot.*"

Jack pondered Babyface for a second and turned to

the set, squinting at the models milling around. He looked over to his lighting tech, who was pretending not to appear concerned as he fiddled absently with an electrical circuit box.

"Steve. Fire up the 12k lights," Jack said. He turned and faced the models. "You guys stand over there and talk to each other. Ask her for her number or something. Banter."

With an echoey click, a bright light bathed the set. Jack calmed himself and studied the tableau thoughtfully, like a painter. He raised his camera, focused, and took one shot. Then another. He inspected the viewfinder, nodded to himself, and handed the camera off to the assistant.

Then he walked toward the large, padded door of the soundstage.

Babyface hissed, trailing him. "Jack? Jack! You can't just walk outta here! What's wrong with you?"

The assistant joined up, and they both watched Jack as he exited through the door. She waited for the right moment and then spoke. "He's been weird for weeks. I think he got something in the mail that set him off."

Babyface turned to her sharply. "Wouldn't have been the break-up message from Annie you handed him by any chance? I have to tell you. In the middle of a shoot? *Really?* Rookie move."

She looked repentant for about six seconds. Then she spoke. "But seriously, I think it had to be something else because, I mean, he breaks up *a lot.*"

Just then, a middle-aged suit from the puppy scrum approached. He spoke almost cheerily, despite the obvious behind-the-scenes drama. "Hey, guys! Guess what? I don't care if he's the best. He's fired." The suit turned and eyed the assistant as if seeing her for the first time. She smiled back.

"Hi. You shoot stills?" he asked.

"Totally. Trained by Jack."

"Interesting," said the suit.

Babyface shook his head and took the camera from the assistant, looking down at the image in the viewfinder. His jaw dropped. He handed the camera to the suit, who studied the image for a long moment. Babyface scratched his ear and waited for the verdict. The suit broke into a wide grin and shook his head. He handed the camera back to Babyface.

"That photo is gonna sell a *shitload* of SUVs."

Babyface exhaled deeply. "That's exactly what I'm talking about! He's fresh, unpredictable! It's what makes him so exciting! So should we go ahead and book the entire campaign?"

"Nope," the suit said as he walked away. "I told you. I don't ever want to work with him again. He's done."

So that was his day.

Jack was spinning out. Spinning out of control. Spinning his wheels. And here he was, pedaling and sweating. Spinning. The instructor of the class, an impossibly fit twenty-four-year-old Brazilian woman, shrieked at them all. "Come on! Fah-ster!! Move dos feet! Eet's all in front of you! *Don't look back!*"

Don't look back? Jack thought.

It came into focus.

Why the hell not?

What's so wonderful about this overpriced bullshit

sweatbox where people paid to ride fake bikes. *Inside.* He reached down and pulled the brake, slowing the free-wheel to a quick stop. His world slowed down as well. He looked around at the class for what seemed like ten minutes but was probably only ten seconds. The scene had taken on the other-worldly sheen of a movie.

He knew.

It was the first moment of clarity he could remember having in a long, long time. Maybe years. He got off the bike, grabbed his gym bag, and for the second time in a day, walked away.

This time, nobody cared.

Heading Up North
August 29, 1999

As Jack drove his rented Ford Explorer up I-75 under dark Michigan skies, he reflected on the past few months of his life. There was no question the letter had set his spiral in motion. It was handwritten in the familiar style of his old friend Foster Duprey. He hadn't spoken to Foster in ten years. But he knew his chicken scratch instantly from the poetry he used to tape up in the men's room stall at the Arnold Line ferry dock.

> *A broken-down lecher named Tupps*
> *Was heard to confess in his cups:*
> *The height of my folly*
> *Was diddling a collie*
> *But I got a nice price for the pups.*

He must have had a book of dirty limericks hidden away somewhere in his shack, deep in the middle of the island. Or possibly he made them up, which would have been even more impressive. But this letter was no limerick.

Jacky-Boy! This is my (in)formal invite to the first and hopefully last dockporter reunion bash taking place this summer. I know, you're a big-shot photographer now and have no interest in slumming with broken-down former luggage monkeys, all with bad knees and ear hair. But since the island ain't the same without you, I'm swallowing my pride (in between gulps of Jack Daniels) and inviting you. Ten years now, old friend. And get this: Erin's going to be on the island. Guess she and your ol' pal Gordon (ha-ha) are getting hitched. Anyway, maybe you can honor us with your presence. I'll order an extra case of beer and bring an attractive sheep with a nametag in case you relent.

Yer former mentor, Foster.

When Jack read the letter, he had to sit, and not because he wanted to process the information correctly. He sat because he thought his knees would give out. She was getting married. *Of course, she was getting married.* She was twenty-nine years old. Probably as beautiful as the day he met her ten years ago. Looks like hers didn't fade. Jack wasn't aware Erin lived in the United States much less Michigan.

But then again, he'd never checked.

———

All this was replaying in his head as he raced past the West Branch exit. It was raining now. His wiper blades slapped back and forth, just moments out of time with Madonna's *Ray of Light* playing on the radio. The song dissolved into crackly static and then into indecipherable snatches of a heated sermon from some central Michigan gospel station. Jack reached down and switched off the radio.

How many times had he taken this route in his life? A hundred? More? His first trip to the island was likely as a seedling in his mother's womb, as his parents, sister and various other friends and relatives headed up for the summer, establishing a ritual that would continue all of his young life.

To Jack, I-75 was a five-hour, 250-mile yellow brick road, depending on traffic. It was not a beautiful drive, at least not at first. Leaving Metro Detroit took way too long. Fighting traffic to escape the city were thousands of other overworked Michiganders with similar dreams for their weekends. Billboards and strip malls. Passing through Flint was a depressing reminder of how the state's fate was dangerously interconnected with the auto business and how, when business was bad, entire cities simply expired. Just another reason to step hard on the gas and leave those unpleasant realities in the rearview mirror.

As you moved north, or as they said in those parts, "up north," cities gave way to farms, and farms to trees. Millions and millions of trees. The winding highway snaked through a forest of white pine like an electric wire connecting Detroit to the Straits of Mackinac. The trees shrouded—then revealed—a sight that elevated his heartbeat, no matter how many times he'd seen it: the

Mackinac Bridge. It towered over the trees, protecting the Straits like a benevolent steel totem pole.

The bridge was an engineering marvel. A five-mile span connecting the upper and lower peninsulas of the Great Lakes State. Longer than the Golden Gate. Massive steel and concrete. Five-hundred-foot towers. A testament to the booming 1950s-era Michigan auto economy. One of the biggest bridges in the civilized world built to make it easier for Detroiters to hunt deer in the Upper Peninsula.

But what was mysterious to Jack about the "Mighty Mac" was that most people in the world didn't even know it existed. How could something so impressive be a relative secret to the rest of the world? It was just another bizarre quirk about the Straits of Mackinac. To Jack, it was an area electrified with strange magic.

He stared straight ahead as mile markers flashed past and the bridge grew closer. Familiar butterflies returned, a comforting reminder: ten years didn't change a thing. Even if he had no idea what to expect, it was still a feeling of coming home.

The Arnold Line ferry dock in Mackinaw City was busy. *Mac City*, the locals called it. Tourist families with worried glances toward the dark sky scurried toward overhangs. The torrents pounding his windshield for the entire ride had finally let up. But by the looks of it, it wouldn't last. The storm was following him. Jack grabbed his bags and backpack out of the car and walked toward the dock.

He took it all in. Mackinaw City had changed in the

last ten years. Most of the regular ferries from his youth were replaced by large, sleek catamarans. Newly painted signs touted a fifteen-minute "express" ride to Mackinac Island. The gift shops were tasteful, no longer hocking the tacky, cheap tourist crap he loved so much as a kid.

For reasons he couldn't pinpoint, he wasn't at all interested in a fifteen-minute ride to the island. He spent his childhood on the slow boats: loud, chugging tubs that rolled with the waves instead of cutting through them. Fifteen minutes was not enough time to get a sense of what the island had in store. The longer trip was a time to slow down and prepare the mind and body for an island with no cars. A place where slowness was a mandate.

Now that he was older, Jack recognized that the ferry line slogan—*Getting there is half the fun*—was probably written by a crusty Michigan marketing pro, selling slow ferry boats that took fifty wave-rolling minutes to go seven miles.

But it was true. Getting there *was* half the fun. Perhaps even the majority of the fun. And, today, he was in no hurry.

He approached the new ticket office and thought back to the many rides he had taken between the island and Mackinaw City in the pilothouse of one of the old ferries, the *Straits of Mackinac II*. His mind drifted to thoughts of Cap Riley.

How old would he be now? Was it possible he was still piloting the same ferry, if in fact it still existed, after all these years?

When Jack was a kid, Cap Riley was already a legend in the Straits area. He wore a proper uniform and a slouching captain's hat that gave him the look of a genial General Douglas MacArthur. Cap Riley had become friends with Jack's parents. As summer residents, they spent a fair amount of time on the ferry docks, riding, greeting, and seeing off friends who had spent the weekend at Wildcliffe, the family cottage. These were the types of bonds that formed in places like Mackinac Island. It made perfect sense. If you lived on an island, even just for the summer, you were likely pals with a ferry boat captain. It was practically table stakes.

Jack's father—Big Jack—owned an Oldsmobile dealership downstate. While the rest of the family stayed on the island all summer, Big Jack drove up every Friday night. He left straight from his office with a beat-up tennis racket and small overnight bag. Cap Riley would occasionally hold the last boat on Friday night for a few minutes, sometimes more, knowing that if Big Jack didn't make it aboard, he would lose out on a night with his family and friends on the island. Big Jack would have to grab a ratty bed at a Mackinaw City motel and take the first boat across in the morning. The party on the porch would undoubtedly go on without him, but nobody wanted that.

So Cap Riley sometimes stalled the departure a little. The passengers would grumble, but the way Cap Riley saw it, if a dad drove five straight hours *after* a long day's work to be with his tribe, he was a man worth waiting for. In return, the McGuinn family invited the good captain to all the front porch shindigs, and everything worked out just as it should.

As soon as Jack was old enough to ride a bike, he would find his way down to the island ferry boat dock during the summers, waiting for Cap Riley to dock. He'd drop his kickstand, hop on the ferry, and head straight up to the pilothouse. The rest of the day, he acted as a pint-sized, shaggy-haired copilot, perched on the captain's wood stool with simple directions: "Aim toward the two radio towers on the mainland."

Cap Riley would grab his coffee, sit on the rear bench of the pilothouse with the *Detroit Free Press* and check up on the Tigers' box scores, only occasionally looking up as Jack gripped the large steering wheel tightly.

The very first time, Jack had looked back, concerned. "Will I get in trouble?"

Cap Riley scoffed, not bothering to look up. "Kid, let me explain something to you. I'm the goddamn captain. My word is law on this vessel. And if I want to peruse the box scores while a midget in Keds pilots my boat, that's exactly what happens." Cap Riley smiled to himself, satisfied with his answer. Still not looking up, he added: "And don't tell your folks I said *goddamn*. It's a terrible word."

Jack would nod solemnly and turn his attention back to the matter at hand: the two radio towers on the mainland.

Young Jack kept his promise, and "goddamn" was not the only word he learned from Cap Riley over the years he spent co-guiding the ferry through the choppy waters of the Straits of Mackinac. Cap Riley was a constant, jovial, profane existence in Jack's life, even years later when Jack worked as a dockporter.

But that part of the story comes later.

———

Jack paid for his ticket at the booth like an ordinary tourist. The old-timer behind the glass took his money without looking up.

"You guys still run the *Straits of Mackinac II*?" Jack asked.

The old-timer nodded and grunted. "Freight boat now. Comes in every two hours for hay and kegs. Locals ride it over. It's the same price as the express boats and it's slow. But no discounts. Policy."

"What about Cap Riley?"

"Riley? Hmm." The old-timer looked away, trying to recall. "Think he went fishing."

Jack felt a rush of optimism. Back then, Cap Riley was known to grab his fishing pole and lures and sneak away between runs to pull a few whitefish out of the lake for dinner. Jack would wait for the slow ferry if it meant seeing his friend again. Maybe pilot the ferry for old time's sake. A perfect way to decompress in preparation for the island.

"… on Marathon Key," the old-timer added. "Six years ago."

Jack's face fell. "Oh. Can I still take the *Straits II* instead?"

"Sure. Gotta wait a while. Tellin' ya, the express is faster. Get you there in fifteen minutes. Old ferry's slow as hell."

"I know. I actually used to pilot …" Jack trailed off. There was no use waxing nostalgic with a ticket-taker who was now totally absorbed in a baseball game flickering on a small, crappy TV next to his cash register. Jack's yarns were worthless to this guy. He grabbed his change and took his ticket. He found a bench looking out over the lake, now streaked with whitecaps, and sat down.

In the distance, he could see the island, shrouded in blue-grey fog. A barely visible green strip of land rising from Lake Huron like a ghost. It looked the same as it had all those years ago. It never changed, particularly when viewed from the mainland. The ancients had called it the *Mishimikinaak* or "Great Turtle" because that's what it looked like: a huge sleeping turtle.

It was only seven miles away from Mac City, but the distance was deceiving. When you crossed over from the mainland, you traveled back in time half a millennium. It had been a gathering place that long. The tiny chunk of limestone was a prism of American history.

The Ottawa, Chippewa, and Potawatomi had settled first, drawn by a strong spiritual pull and even better fishing. But like all the best Native American secrets, it got out. In need of a stronghold for the booming fur trade, the French soon discovered the tall rock bluffs of the island. They arrived in canoes loaded with beaver pelts and transformed a tiny fishing village into a rowdy frontier outpost.

The Brits, always on the prowl for prime real estate in the New World, muscled in next and built Fort Mackinac on the island bluff in 1790. The fort was eventually turned over to the Americans after the War of 1812. The Redcoats had won a few battles on the island but lost the war. And the fort.

After 300 years of trading, fishing, and fighting, the island's cultural stew was now as unique and spicy as anywhere in the United States. It was time for the next transformation of the Great Turtle. At the turn of the 20th century, hotels, restaurants, and cottages sprung up on the bluffs and shorelines. A golf course was carved out of the battlefield. Fudge and taffy overtook fish and fur, and new traditions took root as ships ferried in visitors from all over the Midwest.

The state of Michigan recognized the island as a rare gem, and dedicated 80 percent of the land as a protected State Park. Automobiles were banned in 1898. Sometime in the 1950s, Jack's grandfather, on the prowl for a retreat from the humidity of Detroit summers, discovered the place. He purchased an old cottage on the bluff for a song and named it Wildcliffe.

The Great Turtle was many things. Outpost. Fort. Resort. But for the people who knew it best, it was simply *the island.*

The weather started getting rough, the tiny ship was tossed ...

It was all Jack could think about at the moment. That stupid '60s TV ditty echoed deadly serious right now. The *Straits II* was battling a full-on storm. Jack had spent twenty-plus summers on the island, and this was the worst weather he'd ever experienced. The ferry groaned and rocked, rolling side to side as water poured into the portholes on the lower deck and huge swells banged against the metal hull. He had moved to the upper deck and was keeping shelter with a few other locals under the overhang, hand on the rail.

Predictably, the weather didn't faze anyone else. Once a ferry was converted to a freight boat, mainly islanders rode them, and this crowd didn't give two shits about a little bad weather. A smoke and a Pabst tall boy and they were as solid as Alaskan crab fishermen. Jack couldn't even see the island now, the rain was coming down so hard. *Pissing.*

He removed an aged photo album from his backpack and began flipping through it absently to distract himself. The shots were a collection of what he liked to call his "early work," an admittedly pretentious way of saying "before I knew what I was doing." They were mostly island photos from his late teens and early twenties, all shot with a Kodak Pocket Instamatic camera he'd kept with him at all times.

The dockporter years.

As a bolt of lightning splintered the grey-purple sky, Jack absorbed the photos. They were, he could say now, pretty damn good. He could see the early stirrings of some raw talent. An awareness of composition, lighting, and focus. Something to build on.

But mostly what he noticed were the people in the pictures. The *people* were what gave the photos such crackling, vibrant life. Here, pasted in the aging pages, was a murderers' row of some of the best dockporters in history. Perhaps every dockporter thought the same thing about their years on the docks. But the difference was, Jack told himself, *he was right.*

He broke into a wide smile and took himself back to the summer of 1989. There they were. Sunburned noses, Ray-Bans, brightly colored hotel golf shirts, and cargo shorts. Walkie-talkies. Rag-wool socks in the dead of summer for reasons nobody could explain. Reinforced Schwinn Heavy-Duti bikes with oversized wire baskets made by Wald, loaded up with ridiculous amounts of luggage. The boys, ready to shout out their galvanizing rallying cry: "Tonight we drink, tomorrow we ride!"

Jack let the images wash over him, almost if he hadn't taken them himself. He turned the page. His stomach tightened.

Captured in the hazy light of a place called Horn's Bar was a beautiful woman with jet-black hair, playing fiddle with a sloppy bar band. A series of candids as the wild crowd cheered her on. Huge grins. Mayhem and love. Ecstatic. Beers raised and joyously emptied onto random heads. A moment in time captured perfectly. The photos were raw and energetic, some even blurry from amber droplets of beer on the lens.

She was marrying Gordon?

"Either you're finishing an old album or starting a new one."

Jack broke out of his trance and looked over. A bearded, heavyset biker in full worn leathers and a jean vest was watching him. Jack gave him a small nod. The biker let flow a stream of Marlboro smoke from his nostrils like a dragon.

"You mind if I take a gander?" His voice was husky and he had a slight twinkle in his eye as if he knew a secret. Jack quickly closed the album, feeling oddly busted.

"Oh, come on, brother. It's the slow boat and I'm outta weed. It looks like we're taking the back route. That's an extra thirty minutes. Maybe more. Either get me baked or share your tragic tales."

"Excuse me. I'm just looking at some pictures in my photo album." He heard himself sounding like a little boy, and the biker pounced with a cackle.

"Ha! Right. And what freak browses a photo album during a monsoon?" A beat. The big guy wasn't expecting a sensible answer because he knew there wasn't one. He just stood there grinning, a little too close. Waiting.

"Fine. Truth is I'm here—"

"For a reunion? The old crew? Swore you'd never lose touch, but whaddya gonna do? People move on. Get lame jobs. Take up golf. Mainland shit. Am I right?"

Jack stared at him. Speechless. For some reason, the song *Killing Me Softly* passed through his head. The biker continued. "And you're obsessed with the one that got away. Foreign chick, maybe? Artist? You want what the shrinks call 'closure.' You think moping around the island like some dipshit in a Nicholas Sparks novel will help you forget that *one great summer.*"

Jack felt as naked as a whining newborn. He stared at the biker. "That's exactly right," Jack said.

"Knew it," the biker said, taking another deep drag.

"I can't believe you guessed that with such …"

"—*Accuracy?* What? Fat old bikers can't have, whatchacallit … insight? So, cough it up. Spill the beans. I dunno … " He looked out at the roiling lake, searching for the right words. "… *entertain* me."

Jack followed his gaze. The big guy was right. The *Straits II* was slowly adjusting its course to take the back route to the island. At this angle, coming into the harbor with this crappy weather wasn't safe. They were not in any real danger, but they wouldn't be docking at the island anytime soon.

He had time.

He looked back at the biker, who was flashing a shit-eating, greasy grin. He had Jack right where he wanted him.

Jack set down his photo album and zipped his North

Face jacket up to the very top. He took a seat, putting his feet up on the steel bench in front of him. The ferry rolled heavily, right, then left. Below deck, cargo slammed loudly against the hull. The storm was getting worse. But Jack was no longer paying attention to the weather. If it was going to be a three-hour tour, he might as well tell a story.

CHAPTER TWO

Summer of Fudge
June 1, 1976

When someone asked that famous outlaw why he robbed banks, he said, "It's where the money is." That's precisely how we felt about Ryba's Fudge Shop. *It's where the fudge was.*

It's also where I first met Gordon and Smitty during the long, hot summer of 1976. The rest of the island was going bonkers over the news that the tall ships were passing through the straits later on that summer. Everything was red, white, and blue. All anyone could talk about was bicentennial this and bicentennial that. The fireworks that Fourth of July were beyond memorable, especially when Brody King, the island fire chief, had a few too many cocktails and caught the ex-governor's private dock on fire. A grand finale indeed. But that summer, all we cared about was fudge.

"Will you look at that shit?" Smitty said. He was a real islander, the born-and-raised, year-round type. He was part Chippewa, part French, and all *yooper*. "I'm getting starved just watching this guy," he said, as if consuming chocolate fudge as a meal substitute was a perfectly reasonable idea.

Smitty's lineage went back hundreds of years on the island but he was hardly royalty. His extended family mostly handled maintenance jobs and he lived with his mom, dad, and brother in a tiny clapboard house in a village in the center of the island. I guess, looking back, he was technically "poor" but that was nothing that interested us. The very best thing about being an eight-year-old kid is that your world shrinks to sports, bikes, sugar, and pals.

We were leaning on the wood railing that separated the fudge maker from John Q. Tourist, our heads resting on our arms, watching the glorious work like snobs watch opera. It was perfectly normal that summer for us to meet up at the fudge shop and observe the creation of loaf after loaf of the sugary miracle food. *For hours.* It never got boring.

The fudge maker, a sweaty, skinny guy named Paulie, was half-stepping skillfully around a large slab of marble with an oversized steel paddle, working a firming mass of chocolate fudge. Overhead, a fan cooled the sweet creation and blew the aroma across the shop and out the front door. It was orgasmic, even by the standards of awkward kids with no clue what that word even meant.

The three of us formed a potent crew that summer, and Ryba's was our clubhouse. Our only noticeable gang colors were matching beaded belts from the

Trading Post, one of the many souvenir shops that lined Main Street. They were made of cheap imitation leather, and the bright orange and red beads spelled out "Mackinac Island." They weren't exactly biker jackets, but we wore them with pride just the same.

"I can't believe he gets to do this as his *job. And gets paid for it!*" Gordon said, giddy with the concept. Gordon was nine and from the opposite end of the tracks as Smitty. Like me, he was a summer kid. A cottager. He was what we called back then *preppy*. Blond hair, perfectly combed to the side, and alligator shirts with the collar up. A pint-sized version of James Spader in *Pretty in Pink*. A privileged kid, yes, but he had an easy laugh and was willing to be the butt of any joke. We usually went easy on him, figuring his mom probably picked out his wardrobe.

But our thoughts were not on Gordon's questionable fashion sense at that moment. My eyes never left the slab, my mind racing with a thousand interlocking calculations. Finally, I leaned over to Gordon, speaking in a low tone.

"Bet you your signed Gordie Howe puck I can get us a free slice." (We did a crazy amount of betting that summer.) I wanted the fudge, the puck, and the glory. The bet was a one-stop gambit for all three.

"Fine. But if you lose, I get your G.I. Joe footlocker." He thought for a moment, then added: "with the scuba suit."

It still impresses me that the Hasbro company figured out how to get boys to play with dolls, merely by adding a gun, a buzz cut, a facial scar, and kung foo grip. They are *geniuses*. But I digress.

My grandfather was the biggest Gordie Howe fan on

the planet. If I scored *this* goal, I'd be set for life in his eyes. Straight to the front of the Gramps line, baby. VIP. *Boom.*

With great subtlety, Gordon and I sealed the bet with a handshake. It was a complex *Good Times* meets *Happy Days* hand-slap thing that the three of us perfected that summer. I turned back to the fudge maker, studying him with the concentration of a chess master for a full three and a half minutes. The guys were silent. Respectful. They were giving me space. Then, it was time.

"My sister likes you. Said you're …"

Paulie looked over, now interested. He slowed, waiting for the rest of my pitch. I was caught like a deer in headlights. We locked eyes. I glanced up at the sweat dripping off his pimply forehead and blurted out—

"… hot."

Things were going south fast. *Shit.* I liked that G.I. Joe footlocker with the scuba suit. And I think I just called a fudge maker "hot."

"And she puts out!" The phrase simply exploded outward like snot during a wet sneeze. I literally had no idea what it meant. I'd seen it on a TV show once and it lodged in my head. But the result was shockingly efficient. He stopped short and studied me for a moment, intrigued. He wordlessly cut off a slice of fudge from the loaf with a flat, two-handled knife and wrapped it up in a piece of wax paper. He handed it over carefully, as if cradling a gold bar, never taking his eyes off me.

"Wildcliffe Cottage, yeah? McGuinn's place?" the fudge maker asked, his voice a nasal twang.

"Yup."

"Maybe I'll swing by."

My sister Beth was going to murder me when this guy "swung by" Wildcliffe, but she could handle herself just fine and I'd cross that bridge when I came to it. I leaned in close and gestured toward Gordon and Smitty as if they were a couple of orphans I was responsible for feeding. I spoke in a near-whisper. Man to man. "And how about a little extra taste for those two?"

The fudge maker nodded. No problem. Hell, we were now practically in-laws. He went back to the slab and cut off two more slices from the still-warm loaf.

I could see Gordon, probably calculating the jive he'd have to spin to his old man about how he "lost" a signed Gordie Howe puck. He shook his head, but with a trace of a smile. This particular skirmish was over. There would be others, but we'll get to that later.

———

We weaved our Schwinn Sting-Rays through the throng of bikes, foot traffic, and horse-drawn carriages, savoring fudge and feeling the early euphoria of a full-blown sugar rush.

"Mm. So good. Gotta say, it's almost worth losing the puck," Gordon said. "Besides ..." He started to giggle. "I got three more at home. My dad gets 'em for free."

"You're an asshole, man!" I looked at Smitty.

"Did you know that?"

"Nobody tells me nuthin'." Smitty let out a sigh of ecstasy. "Shit's *unreal.*" His mouth was now stuffed with fudge, a brown sugary mess. We continued our ride, focusing on jamming as much fudge down our young gullets as humanly possible.

The biker broke into the story at that moment. "Wait, dude, back up." He leaned forward toward Jack, who was now standing at the railing. "You're telling me, as a little kid, you pimped out your own sister for free fudge?"

"I didn't know that's what I was doing. Besides. A man's gotta eat."

The biker shook his head with newfound respect. "Proceed."

When I wasn't scamming fudge, I delivered papers. Even back then, the island had its share of wealth, and many cottage owners lived and died by the *Wall Street Journal*.

That was my beat.

Every morning at 7:30, I met the first boat, which was loaded with tough construction workers with lunchboxes and plaid shirts coming over from the mainland to start their day. The island was "older than baseball," as my grandfather liked to say, and in a constant state of disrepair. These guys put the place back together.

Shortly after the workers trudged off the ferry, the deckhands would roll out a cart of newspapers. I'd load up my shoulder bag with a healthy supply of *WSJ*'s and bike off to drop in on island royalty, trading a paper for an extra buck and, occasionally, a stock tip, which meant nothing to me. I'd be a millionaire now if I knew what to do with all that inside information back then. But I was no MBA. Just your average everyday eight-year-old street hustler.

Check that. I *wasn't* average. I was a damn good paperboy. I knew this because Big Jack made it clear he was proud of me, albeit in his usual opaque way. Not with an "atta boy" slap on the back or a gold star. No. He just left his boy alone to do the work at hand.

Big Jack was a bit of a control freak on an average day, and when he saw things going hopelessly pear-shaped, he was known to go hopelessly ape shit. If there were issues about my methods, whether it be my throwing style, aim, speed, or trajectory, Big Jack would have announced it over dinner. He enjoyed dishing out a little public humiliation as much as the next dad. But he never uttered an unkind word about my route, and that was as meaningful to me as a bear hug and a chocolate chip cookie. His boy had a job on Mackinac Island when most summer kids were sleeping off head-splitting fudge highs until noon.

But the real reason for my diligence was more complex than the pride of a job well done. It was less about impressing Big Jack and more about getting noticed.

Specifically, I wanted to get noticed by dockporters.

In India, they call them coolies. On Everest, Sherpas. On Mackinac Island, they're called dockporters. On an island where automobiles are outlawed, these guys had the balance and the balls to move luggage. They'd been doing it this way for the last one hundred years or so. When I was a kid, they were the knights of the Mackinac Island round table. Part athlete, part show-man, they hauled suitcases with their bikes. They made sure every hotel guest was met the moment the ferry spat them onto the dock into a morass of suitcases, bikes, dogs, and, often, horses.

The dockporter's job was to zero in on the guests of their hotel, make them feel welcomed, and send them off. The dockporter would then stack their luggage up in their bike basket, ride it through the streets, and, God willing, pull up just as said guests were meandering into the lobby.

They had to *see it* ridden or the tip was meaningless, nothing but token gratitude based on old, outdated conventions. Skycap shit. Boring. Barely earned. But when a weary traveler saw his or her precious payload arrive stacked sky-high in the basket of a beat-up one-speed Schwinn unscathed, they were impressed.

Making an impression. That was the whole point. That was the unspoken law. Impressive feats were rewarded. With cash. Finskies, hammies, or even, perhaps once a summer, a Benjie. Any dead historical figure would do.

Island skeptics dismissed them merely as "bellmen on bikes," and while there was truth to the label, there was more to the story. These guys were artists. I knew from the first time I saw twenty-year-old Foster Duprey pass me with a massive load of luggage—focused as a fighter pilot behind his Ray-Bans, easing his brake and pushing on the pedal, finding his pockets of air on Main Street—that I was witnessing something special. Foster would never have time to acknowledge some eight-year-old punk paperboy, but we were already distant brothers in my mind. He hauled one hundred fifty pounds of luggage; I hauled one hundred fifty ounces of financial insight. Just a matter of scale.

I would often glide my bike down to the docks between ferry boats, sometimes with Smitty in tow, and hang out. They were a raunchy, lewd, hilarious lot when they were away from guests. They pitched quarters and placed bets on everything from the Detroit Tigers to certain tendencies of certain unnamed waitresses. I drank it all in until I was bursting and came back for more. While the old-timers managed the island businesses, and the rich folks made the rules, the dockporters ran the streets, the hotel lobbies, and the docks. They knew the real score. If there was an island telegraph, these guys were the operators.

My dream of becoming a professional fudge maker was fading, tossed on the scrap heap along with the fireman dream and the going-to-the-moon dream. The best thing about this dockporter dream? *It was mine.*

I bounded up the stairs of Wildcliffe, my family's summer cottage on the East Bluff. It was after five on a Saturday, and the place was already heating up. The house was an aged Victorian with a rambling veranda that overlooked Main Street far below and the bay beyond. A bit of a fading lady from years of island winters, the place nevertheless lit up on weekends. Wildcliffe always crackled with life when Big Jack was on the rock. He and my mom made sure that their downstate friends were always welcome on the weekends, and things got loud, with a crescendoing of music, cracking beers, and howls of laughter.

My dad's dad, the original Jack, my "Gramps," held court with some locals, in the midst of another story about his adventures in Hollywood during the fifties. He'd done some running around in Los Angeles after the war and before he'd formed the dealership in Detroit. There was nothing he enjoyed more than name-dropping to the locals.

Rumor was, he'd once had an amorous roll with Marilyn Monroe, but of course he had no proof. Many of Gramps' juiciest rumors were started by Gramps. Seeing that he was a dirt-poor farm kid just back from fighting in the Philippines, I doubted the veracity of that tale. But not so much that I didn't share it with anyone who would listen.

Gramps, drink in one hand and a bunless sausage in the other, was wearing his worn University of Michigan block "M" cap. He was as rabid a Michigan fan as I'd ever known, even though he never graduated from any college.

"Catch," I said casually, tossing him the newly won Gordie Howe puck. He flinched, spilling a bit of his drink. The puck bounced off his chest and landed in the crux of his arm, the autograph straight up. *Helluva save.* He studied it.

"What the … Is this … *how?*"

"Sure is!"

"No, I mean … *how? How* did you get this?"

"Won it in a bet," I responded. Cocky. The party crew crowded around the prize, impressed.

"Why, you little rogue. Who'd ya get this offa?"

"My friend Gordon."

Gramps lit up. "That's fantastic! The Whittaker boy! I believe your father and his father play a little tennis together. This might add some spice to their bullshit game, know what I mean?"

"Dad! Easy on the language in front of the kid," Big Jack rebuked, looking over from the wicker front porch swing. He watched our exchange, his head cocked. My dad always kept a close eye on Gramps.

Looking back, I suspect he was trying to calibrate just how much unfiltered corruption to allow. He knew that the closer we got, the better chance I would end up like him. Gramps did just fine by the world. He had friends that loved him, money in the bank, and grandchildren that idolized him. But I imagined his skeletons could form a conga line long enough to stretch around the island twice should they ever venture out of his closet.

"Oh, good *Christ*, he's heard worse on this porch."

Gramps looked down at me. As he spoke, he gestured emphatically with the sausage. It was hard not to notice the bouncing, somewhat suggestive gyrations of the thing. I bit my tongue, choking back a laugh.

"Jacky-boy, I sold a lotta cars in my day. *Lotta cars.* I could've blown every dime chasin' skirts, but I didn't. I bought Wildcliffe. And someday, boy, it'll all be yours." He took a bite of the sausage. "On it goes." He loved saying this. There was a moment as he waited for the traditional response.

"On it goes," I repeated solemnly.

"That's right, boy. *On it goes.*" He continued. "Maybe someday you'll be the ceremonial mayor, just like me. You wanna be the ceremonial mayor? Just like me?" He arched one eyebrow and waited for an answer.

I loved my grandfather, and there is not a day that goes by when I don't miss him. But the idea of being the ceremonial mayor of Mackinac Island was *way* down on my list, even further down than being the *actual* mayor. I wasn't sure what the ceremonial mayor did. I'd never seen my grandpa do anything on the island other than host parties, ride his foldable bike up and down Main Street, and listen to Ernie Harwell call Tigers' games on the radio. I thought about it and stated, perhaps a tad too boldly, the truth.

"I wanna be a dockporter."

"Ha! Smart kid. The ladies love 'em, that's for sure." He grew reflective for a moment. "Besides, you don't wanna be the ceremonial mayor. It's mostly, you know … *ceremonial*." The once-jiggling sausage was now steady. I wasn't sure how to respond to the old man's obvious observation.

The moment turned uncomfortable.

He broke into a wide smile. "You missed the funny part, Jacky! It's ceremonial! Of course, it's purely ceremonial!" His crew broke out in laughter. "Damn kid probably thought I went batty on the spot! Okay, Jacky, hop up and smack the sign for good luck."

At that, my father's eyes widened. "Dad, he's gonna kill himself," he said, "and shatter the sign to pieces."

"It's tradition! Let the boy give 'er a whack!" I looked over at my dad. He nodded in approval, resigned but smiling.

I hopped up on one of the beat-up wicker chairs spread around the porch and reached up to the hanging painted sign that read *Wildcliffe Cottage*. Steadying myself with my left hand on the back of the chair, I smacked it hard with my right. As the party crowd cheered, the sign screeched back and forth on the rusty mount. I watched it swing and then gently settle back into position.

How many times had I smacked this sign? How many more smacks to come? How many smacks can one painted front porch sign endure?

If this were a movie, the sign smacks would continue, one after another, symbolizing the passing of island summers. Presidents would come and go, from a football player to a peanut farmer to an actor to an oilman. More cracks in the old wood would indicate the passing of time. Wildcliffe was getting older. The sign would stop swinging and settle.

And it would be thirteen years later.

And I would be a dockporter.

The First Boat of the Day
June 15, 1989

The ferry boat slammed into the dock with force. It knocked me off the luggage cart. I landed in a small dried-up pile of horse shit, face-first. Not surprisingly, it tasted—but didn't smell—a lot like hay. I looked up to see the cart rolling on its own steam toward the edge of the dock, a slumbering waitress aboard. I was strangely confident all would work out. Sure enough, the cart rammed into a tall stack of Hostess Twinkies boxes. The towering cascade of shrink-wrapped pastries toppled onto the prone waitress. Disoriented, she blasted like a rocket from her blanket and assemblage of black and white garb, instantly wide awake. A rabbit in an earthquake. Her dark eyes darted around in a vain attempt to decipher the who-what-when-where-why of the current moment.

She was on a dock. That part was clear. She saw me

looking at her curiously and smiled broadly as it all came rushing back. Big white teeth. She snorted out a laugh and laughed again at her snort. *I knew I liked her.* Without warning, she was as chatty as the night before, her words piling on top of each other.

"Jack, right? The dockporter?" she said. "I remember. You're all, 'I'm Jack. Cottage on the East Bluff.' Then you're all, 'Dad owns a Buick dealership downstate, but I'm not into the family business thing.' And I'm all, 'Awesome, his family's got money, but he shleps other people's bags. Girl, you sure can pick 'em.' Then we started making out." She glanced at her half-undone uniform. "I think I can guess the rest."

I pulled myself to my feet and brushed off, stealing furtive glances toward the far end of the dock.

"It's Oldsmobiles," I said.

She looked at me sideways.

"Huh?"

"My dad sells Oldsmobiles."

"Oh. Sorry to hear that. My aunt drives a Cutlass. It sucks."

An unmistakable voice exploded: "Would some *goddamn* porter catch my *goddamn* lines before we end up docking in Marquette *goddamn* Park!" I knew the voice and what the jarring dock-bump meant. The morning ferry was in, which was fine, except somebody was supposed to be catching the lines, and that somebody was currently dusting off dried horse shit.

"Have a seat, Jack the dockporter. Let's catch up." She patted the base of the cart next to her. Gentle. Like a psychologist or a dog trainer.

"Ummm … I'm supposed to be catching the lines," I said.

"Ummm … I don't care. Have a seat."

"The boat is …" I trailed off.

"You're not going anywhere until you answer a very simple question."

I sat down next to her. She snuggled close, but only for dramatic effect. She looked up at me with her big brown eyes, still a half-smile on her face. The Huntress. "So," she said. *Here it comes.*

"Don't worry, don't worry. It's easy," she lied.

"Great. What's easy?"

"My name. What is it?" she asked sweetly.

I scoffed, a bit too loudly. Fake indignant. My heart was pounding. I may have been hungover and dirty, but I was still a gentleman. I held her gaze for too long, scanning my glitching brainwaves for a flash of memory. Any clue to answer this perfectly reasonable question and be released unharmed to catch the lines and keep my job.

She said she was an Eskimo.

I remembered that part of the conversation from the previous night. We'd been doing shots at Horn's Bar when she wandered in with friends, still in her waitress uniform, and joined us. The talk, as it often did at that particular location, got bleary. Time passed. Open. Semi-intimate. Funny and innocent.

She said she was an Eskimo.

Maybe not fully, but somewhere on the family tree. I laughed, loving the sound of that. I told her I was Irish. Somewhere on the family tree. More small talk. But there was no avoiding the stark truth: We were both Americans in our early twenties. Red-blooded and looking for fun. All this talk of ancestry, all a precursor to something else. Something that may just end in the harsh morning light on a luggage cart on the Arnold Line dock.

Her name. *Shit.* The shadow of a disapproving Big Jack loomed like a phantom. *Don't you remember her name?*

The horn from the *Straits II* blasted. We both grabbed our temples in unison, like a hungover synchronized swimming team. It was there I saw it. Half-pinned to our rumpled blanket and out of her line of sight was the Holy Grail of the moment: *A name tag.* It even had her hometown printed on it.

"Vicky. From East Lansing," I said calmly. *What a perfectly silly question.* I then remembered a detail all on my own.

"And you're a swimmer!"

She leaned back and fixed me with a look, astonished. "Well, Jack the dockporter, I'm amazed and impressed. Even got my hometown right. You, my new friend, are dismissed."

Relief washed over me. I kissed her on the cheek as I tucked in my green golf shirt emblazoned with *Waterview Inn.* She smiled, understanding the score entirely. It was Mackinac Island. It was summer. We were young. As I jogged toward the ferry, I heard her warm cackle echoing across the lake.

"Ha! You read my name tag! Nicely played, Jack the dockporter!"

Cap Riley leaned on the upper deck railing, observing the scene from his perch with regal amusement.

"There he is! You got fudge in your ears? We almost drifted into the yacht docks." He glanced over at a hunched figure with a wheelbarrow full of fresh horse dung, wearing worn state park-issued green coveralls.

This was Rick.

He was a shit sweeper.

Rick the shit sweeper.

"Whaddya think, Rick? Should I have the boy disbarred? Removed from his post? Drawn and quartered?" Cap Riley loved to yell hypothetical questions to Rick the shit sweeper, who was a permanent fixture on the Arnold Line dock. Rick, who rarely responded, was in his fifties but looked older, dark and wrinkled from years in the sun. He still maintained a full head of salt-and-pepper hair, which he kept meticulously groomed, Elvis-style, probably with Brylcreem.

Rick held a shovel and looked out over the calm lake water as if he'd seen something odd. The moment passed, and he went back to shoveling a set of three fresh road apples into his wheelbarrow. Rick had been sweeping horse dung off the same dock for over thirty years at that point. He'd seen more ferry boats pull in than anyone on the rock. He'd watched island tourist fashions change from porkpie hats to deliberately torn jeans. From fashionable fifties' dresses to his-and-hers matching T-shirts that said *I'm With Stupid* and *I'm Stupid*. The world around him kept devolving, and Rick kept shoveling shit.

"Whaddya think, Rick? The kid sleeps on the dock just so's he won't miss the first boat." Cap Riley laughed like a pirate. "On the mainland, they ship brainiacs like this off to law school, but not our Jacky. He likes it right here on the island!"

"He's dedicated to his craft," Rick grunted. He knocked some lingering dung off his shovel into the wheelbarrow.

I was waiting for Franklin, the big-as-a-house deckhand of the *Straits II*, to toss me the line. Seeing my sorry state, he grinned and whipped the heavy rope hard toward my head. It sailed straight through my hands and smacked me hard in the face. My knock-off Ray-Bans were knocked off, and skittered across the dock.

"Nice catch, *dad*."

Franklin liked to call everyone "dad." It was a northern Michigan thing and came out more like "*dahh-d.*"

I quickly secured the bow and the stern lines. Scrambling, I hopped over the precipice to the ferry and pulled the gangway up, joining in a ritual I'd performed many times. I looked the passengers over like a rancher eyeing cattle as they piled off the ferry.

A female voice cut through the normal chatter. It was the Irish lilt that grabbed my attention, very unusual in northern Michigan in 1989.

The voice said something close to "*Fookin'* watch where you're goin' there, boyos!"

That's the first time I ever saw Erin O' Malley. She wore a light-blue sundress and faded Chuck Taylor tennis shoes and hugged three grocery bags as she walked off down the gangplank to the dock as if she was returning from an overnight supply run. With long, raven-black hair, she had sky-blue eyes that looked straight through me. If she was pricing brake pads, she'd have shown more interest. I was air. I instinctively looked around for her father, older brother, boyfriend. Someone.

Some backstory here is helpful. In the early summer on the island, the ritual was always the same. Fathers delivered their college-aged daughters to work as bartenders, housekeepers, clerks, hostesses, and waitresses. They would analyze the scene at the dock with a sinking realization. *How did my precious little girl talk me into this?* Hell, they were young once, and it didn't take a Ph.D. in biochemistry to recognize the potential for antics on this island. Particularly when an eager dockporter offered to "help" her with her suitcases.

But it was too late. She'd landed the gig, the contract was signed, and nobody was turning back.

Payback time, pops.

Yes, some wonderful women arrived on that dock over the previous four summers. But I could recall nothing like this Irish beauty. I stammered out the old standby: "Need some help?" I looked around, realizing I hadn't seen my bike since my rude awakening earlier. "Just need to find my bike. Odd. It was here last night," I stammered.

She didn't slow down. "A dockporter without a bike?" she said. "What does that make you? A bellboy?"

"Useless," I replied.

She stopped. "Your bike. Is it yellow? Big basket? Absolutely banjaxed?"

"Yes! Why? You see it?"

She looked off into the distance. "Nope."

She walked off with her bags. No, this woman didn't need a dad to drop her off. She was an independent woman. Foreign. Adventurous. Different. And what's *banjaxed?*

Cap Riley called down to her. "Stay away from dockporters, Erin! Those boys only have one thing on their minds."

She called back over her shoulder. "What's that?"

"Luggage!" Riley cackled.

I watched her walk off toward Main Street, secretly hoping she might steal a glance back. She didn't.

"Who is *that?*" I called up to Cap Riley.

"That ... is out of your league. Her name is Erin O'Malley. She's a musician at the Grand Hotel." I grabbed my Instamatic camera and brought it up to my eye. I called out. "Erin!" Nothing. I yelled louder. *"ERIN!"*

She turned, and I snapped a shot. I admit it was an odd move. Borderline creepy. She looked annoyed and turned back to resume her walk. I vowed to get the shot developed quickly and check her expression. I sensed perhaps the slightest smile, and I needed proof.

CHAPTER THREE

Dockporters
  June 15, 1989

I slid the Instamatic camera back in my pocket. It was already a pretty eventful morning. Vicky, the swimmer from State. Erin, the Irish smartass. A bike gone missing. I hadn't ridden a single suitcase and already had a few stories for the boys.

I heard a commotion and looked up. The island version of a Mongol horde was approaching, all on Schwinn one-speed bikes with reinforced steel baskets. They weaved wildly, cutting one another off, cackling like lunatics. Bike tires skidded across the dock and bungee cords were spun and tossed like Spanish bolas. It was a loud scene but one that would be repeated boat after boat, day after day, all summer long. These boys did not know the meaning of a quiet entrance.

A long, horrifying skid scattered a family of seagulls

as Smitty, clad in his yellow Woodside Inn golf shirt, made a grand entrance.

Smitty was transformed since our fudge-scamming days. He was now solid and strong, with a long shock of dark hair that often covered his soulful brown eyes. Smitty was an anomaly as a dockporter, as he was the only year-round islander.

For reasons I never entirely understood, most dock-porters were college types, or at the very least, *looked* like college types. It was the unwritten policy of the hotels to hire mainly from Midwest universities. Perhaps it was some delusional pipe dream that today's dockporters would become tomorrow's management, thus creating a funnel for what they used to call *future leaders*.

But to my knowledge, this never happened. Not once. Dockporters hauled luggage and hustled tips. Managers tried, with utter futility, to manage them. It would have been a wholly unnatural career progression, akin to moving from bank robber to bank teller.

But Smitty was no college boy. Unlike the rest of us, he didn't leave at the end of the summer. In the winter, only the toughest of the tough stayed on the island, grinding it out with construction jobs and a lot of Pabst Blue Ribbon, long before it was a hipster cocktail. They rode snowmobiles, which were legal in the winter, and traveled to the mainland and back over an ice bridge for supplies. In short, year-round islanders were badasses, and Smitty owned it with pride.

He hopped off his bike and began unloading luggage from the cart. "What's the word of the day, Jackass?"

"*Money.* Dirty, filthy, beautiful *money.* This is gonna be our best summer ever." Something about the chaotic wake-up call, the vision of the Gaelic Goddess, and the perfect morning air had me elated. The hangover was blissfully evaporating.

"What's the 9-1-1 on that waitress I saw you with last night? Was it Allison? Cheerleader from Central?" He cocked his head. "Was that her name? Andie, right? Allison? Alll ..." He trailed off, visibly contorting, desperately trying to recall the previous night's escapades. I allowed him a moment to twist in the cool breeze, then bailed him out.

"Vicky. And she's a swimmer from State."

"Vicky! Right. I knew it was early in the alphabet." *Early in the alphabet?* That was Smitty. Hardworking? Street-smart? A million laughs? Yes, yes, and yes. But a deep intellect? Not particularly.

AJ Veldachio, crashed the recap, grabbing Smitty in a friendly headlock. "And it's *4-1-1,* Little Einstein!" As we rolled the cart further down the dock, AJ hopped on, hands on hips, posing like a Roman Caesar. With his strong Italian profile and Tyrian purple golf shirt, it almost worked.

AJ worked for the Huron Inn. Yes, he hauled luggage. But in his heart, he was an actor. Two summers ago, he'd driven to Los Angeles to audition for a soap after getting noticed by a local Detroit talent scout. The rumor was, they liked him and wanted to show him off to the network executives. But his old man was sick, plus his sister was having troubles on the homefront, plus it was a heckuva long way from home. *Plus, plus plus.* AJ carried a laundry list of reasons for missing the callback, and we'd heard them all, often after a long night of carousing.

AJ could sing, play guitar, dance, and do impressions. This was before the internet demystified talent and showed us all that it wasn't all that magical. But in conservative Michigan in the late eighties, it was as exotic as a birthmark on your face shaped like Florida. He may have passed on his big break in Hollywood, but he made damn sure to make up for it on the island.

Every night he put on his own show, turning the bars, beaches, and employee dorms into an audacious One-Man Show. Sweating wildly, manic, talking fast, laughing with loud bursts that cut through the night like a steel machete of fun. He could nail Billy Joel's *Piano Man* and croon Sinatra and Dean Martin with a subtlety that was mind-blowing to a bunch of lowbrows who could barely belt out *Wild Thing* on key.

He would often commandeer the drums of the house band. They had no idea what they were getting into until it was too late and their hippy-dippy, female-friendly cover of *Hotel California* morphed into speed metal.

AJ knew he was good. He also knew he might never get a chance to prove it on the Big Stage. But *boo-fucking-hoo*, as the saying goes. There were worse curses than being good looking, funny, and talented.

The guys sauntered to their appointed positions along the dock as if in a rehearsed ballet, as AJ checked luggage tags, scrounging for a score. Maybe something fancy and upscale like Louis Vuitton or Hartmann. Even better? Something tagged with his hotel.

Foster Duprey, the Chippewa Hotel porter, glided to a halt on his beast of a bike, which was adorned with faded, vintage luggage tags. The basket of his bike was a piece of modern art, bent and re-bent, formed like metal clay from the weight of the thousands of suitcases he'd ridden.

Foster was thirty-three now, with the small but solid build of an Apollo astronaut. His sun-creased face showed the mileage of over a decade in the sun, but he still moved like a confident cat, always with a slight smile on his face, as if he was in on an industrial-sized joke.

"Mornin' dipshits," he said.

"Morning, master," we returned in unison. Foster made every dockporter he ever trained promise that— once a day for the rest of their career—they'd address him as "master."

Foster was an enigma. If the rumors were true, a fat family trust fund awaited him when he earned his college degree. All he had to do was strap on the books and graduate and he'd be on Easy Street. But he'd gotten hung up on second-year Spanish.

For ten years.

There were also contradicting rumors that the secret millionaire bit was a bullshit story he and some buddies concocted in a bar in the late seventies. He taught many of us the tricks of the trade and was now content to let us have our time in the sun. While we privately debated what was truth and what was legend, he did his thing. Mackinac Island in the summer and Breckinridge in the winter. He was an old-school resort rat, a picker, following the seasons and harvesting suitcases.

Foster was joined by a tall beanpole of a kid checking over a spiral notebook. This was Spengler. He wore thick glasses and black dad socks pulled up high. With his khaki cargo shorts and bright red golf shirt, it was a ridiculous look, but he managed to pull it off.

Sometime in the distant past, his name was Harold

Riney, but AJ re-minted him "Spengler" after his favorite Ghostbuster. It stuck like glue. The guy didn't look strong enough to ride a lady's handbag, but he surprised us all with his logical approach to stacking bags, and eventually he could hold his own.

Spengler spent his time in the off-season as a journalism major, with dreams of becoming a reporter. To us, this was hilarious, as he always managed to arrive on the scene five minutes late for any reportable event. When President George Bush unexpectedly visited the island for a political conference, Spengler was downstate at a vintage book convention. And there was the time he hauled Detroit rock and roll legend Bob Seger's luggage. Oblivious, Spengler spent his time with Rockin' Bob blathering about the songwriting genius of Bruce Springsteen, Seger's arch-rival. *No tip.*

Lately, he'd been obsessively learning jokes, he said, "to be more like AJ."

"I bought the world's worst thesaurus," he said as he walked up. "Not only is it terrible ... *it's also terrible!*" He giggled hysterically.

Smitty stared at him blankly. "I don't get it."

"Has anyone seen my bike?" I asked.

I detected a few snorts and stifled laughs.

"When was the last time you saw it?" Spengler asked. "Retrace your steps."

"Last night. I gave Vicky a ride and we crashed on a luggage cart over there behind the snack shop."

Pulling up next on a garish, bright red bike was Shawn *Superfly* Karma, "Fly" for short. Fly played up the scrappy Black Detroit kid angle, but it was all an act. His dad was an auto executive. Fly grew up comfy in the suburbs and studied engineering. He leaned his bike on his kickstand and double-checked a notepad.

"The new guy's coming in today. Eddie Bulloski. Plays football at Michigan!"

"Bulloski," I said. "Nice! Sounds like a lineman. Let's call him *Bull.*"

"*Bull.* I like it. I hereby claim him as my loyal protege," Fly exclaimed. "I'm showin' this big homie the ropes. My very own Polish servant. *God be praised!*"

Smitty looked over. "Perfect. We let Bull handle unloading. We kick back and retire in style."

"Retire? Smitty, we're in our prime," I said.

"I'm a luggage-hauling chimp," said Smitty. "Please, Jack. Tell me this isn't my prime."

I blinked. "You're not just some burned-out skycap hustling tips at Detroit Metro. You're a dockporter, man. Have some pride."

"Nope. Did some thinkin'. This is my last summer. I'm moving to Vegas and marrying a stripper. I read that's where they're from."

I shot him a look. I was a fan of the original Batman TV series. For my money, Batman without Robin was just boring. And kinda lonely.

I stood up on the cart. "*This* is where we belong." I gestured to the luggage. "*This* is the stuff these tourists couldn't live without for even three days. *It's precious!* They hand it over to you. A total stranger. And you know what you do?"

The guys responded in unison: *"You ride it!"*

"Right." I was done. "But seriously. Where's my bike?"

They traded subtle glances and, as if on cue, began humming "The Star-Spangled Banner" as they lined up

the bags. Then, as always, AJ took charge, standing tall
with his hand over his heart, looking proudly up at the
flag like a GI on a World War II recruiting poster. Soon
they were *all* facing the flagpole, singing their hearts out.
Automatically, I put my hand on my heart and turned.

There, just below Old Glory and the Michigan state
flag, was my yellow porter bike, secured with Eagle
Scout efficiency by a shitload of sticky black duct tape. It
would take a hatchet to cut it down.

"… *and the home of the braaave*," dissolved into laughter. My mind flashed to the Irish girl I met earlier. *Erica,
was it?* She must have seen my bike taped up there. How
else would she know it was yellow? My respect for the
captivating Celt soared.

AJ spoke up. "I ran across you and Vicky spooning
in the moonlight and couldn't resist."

I looked over at Smitty questioningly and pointed to
my bike.

He just shrugged. "Nobody tells me nuthin'."

Cap Riley looked down at us, amused. "Since we
now know you can't sing worth a damn, any of you
ladies gonna make *real* history this summer?"

A few of us glanced toward the long, two-story
freight shack that ran the length of the Arnold Line
dock. Hand-carved in the red and green wood siding,
partially hidden by a Mountain Dew vending machine,
was a list that went back over one hundred years. The
dockporters' very own Cooperstown. Most of us just
referred to it as "the list." It was the sacred site that
enshrined the top luggage haulers of all time under the
scrawled heading *BLACKJACK.*

"Blackjack," AJ said. Somber.

"Twenty-one in the hopper," added Fly. Reverential.

"It's impossible, Cap!" I called up. "They outlawed crossbars. Nobody's ridden blackjack since—"

"—*1975*. High-Rise Jimmy Oliver," a gravelly voice interrupted.

We all turned to look. It was Rick. He was paused in mid-scoop, eyes far away, as if recalling a moving speech by Vince Lombardi, or Kirk Gibson's epic home run off Goose Gossage in the 1984 World Series.

"You know that load?" I asked.

Rick snorted. "Know it? *I helped him stack it.* And crossbars had nuthin' to do with it. High-Rise coulda rode twenty-one pie-eyed on a big-wheel." Rick resumed scooping a fresh pile for dramatic effect, while I tried to imagine luggage stacked on a big-wheel. Then he looked right at me.

"See, High-Rise? He didn't *have* a crossbar."

A shocking revelation. The science, physics, and insanity behind that legendary load was something we spent years dissecting. We all agreed that it was impossible to ride twenty-one suitcases without custom handlebars, called "longhorns" by the veterans, connected with a welded-on crossbar to hang extra bags. When an island ordinance passed, deeming it unsafe to ride with crossbars, blackjack was considered out of reach forever.

To now hear that the legendary High-Rise Jimmy Oliver, the last name carved on the list, rode an astonishing twenty-one pieces of luggage *without* a crossbar was a collective gut-punch to our pride.

I began peppering Rick with questions. "But how'd

he see over the load? Was it triple-wings? How heavy were the bags? What was the secret?"

But Rick was rolling away. Compared to the Greats on the list, we were all just children in his eyes.

I watched him with newfound respect. "It's like Rick was at Kitty Hawk," I said.

Foster spoke up as he sorted a set of matching bags tagged with his hotel. "Yup. And trust me, he'll never give up the code." He smiled at me. "Don't worry about it. There's 'tip men' and 'load men.' You'll always be a 'tip man,' Jack. A lean, mean, tip-scoring machine." He turned his attention back to the bags.

I pondered the comment, not convinced Foster meant it as a compliment. *Tip man?* What did he mean by that? I'd ridden plenty of big loads. Just because I also understood the subtleties of the gratuity phase of the process shouldn't diminish my accomplishments one bit. Hell, that's why we did it, right? For tips?

But if that were true, why wasn't there a century-old, hand-carved list honoring the biggest tips?

———

Later that day, I was organizing a wad of cash on the dock when I was distracted by the high-pitched whine of an electric engine. Heads turned toward the source. Driving toward me in a bright green golf cart tricked out with a flatbed was Gordon Whittaker. In the passenger seat sat an unsmiling forty-something dressed in a black button-down shirt under an expensive-looking black blazer. His face was pale, as if he hadn't been in the sun in ages.

Gordon was not the same loosey-goosey kid he used

to be, although his fashion sense remained consistent. He was wearing a pink pastel shirt and a light blue tie, his blond hair neatly combed and groomed. I walked to the cart, curious.

"What the hell is this ugly beast?" I asked. It occurred to me that Gordon and I had not spoken once this summer. To say our paths diverged since the old days would be an understatement. Gordon ran many of his father's businesses—real estate, development, and upscale shops in the northern Michigan towns of Harbor Springs, Petoskey, and Mackinac Island. He was, I'd heard, damn good at it. Meanwhile, I'd become skilled at organizing sweaty, crumpled, one-dollar bills into tidy green stacks.

I guess everyone has a calling.

Gordon smiled. His perfect white teeth gleamed in the bright island sun. He gestured to the cart. "It's the future. Beautiful, right?" He leaned into me, sniffed and grimaced. "Jesus. You smell like a brewery."

"The future of *what*?" I said.

"Luggage! New revenue stream. This is the proto-type. Hauls forty bags, it's fast, and never tries to sleep with hotel guests."

"It's *motorized*, Gordon. You can't legally drive this on the streets."

"We're on that. Next summer. Here's the thing. We're proposing a baggage service. Found a crazy loop-hole in the city's written charter." He looked over at the man in black, now playing the expert. "City charter reads like a third-grader wrote it. Just *full* of vague claus-es." The man in black nodded, but it was clearly obligatory.

I needed a moment to process this. Gordon was,

understandably, not up to speed on the legacy of dock-portering, and even if he was, he'd probably find it all a bit childish. He was just sharing a statement of fact, unaware of how this might affect me and my brothers-in-arms. *Just business.*

He leaned in close with a salesman's winning grin. "Maybe you want to run it for us, Jack. Management track. Who knows the docks better than you? Make your old man proud."

"A luggage service that puts us all out of a job?" I shot back.

"Well. Everyone but you."

I took in a deep breath and exhaled. "A golf cart can never replace a dockporter. *Never.*"

A light smile touched his lips. He was unfazed. He fired up the cart and began a slow roll down the dock. Then he stopped and turned to the man in black. "Technically, he's right. We can't leave the dock. Let's walk. I'll show you around the offices. My dad's waiting."

The man in black looked around the dock with vague disgust. He pinched his nose from the aroma of distant horse crap. "This place stinks."

They climbed out of the cart and headed toward town. It occurred to me that Gordon's metamorphosis from unsteady, towheaded island boy to this streamlined force of nature was both impressive and sad. He just threatened the entire dockporter ecosystem while simul-taneously reminding me of my strained relationship with my dad. He may have become a jerk, but he was not an untalented jerk.

AJ approached from behind and put a brotherly arm on my shoulder. "Don't sweat it, Jacky," he said. "Every summer, the Whittakers try to get rid of us. And every summer, we magically reappear. Like that bad penny from *Somewhere in Time."* He acted out the scene. 'Richard? Richard! Richaaaard!!'"

AJ loved *Somewhere in Time* references and weaved them into conversation any chance he got. The movie was filmed on the island ten years earlier and was probably the closest he'd ever been to a real movie set.

Fly looked over. "Jack, you know that blond shit-bird from when you were kids. Why the disrespect?"

"I'm guessing the Whittakers think dockporters are out-of-control maniacs that threaten the classy veneer of the island." Fly took it in for a moment. "I can see that."

Spengler chimed in. "I think that's a gross misrepresentation, personally." Smitty called over. "So's this." He let out a long, loud, wet fart.

Jesus, I thought, *the Whittakers are right.*

I looked over to Spengler, who was watching Gordon and his mystery friend trot down the dock, deep in business chatter. He removed his notepad from his pocket and jotted down a few observations. He saw the same thing I did. The guy in the black jacket was, as we liked to say, "not Mackinac." We shared a look. Spengler was on the story. Whatever it was.

The 1:30 Boat from St. Ignace
  July 1, 1989

The dock was, again, awash in tourists. Every half hour, all day long, was a brand-new one-act play called *Tips.*

AJ, the actor, was devoid of any morals when it

came to charming hotel guests. I watched him from the corner of my eye as he appraised the approaching crowd of tourists like a master chef inspecting fresh produce. He reached into his pocket and pulled something out. He began talking to himself as if he were rehearsing lines backstage before opening night.

He pinned a plastic name tag to his hotel golf shirt. It read, *"Carlo Bologna: Bologna, Italy."* He took a deep breath. His face magically transformed from the cocky East Detroit Italian kid he was, to a forlorn immigrant boy. The toothy grin dropped, and he looked out toward the lake, willing himself to start missing his mama and papa in the Old Country. All that was missing to complete the act was a warm loaf of Italian bread in a leather rucksack.

AJ approached a family of four as the father, a balding man in a purple button-down, was reaching for a suitcase.

"Ello! You stay at Huron Inn?"

The man looked up. "Yes, we are."

"Benvenuta! My name is Carlo. I from Bologna, Italy. I haul the, how you say, sooot-cases? *In mi bee-ca-cleta. Inna da basket.* No?"

He pointed to his porter bike. The wife, a cute tennis mom, beamed, charmed instantly. In the late eighties, most Midwesterners didn't travel much. The idea of a real Italian to help them with their bags was nine levels of quaint, absolutely something to tell the downstate neighbors about when they returned.

"Oh, honey, look. Carlo! *He's Italian.*" Then to AJ, "Yes, these are all our bags."

"Bene, bene. I take them for you. You no worry. This issa my job. Go up to the street, turn right, pass-a

through town and the hotel is, ahhh, how you say it?" He looked over to me faux-helplessly, struggling for the phrase, forcing me to become an unwilling accomplice to his con-job. "Jack, how you say … I … my English is not so good."

I answered, without making eye contact with him to avoid breaking out in laughter and ruining his carefully constructed scene. "It's on the left past the Yacht Club. You'll see the sign," I called to the family, playing the helpful American friend.

"Essactly! On the left, past the Yacht Club! You see a sign. You go now! I catch up. *Go, go!"*

They smiled and shuffled off as AJ grinned, his eyes lingering for a moment too long on the long-legged collegiate daughter. She flashed a smile at him as she passed.

Carlo turned to me, satisfied, waiting for them to move out of earshot. "Aaaaand … *scene!*"

The boys gave him a respectful golf-clap and he took a bow, thanking his fans. "Grazie … grazie … grazie."

I turned away and quickly glanced down at my own notepad for today's check-ins. Unlike many of the other hotels, quaint inns, and guesthouses that sprung up like lilacs, my hotel was, well, a bit of a dump. But the price was right and, for many on a budget, it worked just fine. The Waterview Inn and Boarding House, affectionately known as the "WibHo," was unabashedly "old school" in every sense of the word.

The only time it ever became an issue was with honeymooners. Pre-internet, there was no checking a place out online. No posted reviews. No message boards. And for honeymooners—an uptight, horny demo-graphic on a good day—things could get dicey. When they realized that the room they'd be making sweet love in for the next three to five days housed a peculiar odor and rust stains in the bathtub, things sometimes got awkward.

And, of course, the first check-ins today were honeymooners. *The Wheelers*, according to my notes.

I spotted them instantly. Unlike most of the other couples, wandering and dazed, the Wheelers looked to be in love, with no hint of that married thousand-yard stare. I closed my eyes and threw some air punches, loosening my neck muscles like a boxer.

It was time for *me* to make some money.

CHAPTER FOUR

The Bet
July 1, 1989

I approached the Wheelers, feeling confident.

Unlike AJ, my bullshit was *real*. "The honey-mooners, right? The Wheelers?"

A woman with teased hair, wearing red plaid shorts and a pink blouse, smiled and nodded. "I knew it. You're glowing. Seriously! The island temperature went up ten degrees when you two got off the boat. I'm Jack. Welcome to Mackinac Island."

I shook the groom's hand sincerely. He looked to be in his late 30's. *Second marriage or a late starter?* Aside from a conspicuous toupee, he appeared a genuine sort of guy, just trying to give his new bride a taste of what was in store for her: a life of sunny summer getaways, responsible choices, and manly handshakes. I gave the Wheelers directions to the WibHo and pulled their luggage aside. All business. All charm. While Foster's assessment of my skill as a "tip man," not a "load man" may have stung at the time, I quickly moved past it. Hell. I *was* a tip man. If hospitality and first-rate service was a crime, then color me guilty. Ultimately, blackjack was just a physical act. A stunt, really. Like weightlifting or walking a high-wire. No finesse. All brawn, no brains.

As I sent the Wheelers off, I felt the presence of someone to my left, just out of my eye-line, blocked by the metal rim of my sunglasses. I turned to look. There, standing far too close, was a skinny kid wearing a blue University of Michigan T-shirt. His pale arms emerged from the sleeves like two popsicle sticks. He looked at me blankly as if waiting for enlightenment.

"Who are you?" I asked.

"I'm um … the new guy."

"The um … new guy?" I thought for a minute. The new guy? Were we expecting a new guy? I mean, there was the big Michigan football player, but this kid was— *ahh, shit. Tell me this isn't Bull.*

"You mean the new porter? That's impossible. The new porter plays football at Michigan."

"That's me!" he said cheerily. "Edwin Bulloski."

I looked him over. A stiff island breeze would have blown him right into Lake Huron. "No. Bull's a line-man. A big guy. You're just …"

"I'm a placekicker. Well, a backup. Well, a *walk-on* back-up." He reached out to shake my hand. I took it. It was as clammy and moist as a whitefish. I instantly scanned the dock, looking for Fly. He was in the process of configuring a massive load of luggage in the basket of his bike.

"Fly! Here he is! Your very own servant. Show *Bull* the ropes!"

Fly peered from behind the suitcases and stared dumbly at the skinny kid for a full seven seconds, as did every other porter on the dock. A fresh, warm stench of disappointment wafted over the team.

"That's Bull?" asked Fly. He looked closer at him. "You're Bull?"

"My name is Edwin."

I patted Bull on the shoulder, grinning. "Show him the ropes, Fly," I said. "He's rarin' to go."

Fly shook it off and resumed loading up, down-shifting effortlessly into backtrack mode. "Ropes? Dude, I said that *ropes* shit when I thought he was a big ol' Polish-ass *My Bodyguard*-lookin' dude. You named him; you own him. Bull meet Jack."

Fly attached the 'over-the-topper' bungee cord and kicked off with his luggage, muttering to himself as he hopped on the seat of his bike.

"Lil' shit ain't goin' anywhere near *my* ropes. My ropes are precious. These are my ropes. I ain't givin' away my ropes. *Shit* …" And off he went on his bike, rambling on about *ropes*.

I placed the last of the Wheelers' suitcases in a small pile and looked them over. Bull hovered. My bike was still duct-taped to the flagpole, so I pulled out a Swiss Army knife from my pocket and handed it to him.

He looked at it blankly, likely wondering what the hell he'd gotten himself into when he filled out the job application last winter and blindly checked 'dockporter.'

"Cut my bike down." Bull followed my gaze. He took it in and nodded solemnly, taking the knife and trudging off toward the flagpole.

I thought to myself: *Well, at least he's obedient.*

Some moments that unfolded that summer came alive only through the retelling. AJ's love affair with the actress was one of those moments. I wasn't there, as I was occupied with riding the Wheeler's luggage to the WibHo. But I'm told it went something like this:

After AJ sent off the family of four with his immigrant boy act, he wandered back to the luggage cart for scraps. Maybe a redcap.

A redcap was an open load, an untagged piece of luggage not marked for any of the island's main hotels. This luggage was destined for one of the smaller hotels or inns that didn't have a full-time porter. Occasionally a redcap was headed for one of the sprawling cottages on the West Bluff, where the fattest wallets resided. These were the *real* prize loads.

Mackinac Island dockporters were brothers. But brothers fight. A redcap load could mean the difference between a decent day, financially speaking, and a *great* day. Most of these maniacs were putting themselves through college or paying off some future gambling debt. So, when untagged luggage rolled up, small fangs emerged with an audible *shhhk*.

Money turns honorable men into jackals, and we were no exception. Rookies were tossed into the lake for pinching redcaps from veterans. Teeth were dislodged, and porter bikes systematically dismantled as retribution for redcap larceny.

AJ spotted a beautiful set of matching Louis Vuitton,

seemingly brand new, with no hotel tags. His heart skipped three beats, and he quietly began singing the familiar Kingsmen tune, which had a different meaning for luggage handlers: *Louie Louie.*

Louis Vuitton was the cream of the crop and a rare sight in the eighties. When an iconic brand like Louie revealed itself, radiant among the dull pile of scuffed Samsonite and faded duffels, their iconic golden logos had the same effect on us that gold nuggets must have had on stinky California prospectors in 1849. *Mesmerizing.*

Anyone who traveled with Louie had money and wanted people to know it. *Big tippers.* AJ was salivating. He pulled the precious bags off the cart and stealthily slid them behind a bale of hay, out of the eye line of his greedy pals. It was a questionable maneuver, strictly speaking, but we all did it.

AJ waited for his connection, practically quivering with anticipation. He scrutinized the passengers, looking for the telltale pink Izod shirt or salt-and-pepper rich-man hair of the vacationing industrialist. *Nothing.* This was an average-looking boatload of passengers, and they were dwindling. Who would pack this kind of luggage and not claim it quickly? He checked his watch. He was behind. The clock was running out on this score.

Then, through the crowd—in slow motion and illuminated by a perfect, golden backlight—emerged an *Actual Movie Star.* Even under a floppy straw hat and sunglasses, AJ recognized her. His jaw dropped. Without hesitation, she walked straight up to him. She was chewing gum and talking fast.

"Hi. Have you seen five pieces of Louis Vuitton? I'm renting the Hammond Cottage. Do you know it? I know,

I overpacked. But I didn't wanna freeze, I didn't wanna sweat, and I needed the knock-around resort wear but didn't wanna be too matchy-matchy. I got confused. So, yeah." She looked him over. "What happens now?"

AJ finally spoke. "You're … Candace Layne." Then, whispering, *"The actress."*

She smiled conspiratorially. "I am? Because I read in the Hollywood trade papers that she was in seclusion after a string of terrible reviews, one that called her acting 'comically tedious.' Feeling me?"

"Um. No," responded AJ.

She smiled. It was dazzling. "You're cute. And dumb. I like that. What I'm telling you is to keep your mouth shut. I'm here to escape, and Santorini was booked. You spill the beans about me on this island, and we're never going to be friends. Feeling me now?"

AJ took a deep breath and threw caution to the wind. "I'd like to be feeling you now."

"That's just a *really* offensive line. You're hired." She pointed at the pile of Louis. "Those are my bags."

AJ got to work. "I'm an actor too," he said, as he placed her bags in a line and straddled his bike. She was inspecting her surroundings, taking in the island for the first time.

"And how's that going?" she asked, absently working her gum.

"Good. I do local theater. Extra work for the news. Some hand modeling." AJ began loading her bags. She watched him, intrigued, removing her sunglasses with a flourish and a grin. AJ noticed the move. It was the exact same gesture he'd seen in one of her movies, a miracle of perfect teeth and sparkling energy.

"I know that move," said AJ, hoisting up another

suitcase. "*New York Dream.* When you first meet the sarcastic Aussie at the Chinese underground chess tournament."

"Yes! That's exactly right." She put her shades back and repeated the move with even more flair, this time with her signature line from the film. "Should I call this … *check-mate?*"

"That's it! You were fantastic in that movie," said AJ, lifting the final bag on the load, plopping it on top and attaching a bungee cord. She was shading her eyes now, watching him, charmed, her actorly ticks and false bravado melting away. They locked eyes for a little too long.

"I think I like this place," she said, nodding. And for the first time in longer than she could remember, her smile was real.

———

Meanwhile, I was riding toward the WibHo, trying to shake Bull but knowing, as Fly had wisely pointed out, he was my problem now. Bull was riding hard on a red Raleigh ten-speed with drop-down bars, weaving through the Main Street traffic, terrified but exhilarated. I focused on getting far enough ahead of the Wheelers to execute a quick pit stop for some small-time hucksterism. I pulled out my walkie-talkie as I rode.

"Foster. It's Jack. Prep some dummy bags, I got a *triple L.*"

Bull looked over, curious. I filled him in. "Triple L: *light-looking load.*"

"I see," he said, as if it meant anything to him.

Three minutes later, I glided to a halt in front of the Chippewa Hotel, halfway to my destination.

Bull watched, fascinated, as Foster effortlessly manipulated the suitcases in my basket. He added four more bags and handed me the over-the-topper bungee. Bull continued to observe.

"Wow. You're strong," he said. Foster looked over. "These bags here? They make looking strong easy. *They're empty.* Because Jack here doesn't like pulling up with a dinky load in his basket. No, our boy is in it for the show."

"No. I'm in it for the *dough*," I shot back.

"It appears your new mentor is also a poet, Bull." He patted the load twice. "*Go.* Stick the landing."

I pushed off and quickly slid my ass onto the seat. I was back on the road with a load of suitcases that was far more tip-worthy. I continued my lesson. "I'm taking this to the WibHo. That's where I work. The brochure calls it 'quaint.' That's a stretch. Scoring tips is tough. This brings me to lesson one: They gotta see you ride it. That's where the cash is."

Bull nodded. If he could've taken notes while riding a ten-speed, he would've. The kid was a sponge.

I glided to a halt in front of the WibHo. The place was built as employee housing in the late 1900s and existed in various incarnations ever since. For decades it endured the wicked abuse of thousands of drunken, rowdy college students living on the island to make some money for the summer. This crowd worked hard and played harder. The WibHo was legendary for its loud, late-night parties and became synonymous with island debauchery.

Sometime in the early 1970s, it fell into the hands of

Trina LaFromme, a French-Chippewa local. She inherited the weathered, rambling house from her husband, who was killed in a hunting accident when she was just seventeen. With no other source of income, she quickly kicked the college kids out, patched up the holes, slapped up some floral wallpaper, and rebranded the place as an "inn." She still rented a few rooms to select summer workers, but mostly it was a hotel. An old, shitty hotel.

"I mistimed my arrival. But I got the owner, Trina, trained like a Golden Retriever," I said to Bull. "We go back."

Moments later, the Wheelers, accompanied by Trina, came through the squeaky, spring-loaded front door to watch. Trina was a purple vision in scarves and red lipstick, clickety-clacking on high heels, even though her days of wearing high heels should have been long over. I could always count on her to usher the guests out at the exact moment I pulled in. She may have been seventy-something, but she understood the nuances of the hustle better than any dockporter ever would. It was no accident Trina held onto the place this long, despite a myriad of economic downturns for both herself and the state of Michigan. Plus, she liked me. Rumor had it, she and my grandfather had a summer fling back when they were both young and wild, but I was never going to follow up on that story. *Way* too weird.

Mr. Wheeler pulled out his camera and took a few pictures as I pretended to struggle to unload the light-as-air dummy suitcases, followed by their bags.

"Got a light?" He laughed out loud at his own lame joke.

"Ha! That's a good one, Mr. Wheeler. But no, I don't smoke."

"It's amazing you rode all that luggage on your bike!"

"All in a day's work." I turned and flashed a smile. "It's what we do."

A sideways glance behind my shades was positive confirmation. Mr. Wheeler absently patted his left ass cheek wallet pocket. It was a critical tell.

The Wheelers followed me up the stairs to their room. The WibHo hadn't changed much in the hundred years since its construction. The wallpaper was stained, the carpet was worn, and the entire place was covered in the dusty, fine sheen of something ancient.

The room key was bent, and unlocking the door took the patience of a safe-cracker. I made small talk and gently coerced the key, willing it to surrender the familiar "slide-and-click" sound. Bull followed us up and was hovering back, watching the scene unfold. It was odd, yet somehow endearing. *Learn on the job.* Poor kid hadn't moved his gear into employee housing, yet here he was, observing my intimate tap dance with the Wheelers.

Finally, I hockey-checked the door and it flew open. I burst in, Kramer-style. The Wheelers walked in slowly after me and looked doubtfully around the tiny room, solemn as pallbearers.

"This is the honeymoon suite?" asked Mrs. Wheeler. She was now looking at her groom with rising anguish. He glanced out the window, avoiding her withering gaze.

"Indeed, it is," I replied, seeing that this was *not*

going to be an easy close. No two ways about it. They were appalled. Something needed to be done, and fast.

"The room was recently redone by a world-famous Asian designer," I said. "He's a minimalist. His name is …"

I trailed off, unsure from what black hole the lie had sprung. *Asian designer?* I glanced over at Mr. Wheeler's lousy hairpiece.

"… Mai … ummm … Topai." *My toupee? Shit!*

Mr. Wheeler looked over, unsure if he heard me right. He shook his head and let it go. He had more serious issues to deal with. "The brochure showed a water view," he said.

"Of course! Right over here." I led them to a dirty window and pointed. "See that strip of blue over there? Past the roof?"

Mrs. Wheeler leaned forward and looked out the window, her nose nearly smushing against the glass. "That's a rain tarp," she said.

"No, no," I said. "To the right. See it sparkling? Right above the dumpster over there? See it?"

"No. I don't."

It was all going south. It was an eternity since Mr. Wheeler touched his wallet pocket. There was no choice but to dust off an old chestnut. A spiel that was passed down from dockporter to dockporter for a hundred years. It was a standard, run-of-the-mill hail Mary, but it was worth a shot.

"How much time do you spend in your room anyway?"

Wheeler turned and stared as if he were dealing with a three-year-old. He spoke slowly. "This is our *honeymoon.*"

The tip, so carefully cultivated, from the light bags, the theatrics, the banter, Trina's coordinated timing—all of it was circling the drain. But Bull was watching and, if nothing else, I needed to impart to the rookie the importance of perseverance.

I turned to the Wheelers. "Okay. So the room's ... *unique*. And you know what? So are you. You two don't do it like everyone else. Same bullshit 'honeymoon special' every other couple gets. Same beach in St. Barts. Same fruity drinks. Same weirdo snorkeling guide with the three-legged dog. You come home, you take a look at your pictures, and they're exactly the same as every other honeymoon couple's."

They were warming up. The rap was working. I charged ahead.

"So, the room's different. You know why? *It's alive.* Full of energy. Full of spirits. History. Magic. Can you feel it?"

Mrs. Wheeler looked at her new husband with eyes wide. "I think I do," she said.

"Bull, you feel it?" They looked over at Bull, who was standing in the doorway. They hadn't even noticed he was in the room.

He gave me a *who, me?* Then two thumbs-up. "Actually, yeah. I do. I mean, yeah. It's really like ..."

"That's enough," I said, cutting him off before he said something stupid and blew the moment.

"So, forget about the lake view, the crappy carpeting, the door lock that never works. That's all part of it. I've spent every summer of my life on this island, and I can tell you, you're now a part of this place. Forget the flaws. *Tap into the magic.*"

Boom! They were sold. It was time to take a bow and

exit stage left. Mr. Wheeler pulled a twenty from his wallet and handed it over. I pretended it was too much, took it anyway, and got the hell out of there. Mackinac Island was taking hold, and the honeymooners needed some alone time.

I gently closed the door until I heard it click and turned around. There, standing in the hallway, was the beautiful Irish woman from the dock. Bull had propped the door open, and she stopped to listen to the tail end of my spiel from the hallway.

"Do you believe all that ..." she struggled for the right words and then fell back into her Dublin slang, "that ... holy show? About the magic and the history?"

I shrugged. "I may not believe all that." I held up the twenty-dollar bill. "But I believe all *this*." I pulled the twenty tight with a snap. "You live here?" I asked.

She nodded and pointed at the next door over, pulling out a set of keys. "It's the Waterview Inn and Boarding House. I'm boarding." She unlocked the door without a hitch and turned back. "By the way, it's rude to take people's pictures without their consent." She turned around and disappeared into her room, shutting the door behind her.

Bull looked at me, raising his eyebrows. For some reason, I felt the need to explain. "We know each other. I took her picture because ..."

Bull raised a stalling hand. Then he slowly pointed toward the door of the honeymoon suite. We could both hear the telltale sounds of bedsprings starting to creak.

"Can we ... *leave?*" he asked.

As I came down the stairs, I could hear the very agitated voice of Trina. "I'm not selling. This is my *home!*"

I peered around the corner. Standing in the lobby holding Trina's phone was the island's newest entrepreneur, Gordon Whittaker, a Ralph Lauren sweater tied casually around his waist. Sitting on an old leather sofa was the same out-of-towner, the man in black from the golf cart earlier in the day, inscrutable as ever. He wasn't quite pinching his nose this time but looked vaguely bored as he watched Trina click-clacking across the oak floor. His head was cocked to the side and he was absently tapping a rhythm on a leather briefcase on his lap.

Gordon held Trina's rotary phone in one hand, nearly chasing her around the lobby, pleading, the phone cord restricting his attack range like a pit bull's chain.

"Trina. A woman your age should not be washing linens at a broken-down boarding house—one sec." He spoke into the phone.

"Tell him no hard feelings but he needs to *grow balls*." Then back to Trina. "Sorry. I have a deal in Harbor Springs that's gone just silly. Anyway, I have a party interested in this place. They want to take it upscale."

Trina was appalled at the implication. "This *is* upscale!"

Gordon glanced over at the man in black, making a show of rolling his eyes.

"Upscale. Right. Maybe in Manila. One sec—" Back into the phone, livid. "You're a child, Jonesy! Tell that partner of yours that this is *my* deal. If he wants to set up shop in Traverse City, he should break ground

there!" Then, he switched back to Trina, instantly serene as a Buddhist.

"I know all about your tax issue. Do you want to
hand this place over to Uncle Sam?" He effortlessly
shifted into empathy mode. It was convincing as hell. An
Oscar-winning performance. "I'm just trying to help
you."

Gordon noticed me standing on the landing. He
instantly brightened. If anyone could vouch for the
dicey economic realities of Trina's precious little dump,
it was me. "Jack. Explain it to her."

I walked down the stairs slowly, Bull trailing. "He's
right," I said.

Gordon nodded, smiling. "Listen to Jack, Trina. He's
a smart guy."

I walked toward her. "You work too hard to let
anyone take it away."

"That's exactly what I've been telling her." Gordon
positively beamed.

"… particularly the Whittakers," I added.

Gordon spun around and glared at me, then turned
back to Trina.

"Don't listen to Jack, Trina! He's just a goddamn
bellman on a bike! What does he know about taxes or
property values or profit-loss scenarios that might affect
…"

But it was too late. He'd opened the door. I simply
strolled through it. "You provide a service, Trina," I
said. "Not everybody can afford the fancy hotels. Listen
to them up there." The sounds of moans and bed creaks
from upstairs were now impossible not to notice. The
Wheelers were not wasting any time. I continued, "You
hear that? You probably helped spawn a generation in

those creaky old beds. Someday they're going to bring *their* kids to the island. And their kids will bring *their* kids. On it goes, right?"

With that line, I knew I had her.

On it goes.

It was a line Gramps uttered hundreds of times. To anyone with deep connections to the island, it was a phrase loaded with meaning. Mackinac Island was as precious as fine china, passed down with caution and delicacy, and only by people who loved it. That's how it survived so far. But we all knew nothing was guaranteed. The future was a big, dumb monster, lurking just seven miles across Lake Huron, waiting. Ready to pounce and smash it all to pieces.

Trina softened, looking through the smudged front window as a team of horses clip-clopped past, pulling a buggy full of tourists. She turned to me. "How is the mayor?"

"He sends his love."

"He's a good man, your gramps. A damn scoundrel, but a good man." She walked over and touched my sunburned cheek lightly.

"You remind me of him."

"The 'good man' part or the 'scoundrel' part?"

"Good question. Both?" She smiled, then turned away and wandered to a dusty bookshelf, stopping to take in a framed black-and-white image of her younger self. 1930s maybe? No more than twenty, young and wild, sexy even, dressed in flapper fashion and ready for a night out. She picked up the frame and considered it.

Gordon covered the phone and watched her, cautious, awaiting a response, a frozen smile on his face.

She carefully set the frame back on the shelf and

turned toward Gordon. Almost sweetly she said: "Outta my hotel, you quiche-eating little turd." She pointed at the man in black. "And take Johnny-fucking-Cash with you."

Outside the WibHo, I meticulously reattached a stray bungee cord to my basket. A dangling cord tangled in the front spokes while in transit could mean an ugly face-plant, and an uglier moment at the bar later trying to explain it all. Gordon burst out the screen door and charged at me, his face flushed.

"Thanks for the backup, pal! You know she has to sell. If you don't want to help her, you could at least stay the hell out of it."

I continued the reattachment process, not looking up. "I never imagined you harassing old ladies. What happened to you, Gordon?"

He looked at me incredulously. "I grew up. Joined the family business. You should try it."

"What's next? A bullet train to Fort Holmes? You and your family are going to sink this place."

I looked back down to arrange more bungee cords. What was it about *change* that hung me up so much? It was almost an obsession. From my earliest memories, I had never taken the unique charm of the island for granted. When we were kids, everything on the island was a little faded and cracked. Buildings sagged a little. It was a tourist island to be sure, but it was a tourist island with dirty fingernails. Other than Grand Hotel, which catered to the affluent, Mackinac Island was like a friendly, unkempt best friend. Gordon represented my worst fear: that well-trained, MBA-infected business minds would upgrade my island, and in the process paint over my memories.

Gordon shook his head. "You're the wrong guy to be giving the eco-warrior speech. Look at you." He gave me a dubious once-over. "Hungover. Bar stamps up to your elbow." I didn't look up, so he continued. "You know, a couple hundred years ago, the Chippewa were smoking peace pipes in teepees right where we're standing. Now look." He indicated the WibHo. "It's a hotel. And you seem fine with that. You know, you draw a pretty convenient line in the sand where everybody else has to stop what they're doing. But guess what? That's not the way it works."

Was Gordon taking philosophy classes at Yale? I didn't recall him ever being this insightful.

He looked at the remaining bags in my basket and randomly grabbed the handle of a large suitcase. It weighed nothing. He rolled his eyes. "Empty bag. Typical. You were always a bit of a bullshitter. Think you'll ever ride blackjack, or is this little con-job enough?"

I turned to face him. "Leave Trina alone."

———

Bull, who was quiet the whole time, rode next to me. The kid witnessed some solid drama and didn't even have his name tag yet. I still didn't know much about him, but I felt oddly close after this last skirmish. I stood up on my bike pedals, coasting for a stretch as we passed Ste. Anne's Church. A gang of seagulls congregated on the veranda of the old wood edifice and scrounged for scraps.

Finally, Bull broke the ice. "Is that guy back there a friend of yours?"

"We used to be great friends." We rode a little further as the words hung in the air. In the distance, the cannon suddenly *boomed* like it did every hour on the hour. Bull, spooked, swerved.

"What the hell was that?"

I smiled. "That's the cannon demonstration at Fort Mackinac. They have it all up there. Cannons, muskets. Guided tours." I looked over. Bull was taking it all in as we passed Victorian homes with sprawling views of the harbor.

"This place is pretty fantastic so far. I can see why you like it so much."

"You're right. It is fantastic. You're gonna have the best summer of your life."

We rode on, past the broad expanse of green grass that made up Marquette Park. A 25-foot statue of the legendary missionary and explorer kept a watchful eye over a mix of tourist families and summer workers on break flinging frisbees and kicking hacky-sack footbags. Ferry boat horns honked. Little kids shrieked. The sky was impossibly blue.

Suddenly, I swerved in the middle of the street, nearly cutting off a young couple riding a tandem. I called back to Bull. "Go get yourself situated. I need to do something!"

I pedaled hard back to the WibHo. Gordon was still standing outside, chatting with the man in black. I rode straight toward him, laying down a screeching skid, and stopped inches away from the curb. He looked up, unfazed.

"Hey, look who's back. The dockporter. Forget an empty suitcase?"

"You wanna play blackjack? Let's do it. A bet. Like the old days."

Gordon was listening. "Continue."

"I ride twenty-one bags before the end of the summer, dockporters stay on bikes and you leave us alone. No golf carts. No luggage service. Ever."

He looked at the empty bags in my basket. "Twenty-one *legit* bags," he scoffed dismissively. "You know, with stuff in 'em."

"Of course," I said.

"And if … sorry, *when* you don't ride twenty-one?"

I took a deep breath. Time to cross the Rubicon. "Next summer, I'll run your luggage service, just like you asked. You're right. You'll need an experienced dock-porter to make it work."

"Suit and tie, Jack. This is a desk job. You're clear on that?" Gordon looked at me sideways, searching my face for a tell. There wasn't one.

"Yeah. I'm clear."

Gordon nodded. "You're on. But if anyone finds out? Bet's off. My dad hates it when I gamble with a sure thing. This bet stays between us."

I extended my hand. We shook. Instinctively, it was the same *Happy Days* meets *Good Times* handshake from the old days, betting on fudge and hockey pucks.

But this time it was grim.

As I rode away, it dawned on me what I had just done. I was gambling with something precious. If I didn't ride twenty-one bags, it was all over. I'd take the miserable management position with the Whittakers and run their stupid luggage service. After my tour of duty in a jacket and tie, I'd likely head off to the mainland to do ... *who knows what.*

And just like the fisherman, the tribal chief, the fur trader, and the fort soldier, the dockporter—as an occupation and a way of life—would vanish into the fog of island history.

And it would all be my fault.

CHAPTER FIVE

Studying
   July 5, 1989

I wasn't much of a student, but riding twenty-one bags would take next-level knowledge about weight ratios and physics. If I was going to be a *load man*, I'd have to learn how. And fast.

Per my promise with Gordon, I kept the bet to myself. But my increased interest in riding bigger and bigger loads caught the crew's attention. The topic of balance permeated conversations in the morning, cutting into the normal quarter-pitching, time-wasting antics. What's the secret to countering the weight of twenty-one (full) suitcases in the basket? How do you avoid being launched into a steaming pile of horse shit the moment you push off? It was a quandary. I weighed 165 pounds, solidly average, and gorging on Ball Park Franks would never transform me into a suitable counterweight. Besides, we rode a good fifty miles a day on one-speed bikes. Even with our beer consumption—which was substantial—nobody on this crew was gaining weight.

In the beginning, our balance technique studies focused mainly on the developing world. Spengler brought in a stack of dusty, faded *National Geographic* magazines he found in the Murray Hotel's storage bins. He earmarked articles featuring indigenous tribes of sub-Saharan Africa, with women balancing all manner of items on their heads, on poles, and on their backs.

We passed the magazines around between boats, debating the methods these acrobats employed, trying in vain to avoid getting derailed by the fact that they were often topless. While we prided ourselves on being gentlemen, it was difficult not to comment. Then we moved into a Sherpa phase. The Nepalese madmen who lugged gear up Mount Everest contained something in their DNA that made them superstuds. If a Nepalese Sherpa moved to Mackinac Island to become a dockporter, he would be the top tip-earner every day of the week and twice on Sunday, and the blackjack list on the side of the freight shack would be carved up with names like Aapu, Yamit, and Jagbir. That depressing reality was of no help, but it was interesting to ponder.

Foster had been to the Philippines. He showed us a series of Polaroids he took of locals on motorcycles loaded with entire families plus food supplies for a month. Generations piled on a decrepit Honda, heading up a mountain road. Tiny kids, grandmas, the whole lot. If they could balance nine people on one motorcycle, there might be hope for me.

Fly was an engineering student and showed up one

morning with a schematic he'd drawn up in a late-night burst of inspiration. We studied the onion-thin paper with the perfect lines and arrows in awe. Smitty took in the intricate drawings. "Fly, you have the best hand-writing I've ever seen in my life."

"That's pretty much all you learn in engineering school, Smitty. How to make perfect capital letters." He stood up on the luggage cart, pretending to lecture to an imaginary class full of MIT eggheads.

"Now class …" he announced, mock professorial. "Freehand lettering should be in the gothic style, and the line thickness should be consistent. Either straight gothic with vertical strokes perpendicular to the baseline, or inclined gothic, with vertical strokes at seventy-five degrees. Why these rules? I have NO idea."

He hopped off the cart. "I swear, my brothers, someday I'll do something interesting with these useless skills."

Spengler frowned. "Looks good on paper. But I don't think it'll ever work. Too top-heavy."

Fly nodded, not bothering to disagree. "Yeah. I just felt like drawing something." We collectively threw our hands up and walked away, our time sufficiently wasted.

One of the guys constructed a huge, homemade Jenga puzzle out of discarded two-by-fours, theorizing it might help us master balancing skills. It soon took over the usual quarter-pitching rituals, although we still bet a five-spot on every round. The problem was, every time it collapsed, it scared the crap out of the draft horses. Literally. An agitated Rick made us stop the game, as he was the one charged with scooping up the mess.

It all helped. I started to look at the world differently. I never paid much attention to the way things fit together. A house was a house. You lived there. A bike was a bike. You rode it. But this amateur immersion therapy made riding twenty-one suitcases feel possible.

———————

Dumps
   July 13, 1989

Bull had the spark. Beating deep in that skin-and-bones facade was a real dockporter heart. I could see it in his intelligent eyes. He was a learner, and for a talker like myself, that was critical. Sure, we all wanted a big, strong lineman type to do the heavy lifting, but Bull was finding his own way. How can you not secretly pull for a back-up kicker?

Mid-afternoons, when check-ins were pouring off the ferries in D-Day-like waves, I worked with him, demonstrating the right way to self-load. The lingo. The pitfalls. The tricks.

"These are wings. They hang off to the side. They make an unbalanced child like you into a tank." I helped him hang two suitcases on the side of his empty basket, using a bungee cord to attach them to the metal wire of his too-new, hotel-issued porter bike basket.

"Feels heavy," he said, eyeing the two bags doubtfully.

"No. It's perfect. A work of art. And a perfect load rides itself. You'll know when you got one. The sun shines brighter, the sky's bluer, and those college girls look at you in a whole new light."

Fly chimed in as he loaded up a large bag. "Art?

Naw, man. It's engineering. Dynamic equilibrium. Basic physics and weight ratio. Shit like that."

Bull looked over. "Where'd you get so smart, Fly?"

"MIT, Bull-dog. Hundred and sixty pounds of skinny-ass engineering meat." He broke into a laugh and rode off toward Main Street to test his theories on Newtonian physics. Or was it quantum?

I handed Bull the longest bungee cord, and he pulled it over the load of bags, attaching it to the stem of his handlebars. "Two riding positions in this game," I said. "Position one: ass-on-seat, arms-on-bars. Position two ..."

A few other porters piped in: *"Dead!"*

I looked Bull straight in the eye. "Once you push off, get your ass on the seat quick, or you'll be chewing Samsonite. If you have any teeth left."

He nodded, compliant as a Marine recruit, and pushed off. He wobbled until he got moving fast enough to compensate for the nuance of gravity. I followed him with my eyes like a proud drill sergeant. Yup, the kicker was going to be okay.

I began loading up my own ride.

"Reminds me of another greenie I trained four summers ago." I looked toward the voice. Just inside the freight shack, Foster was lounging on a makeshift La-Z-Boy he'd crafted from four bales of hay left behind by one of the horse-drawn freight carriages, known around the island as "drays." Dressed in his teal blue Chippewa Hotel polo and cargo shorts, he was scanning a hand-written letter. Arranged neatly on another hay bale was a can of Vernors ginger ale, a half-eaten Twinkie, and an open roll of Velamints.

"I was never *that* scrawny," I said.

"Maybe, but I bet you can't boot a football forty-five yards either. Technically speaking? He's better than you."

"That's true," I said, hooking the end of the bungee around the stem of my handlebar.

"That's true *what?*" he added with a smile.

"That's true … *master,*" I responded.

"Why thank you, grasshopper." He looked up. "Remember that Latina maid from the Chip a few summers back? Real spicy. Didn't speak any English?"

"She got deported, right?" I asked.

"That's the one. Fake green card. Anyway. We had a little fling. She taught me how to make guacamole. Among other things. Now she's sending me letters." He waved the letter like a flag.

"What's she got to say?"

"I don't understand a word of it," he said. "I still can't speak the most basic Spanish. But I got a hunch Señor Johnson might be bilingual." He grabbed his crotch and cackled.

"You're an indecent man, Foster," I said.

"That I am, Jack. That … I … *am.*"

Foster returned to his missive as Smitty moved over to help me.

"Give me the two train cases," I said. "I'll go double wings. The clubs can sit in the V."

Smitty finished the job. "Nice one, boss. Where ya headed?"

"The Annex, by way of the West Bluff."

"Ride a load," he said. It was a standard call.

"Buck a bag," I responded. It was a standard response. I pushed off. The mountain of bags began to move.

I meant what I said to Bull. It *was* art. It was something the Gordon Whittakers of the world would never understand. Dockporters painted movable landscapes that reached to the sky. Our canvas was a Schwinn with a basket and the strongest bungee cords money could buy. The paints? American Tourister, Samsonite, Hartmann, Louis Vuitton, Eagle Creek, Travelpro. We hauled it all.

So the question was simple: Why would Gordon, or anyone else, want to rid the world of such a profoundly inspired creation?

I pedaled down Market Street and made the curving right-hand turn past the drive-it-yourself buggy rental toward the Annex by way of Grand Hotel. For obvious reasons, every load that summer felt like the last. Who was I kidding? I wasn't a Sherpa. I wasn't ushering climbers up Everest. I was delivering hinged, rectangular-shaped containers full of shorts, flowered shirts, undies, and aftershave.

Behind my scratched, fake Ray-Bans, my eyes were burning from the sweat dripping off my forehead. But taking a hand off the bars even for an instant to wipe it away would mean almost certain death. The hotel got closer, and I could hear the familiar clinking glasses and tasteful murmuring of the after-lunch cocktail hour.

Grand Hotel—or simply "the Grand" to locals— was a legendary hotel in the Midwest. Built at the turn of the century, its stunning six-hundred-foot-long porch overlooked the straits. Five Presidents had stayed there. So had Madonna, Thomas Edison, and Mark Twain. It was, quite simply, one of the most beautiful hotels in the world.

But for dockporters, there was a flip side. It could be, as Smitty liked to ungracefully put it, "kind of a snob-atorium." A totally unfair assessment, and as I got older, I began to appreciate everything about the place. Its traditions, all from another age and refined from a century of success, were pure.

Perhaps the real issue underpinning our judgment was much simpler: The Grand didn't hire dockporters on bikes. Instead, they transported luggage with private, horse-drawn drays branded with the fancy *GH* logo.

It made perfect sense, really. Their old-world sensibilities didn't exactly mesh with ours, which was more street hustle than champagne and strawberries. A buck a bag. Hell, we'd haul a rucksack of rotten eggs if we could strap it down and the price was right.

The Grand? They had a no-tipping policy. *A no-tipping policy?* What's the point of getting up in the morning if there's no tip in your future? So, we pricked, poked, and prodded whenever possible. It was all a pretty silly, *Caddyshack* stance looking back. We were just annoyed we'd never get our greedy mitts on all that expensive, tip-generating luggage.

What a complete waste.

I pushed hard up the hill that led toward the West Bluff and calculated my route. The hotel controlled the road that ran the length of their long veranda. The last thing they wanted was a sweaty downtown dockporter doing a circus act in front of the afternoon guests.

So, obviously, that's the route I chose.

Quickly avoiding the hotel guard, who was preoccupied giving directions to a family of four, I swerved right, swerved left, and was in the clear. He may have seen me through the corner of his eye, but he didn't give chase. Pedaling past the porch, I caught a glimpse of guests promenading eight feet or so above street level. It was mostly feet I saw. Loafers. Pink socks. Sperry Top-Siders. I was also immersed in the sound of classical music.

It was lovely. And yes. I just said "lovely." There is no other word to describe what I heard that day. I craned my neck, now intrigued, to get a glimpse of the source of this magical sound. It was oddly familiar, an echo of something I recognized. I knew this song, which was odd, because I wouldn't know Mozart if he played second base for the Tigers. Then it hit me.

It was *Metallica.*

As this was the Grand, I was reasonably sure not one person on that porch recognized the tune. Whoever was playing it was pulling off a magnificent fast one, in a Mackinac Island sort of way. It became critical that I see this rebel, perhaps even more critical than the luggage I was being paid to deliver in the basket of my bike.

I stood up on my pedals as I rode, but the pillars blocked my view. I was now splitting my attention between the porch and the road, a technique generally not found in any dockporter manual under "best practices," but I'd done it a thousand times. The music got closer and more distinct.

And there she was.

The Irish woman from the dock, playing … something. It looked like a large violin. A cello? She was deep into the music, wearing a simple dress with a red scarf and classy shoes, her ebony hair pulled back. And *sunglasses.*

I watched her play, entranced, no longer paying the slightest attention to the road in front of me. She happened to glance down to the road. She was seeing me in my element, loaded down with luggage, struggling but totally in control. An athlete of sorts. If you squint. And I was seeing her. An artist, playing her music the way she wanted to. Rebelling, but in her own personal, exceedingly sexy way. There was a bolt of electricity that passed between us, the likes of which I've never felt again.

At least that's the way I remember it.

"Look out!" I heard a kid scream. Then a thud. The impact was shocking but not life-threatening. A blond boy on a Sting-Ray coming from the opposite direction bounced off my basket, lost his balance for a moment, and continued on his merry way. I never saw him coming. But of course I didn't. I was too busy flexing my latissimus dorsi muscles and struggling to appear both cultured *and* virile.

The damage was done. The little maniac grazed a load of luggage that was meticulously stacked and balanced. The slightest impact would send it spinning off into its own orbit. And spin off, it did. I leaned left to compensate. Too much. Then to the right. The cooler slipped. The weight pulled me hard in the opposite direction.

I turned again to regain balance, getting off my seat. *Terrible idea.* It felt like slow motion, which, incidentally, all great luggage dumps do, but it probably took only seconds. I was now riding a bike on my front wheel only. It didn't last long. One pedal stroke later and I was in the air, launched. The bike and precious payload landed with a crash of metal and luggage, locking me into place in a horrible snarl.

It was a pretty spectacular dump. The front porch crowd gasped. The young kids laughed and pointed, and the older ladies tossed out a few *oh, dear me's.*

And the music stopped.

I couldn't move. My right leg was bent backward, my left arm tangled between the bike's frame and a large piece of lime-green American Tourister. I struggled to escape, then paused, thinking back on a documentary I'd seen on Houdini, which suggested that relaxation was the key to his success as an escape artist. Or was it an early Woody Allen movie? Didn't matter. I was trapped.

When you've been in the game for more than a few summers, "dump stories" can take on the golden hue of legend. Die-hard porters will never let a good dump story go to waste. They circulate them at the bars and docks until they calcify around you like a necklace made of hardened dog crap. But after two seasons, dumps were no longer acceptable.

Rookies dump, not crusty vets.

"So. You found your bike." There it was again. *That accent.*

I turned my dirty face toward the sky and was blinded by the summer sun. How does one hold a casual conversation in that position? I did my best. "Yeah, as a matter of fact, I did. The guys taped it to the flagpole. *Ha-ha.*" I laughed weakly.

"I saw it. Didn't know it was yours." She reached down and pulled a suitcase off the pile. She tugged at a tangled backpack wrapped around the front wheel. "Interesting tactic, by the way. Instead of impressing me with your skills, you went the 'inept moron' route, thus appealing to my caring side."

"Thanks. Was that *Seek and Destroy* you were just playing?"

A warm smile lit up her face. "Brilliant! You noticed!" she said. "Later, I do a rather languid version of *Anarchy In the UK*. But don't tell. I don't think management goes much for Sex Pistols."

"I'll keep it our little secret." I slowly untangled myself, stood up, and began reloading the bags.

She surveyed the bike and suitcases. "What's the story? Why not just use a cart?" she asked. "I mean, what exactly are you trying to prove?"

"A cart? *A cart!?*" I smiled. "That would defeat the whole purpose. Tell me." I gestured toward the porch. "Why do you play that … that big fiddle type thing?"

"Cello," she responded.

"Cello. What exactly are you trying to *prove?"*

"Fair question," she said. She bit her finger lightly and looked to the sky, contemplating a suitable response. "Maybe that my family didn't waste all that money on music school?"

"Hand me that," I said. Erin passed me a small suitcase, and I placed it carefully on the pile. "See how it all fits together? Each bag creating its own gravity force?"

She stepped back like an art critic in a museum, her finger on her chin. "Okay. I think I see it. Sort of Cubist meets, I dunno, maybe Constructivism?" I had no clue what she was talking about, but she was utterly adorable when she said it.

"Yeah, that." I continued. "And balance. Weight cancels out weight until it's weightless. Then we—*shit!"*

Smash! The load crashed to the pavement again. She was startled, then threw back her head and laughed.

"And there ya go. Arseways yet again! Have you even *done* this before?"

It was humiliating, but her reaction was infectious, and I found myself joining in. I righted the bike yet again and tossed the last train case in the basket. I checked my watch. "Shit. I'm so late. Don't tell anyone what you saw here today, okay? The dump. It could ruin me."

She smiled slyly. "I'll think about it."

Later that night, after my shift ended, I bounded up the Wildcliffe front steps and hopped up to smack the sign.

This time, instead of swinging with a creak, the sign splintered into a hundred pieces. Wood shards exploded around my head like a small bomb. I blinked away dust and picked a few tiny slivers of wood from my hair. I picked up a chunk of the sign and inspected it. Looked like termites.

How many front porch parties had this old chunk of pine stood watch over? Considering the house was nearly a century old, quite a few. But it was trash now.

I glanced around the porch, taking in the details. It had seen better days. The paint was peeling around the sills. The crack in the smudged window from a wild pitch when I was a kid had grown longer, snaking upward like a Michigan river. Stray boards poked up from under the worn red carpet. The wicker chairs sagged. It occurred to me that we'd never given the place a proper facelift.

To me, it was perfectly acceptable to let the lady go a bit as she eased into old age, but now that the sign was down, I saw it with fresh eyes. Take Wildcliffe Cottage off the East Bluff and plop it somewhere downstate, remove the echoing laughter of revelers, the kaleidoscopic family memories, the blue-green view of the Straits, and the comforting smell of old pine, and the place was … well, a bit of a dump.

There were reasons for the lack of upkeep. Big Jack was exceedingly busy with the dealership. He was also distracted by other, more personal things. My mom, the North Star to all of us, passed away two summers previous. Breast cancer. Evil fucking disease.

We each handled her death in our own way. My older sister Beth achieved a sort of zen sarcasm that was biting and hilarious, and undoubtedly helped salve her grief. Although it wasn't a conscious choice, I dealt with mom's death by becoming more like her.

While on the surface, mom appeared every bit the traditional Midwest homemaker, she possessed a gypsy's spirit. She loved to host parties and stay up late with the rowdiest rowdies, often ending up at the old piano in the parlor singing show tunes.

More than once as a kid, I groggily stumbled downstairs on a late summer night to find my folks and their friends in the midst of a head-stand competition in the Wildcliffe kitchen, drinking wine and eating chocolate chip cookie dough straight from the bowl. While Big Jack ran the business, my mom ran the fun. She once told me her favorite book was *The Electric Kool-Aid Acid Test* by Tom Wolfe. I thought it was a kid's book until I finally it read when I was eighteen.

Then it all made sense.

Born too early,

Gone too soon.

After she passed, the dockporter scene was the perfect way to distract myself. Brotherhood, bags, and bars. It wasn't precisely therapy, but it was all I could think of.

Dad, for his part, kept his chin up and kept the Mackinac scene alive as much as he could. But it's a helluva lot easier to be a king when you have a queen, and I could sense him retreating deeper into the complications of the auto business.

I grabbed a wrench from the toolbox on the porch and headed to the yard. I flipped my bike over and gave the rear wheel a spin, which was wobbling a bit. I was no mechanic, but I knew how to keep a porter bike on the road. I unscrewed the bolts, taking in Wildcliffe again. From this angle, the house looked almost human, a benign presence looking after us all. I reminded myself to snap a photo from that angle later.

"You're a thinker."

I looked over with a start. Gramps was sitting in his favorite wicker chair, holding a martini, wearing his ever-present Michigan ball cap, watching me with a smile.

"You scared the crap out of me, Gramps."

"Well, at least you didn't have to fly Helldivers against the Japanese. Now *that* was scary."

"You win."

"Damn right. Good day on the docks, boy?"

"Every day is a good day on the docks, Gramps. I took a nice load past the Grand." I replayed the scene while adjusting the crank. "I think I saw an angel."

"An angel, huh? Was she playing the harp? I know angels love those harps."

"I think it was a cello," I replied.

"Hmm," he responded, stirring his cocktail thoughtfully as if to say *so angels now play cellos. Who knew?*

Big Jack, up for the weekend, emerged through the swinging porch door. He wandered over to the railing to watch me work on the bike below. "Whatcha calling this one?" he asked. "You always loved naming your bikes, ever since you were a little punk."

"I call this one James."

"*James?* Why James?"

My dad picked up the toolbox and wandered down the few steps to where I was working.

I was now oiling the chain. I hesitated and then barreled ahead. "Well. I named this one after High-Rise Jimmy Oliver, the last dockporter ever to ride twenty-one suitcases in his basket. I never met the guy, but to dockporters, he's a legend."

"Wait a minute, brother."

The voice roused Jack out of his reverie. It was the biker. He was engrossed, but in need of clarification.

"You mean to tell me you named your porter bike after some dude you never met because he rode, what was it, *blackjack*?"

Jack looked over, having almost forgotten where he was. "The man was a legend," he explained. He waited for a few seconds, thinking it over. "I dunno. I guess you had to be there."

The biker leaned back, grinned, and coughed. "I guess you did. *Proceed.*"

My dad handed me a different set of pliers, seeing that I was struggling with resetting the rear wheel. The truth was, he and I didn't talk all that much. He appreciated my spirit, but there was always a sense he was waiting me out, checking his watch, impatient for me to join the race.

"The Wildcliffe sign is shot," I said. "Can you hand me that nine-sixteenths."

He handed me the wrench from the toolbox. He watched me work in silence for a while. Finally, he spoke, cutting to the chase I knew was coming.

"You thought any more about our talk? *McGuinn and Son Oldsmobile?*"

It was a conversation that came up frequently over the last year, and one I was always eager to avoid. My lack of interest in enrolling in college. My growing interest in photography. To a man like my dad, it all had the odor of an interest in something "creative." To conservative Michigan business types of the time, this sounded like trouble, akin to majoring in women's studies or taking up the didgeridoo. Foreign and useless.

My dad dutifully took his place in Gramps' dealership when he graduated from college and never looked back. He grew the business steadily, keeping up with the new models and expanding the inventory. His success allowed Gramps to retire and spend more time on the island, eventually becoming a respected, eccentric elder.

But Big Jack sold Oldsmobiles, and lately, the

Oldsmobiles weren't selling. I sometimes wondered: Was it the economy, or was he on a cold streak? And what did it say that a family that prospered by selling new cars spent their summers on an island that outlawed them?

"Dad, I don't want to be *and Son*." I yanked on the wrench. The rusty bolt wasn't budging. "It worked for you, but not for me."

Big Jack glanced over at Gramps, who was looking over the harbor through binoculars. He lowered his voice. "I could use you on the floor, kid. The way you wheel and deal on that dock? You could use those same skills and make *real* money in a *real* business."

"Jesus. Don't pressure the kid. Let him enjoy himself," Gramps interjected.

Dad shot back, clearly annoyed. "Why not? You sure as hell pressured me."

"I did. And I never should have. If I remember correctly, you wanted to work on a fishing boat off … was it Sitka, Alaska? You had the trip all booked and were ready to go."

"That was a long time ago. And it was a stupid lark anyway," Big Jack called up.

"Yup. Stupid lark. But I should have let you go anyway." Gramps stood up slowly, groaning a bit. "Jesus, these old knees are shot to shit. Never get old, boys. It's no party. I'm a quart low. Time to change the oil." He held out his empty glass as proof and strolled to the porch door. My dad shook his head, irritated.

"Thanks for the help, Dad."

Gramps called back. "Anytime. That's what I'm here for. Settling family squabbles." The screen door swung shut behind him.

I turned back to my dad. "I admit it. I'm a freak," I

said. "The only living soul in the state of Michigan who hates that 'new car smell.'" I leaned into the bolt. It finally gave way and I lurched forward.

"A kid with your people skills can do anything. Instead, you ride around with other people's suitcases in the basket of your bike."

My dad's lack of understanding made me feel lonely, so I focused on the wheel, spinning it lightly to get alignment. "And you," I said, "work like a dog just to afford a few days off during the summer to see us. End of the day, I count my tips. I know what I did. And it's satisfying."

"It's simple," he said.

"Exactly. It's simple. And what's wrong with that? Do you know how much you made today at the dealership?"

My dad looked away grimly, stealing a glance over the harbor. For the first time I could ever remember, he looked old. "Not enough."

"Well, I do. It's in my pocket right now. Ninety-three dollars. You know what else? This summer, I'm riding twenty-one suitcases, which will put me at legend status. Nobody's done it in *decades*. I'm going to carve my name on the list. *Simple*."

My dad didn't bother responding. I was speaking another language.

The work was done on the bike. I flipped it upright. He helped me. I leaned the old Schwinn against the side of the porch, and we inspected it together, standing side-by-side.

"James the bike." He nodded. I put an arm on his shoulder, grateful for any gesture of understanding.

"A beast of a ride," I responded.

"You got a loose spoke." Big Jack pointed. "That's dangerous. Here, steady it." He grabbed a small T-shaped wrench from the toolbox and crouched down. I watched him work on tightening the loose spokes, one-by-one. Despite our differences, I could watch my dad work a wrench for hours. And as a kid, I often had.

"I just don't want you to get left behind," he said, not looking up. His words hung in the air.

Left behind.

What the hell did he mean by that?

CHAPTER SIX

Leaping
   July 18, 1989

I found myself aware of the weight of the bags and the burn of the summer sun on my arms and neck as I rode. Weird shit. I suppose you would call it a *growing sense of self-awareness,* but I wasn't into that psychology crap back then. I just felt different.

Everyone had a mission. Spengler was investigating the "man in black," Gordon's grim, mysterious friend, sensing a story. I suppose that's what aspiring journalists do. Trust their instincts and let the cards fall where they may. Other than the occasional obituary or ice-cream social announcement, Spengler never published much, and the *Island Gazette* wasn't looking for hard-hitting reporting. But, hell, why not try?

Foster consumed his extra moments on the dock translating the letters he regularly received from his señorita in Vera Cruz. He'd read them aloud to us between boats in a mangled Spanish that was, incrementally and day-by-day, improving.

Smitty and Fly kept up a steady banter regarding the feasibility of riding twenty-one bags, presenting new creative—albeit ill-advised—approaches daily.

AJ was harboring his starlet at the Hammond cottage (we'd all find out later), and despite his canary-eating grin, we had no idea what they were up to.

As for me, I was obsessed with the moronic wager I'd made with Gordon, which added a touch of melancholy to the antics on the docks. *Was this the last summer?*

And through it all, Bull continued to learn how to ride loads.

———

I returned to the dock, gliding in after a run to the WibHo. Bull was straddling his ride with a massive load of luggage, made more impressive when set in stark contrast to his spindly physique. The others huddled around a raucous oversized Jenga duel, and nobody noticed that Bull was about to die young.

His face brightened when he saw me approach. His whole body was quivering like a piano wire and his face was bathed in a light sweat. "Look! Blackjack, Jack!"

Foster glanced up and chuckled. *"Look! Blackjack, Jack!"* he said, mocking the kid gleefully. "Looks like your baby's taking his first steps."

"And his last," Smitty chimed in.

I parked my ride and jogged over to him. "Did you load this up yourself?"

"AJ helped," he replied.

"I'm sure he did. And then I bet he split."

"It's fine. He had a run."

Bull couldn't have known that AJ was infamous for stacking up a rookie's basket with a wildly unbalanced load, just to watch said rookie dump. For him, it was a basic rite of passage.

"You're not ready for something this heavy." I inspected and readjusted the suitcases. I admired his guts, if not his intelligence. There was no way he could ride it. It was a great photo opportunity, but it wasn't going anywhere. I pulled out the Instamatic and snapped a few shots. Bull noticed, pleased, and posed like a fisherman with a huge marlin.

"Taking my picture? Must not be *that* unsafe then," he beamed.

"This is for the lawsuit," I shot back, sliding the camera back in my pocket. "First of all, it's not technically blackjack. You need twenty-one FAA-classified pieces of luggage. These sleeping bags don't count." I coached him as I pulled off bags. "It's also too top-heavy. Did you even check the weight distribution on the wings? And these bungee cords are crap. Fly'll set you up. He invented his own." I made a few more quick adjustments.

Bull leaned in close. "Jack. Fly's bungees are expensive. I think they're …" He lowered his voice. "… *kind of a gyp.*"

Fly was in earshot and looked over, instantly irate. His bungees were state-of-the-art, and everyone knew it.

"Gyp?" He said with a menacing scowl, approaching Bull. *"Gyp?"* Fly held up one of his cords like it was a sleeping but dangerous python. "This shit is nylon outer sheath. A cobalt-coated, stainless-steel hook, designed in a lab at MIT. *MIT, Bull!* You could leap off the Mackinac Bridge with this stretchy lil' bitch and bounce back in-*tact!*"

Fly, done, turned away, calling back over his shoulder, "The dockporter game is just like life, Bull-dog. You get what you pay for. And your price just went way up!"

As if Fly scripted the scene, the cheap, bargain-bin bungee cord hook that secured Bull's load to the stem of his handlebars was slowly starting to bend outward. I saw it.

"We got trouble. Bull, we need to unload this shit. Take that cord off and let me—" Too late. The cord *snapped* and sling-shotted across the top of the luggage. The hook smacked Bull square in the nose, and the load instantly self-destructed, sideways and outward. Bull instinctively grabbed his bloodied nose instead of securing the bike.

"Ah, shit!"

Smash. It all went down. A convention of seagulls scattered in terror, their wings stirring up manure dust and popcorn remnants. Tourists glanced over with alarm. It was the wrong moment to dump, especially with sharks like Gordon circling, smelling blood, searching for an excuse to devour the dockporter system in one greedy gulp.

Like a clean-up crew at the Indy 500, the guys rushed into action to scoop Bull, his luggage, and his bloody snout away from prying eyes. I grabbed the basket of his prone bike and yanked him up by the hand while I eyed the ticket booth to see if we were causing a scene. There, wearing a baseball cap but impossible not to notice, was the Irish woman. I immediately let go of Bull.

"Hey!" he shouted as he hit the deck for the second time that minute with a fleshy thud.

"Sorry there, Bull," I said without meaning it. "Boys, help him out. I need to … ummm …" I wandered away without finishing the sentence and approached Erin, who had a ferry ticket in her hand.

She saw me approaching and smiled. It was open, but a touch vulnerable. I hadn't seen this smile on her before.

"You're leaving?" I asked. I noticed her luggage and a large, scuffed cello case.

"I am," she replied. I felt an undeniable wave of disappointment.

"We have twenty-five minutes until the next boat pulls in. Explain."

She laughed as if I'd said something stupid. "All I need is twenty-five seconds. My boyfriend, who dragged me to this rock, morphed into an asshole right before my eyes. It was a magical transformation, I have to say. I've got no money saved and I'm stuck in the back arse of nowhere. So it's back to Dublin for me. Guess I'm *fucked.*"

With her accent, it came out as *fooked* and sounded less like a dirty word and more like poetry. I fumbled for a witty response. "How is it that Irish people make that word sound so cool?"

"We *fookin'* practice." I looked over to her cello case. Something inside me was bubbling up, and it felt a lot like *don't leave.* Instead it came out a lot like stammering. "You should … I mean … there's some … maybe you could …" She looked at me sideways, waiting for a complete sentence.

"What if I could guarantee you a hundred dollars

cash in fifteen minutes?"

"Ha. Well, I'd ask you if it was legal."

"Play for us. One last time." I pointed to her cello.

"Oh no. My buskin' days are over, boyo."

A few of the guys sauntered over. Smitty piped in, "We love the cello."

Spengler filled in the awkward pause. "A member of the string family, if I'm not mistaken."

"Guys, this is…" *I couldn't remember her name.* My face felt flush.

"*Erin*," she said. "And I'm seventy-five percent sure I told you that last time."

I cleared my throat. "This is *Erin*. Erin, these are the dockporters. She's going to play for us."

She looked at me sharply. "I didn't agree to that!" She inspected the sheepish gathering and glanced at her watch and then at her cello case, calculating her next move.

"Guarantee a hundred dollars in tips," she said, indicating the cello case with a pointed finger. "Or that beast of an instrument never comes out of its shell. If the tourists' tips here don't hit the mark, you lads make up the difference. Got it?"

"Deal!" Foster piped in, strolling over for the show, intrigued by this sexy stranger with the brash negotiation skills.

Erin looked around the dock, evaluating the scene. A handful of passengers waited for the boat, absently feasting on maple-flavored fudge. She looked toward the sun, squinted her Irish eyes, and turned toward us.

"Somebody get me a hat." She pulled the bill of her own hat down low. "I'll be damned if I'm layin' this one in the shit. It was a gift."

The gang erupted in a small but mighty cheer. Smitty sheepishly wandered up to her, peeking at me over his shoulder as if he were doing something wrong.

"Um. *Erin?*" Smitty asked.

"Yes?"

"Do you know *Free Bird?*"

"Fine plan! *Free Bird* it is!"

Smitty turned toward me, beaming like a proud little leaguer who just scored the winning run. He gave me a sneaky double thumbs up and silently worded: *she's HOT.*

Soon, we were all experiencing the most heart-wrenching version of *Free Bird* any of us ever heard, or ever would. That was the exact moment I fell for her. Her acerbic exterior vanished, replaced by the sights and sounds of a lonely girl far from home. Melancholy reverberated with each draw of the bow. For that five minutes or so, life became a sad, beautiful montage, and I felt aching déjà vu for moments that I'm pretty sure never happened.

I was confident there would be no issues with her hitting the hundred dollar mark.

A crowd of tourists watched, transfixed, as she played. As the song reached a crescendo, I looked over at Smitty. I swore I saw a tiny tear tracking down his face, glistening in the sun.

I pointed my finger directly at his cheek, almost touching it. "Wait. Is that what I think it is?"

"Oh, hell no!" he said, pulling away from me. "I got a gnat in my eye." He quickly wiped it away, sniffed, and crossed his arms, his posture quickly switching to defiant indifference.

I took in the scene. Tourists, dock workers, the grizzled teamsters, even the snorting draft horses savored the moment.

I stood with Erin as she counted out a healthy stack of cash. "Looks like maybe I've been hanging out with the wrong crowd," she said, straightening out the bills.

"We *are* the wrong crowd," I said. "And I'm pretty sure I would've noticed you."

Cap Riley leaned on the railing of the upper deck. "All aboard!" he called down.

Despite the fat wad of cash she clutched in her right hand, she looked a little lost. She looked at me directly, her deep blue eyes sincere and unblinking.

"Thanks, Jack. You're a good guy. Enjoy the rest of your summer." She moved toward the ramp. "Try not to dump anymore."

She walked up the ramp to the boat. I stepped away, allowing the other passengers to pile on. Foster sidled up next to me and stood uncomfortably close, looking straight ahead at the ferry as he spoke.

"I agree with you," he said.

I looked over at him. His eyes remained forward. "Nice. But I didn't say anything."

"A woman like that could screw up your master plan."

"I don't have a master plan, Foster. You know that."

But he wasn't done. "She's a three-course meal. You're a fast-food guy."

We stood in awkward silence, but I knew he was just warming up. "She's like one of those comets that shoots by every thirty years or so. Better to just stand back and watch 'em pass. And you? You're a *tip man*. Why deal with that kind of heavy lifting."

Again, a long silence. I squinted to catch a glimpse of her through the ferry's porthole, tuning out his babble.

"She's like a finely tuned, sort of—"

"Stop," I said.

By now, the other guys joined the vigil, staring glumly at the ferry like a losing baseball team watching the final pitches of a big game.

Foster spoke again, this time quietly. "That's good. Because I was running out of, you know …" He trailed off.

"Metaphors?" Spengler asked.

"Exactly," Foster said. "That's the word. *Metaphors.*"

Then it was Smitty's turn.

"She was really special." *Really special?* What did these idiots want from me? Some Irish chick plays *Free Bird,* and I'm supposed to go all gooey? Restructure my life?

Even so, they were getting through. I spent four seasons working on the docks and I met a lot of summer girls. Some loved Depeche Mode, some loved heavy metal, some were awesome, some were annoying. But they all had something magical in common: They took a risk.

It was always easy for me. Wildcliffe was in my family. I had a porch and a bed, and when my mom was alive, scrambled eggs and toast. Hell, I was practically *conceived* on Mackinac Island. But summer girls owned an adventurous streak that far outweighed mine. They took the leap and left the safety of their downstate homes. They strapped on black polyester-blend waitress garb and got busy having the time of their young lives. *I loved summer girls.*

But Erin? She was more.

I turned away and walked toward my bike. The ferry was revving its stinky diesel, preparing to back away from the dock. Franklin slid the ramp up with a grind. I looked toward where Erin had just been playing her cello. A lone purple scarf lay on the ground. It billowed slightly, fluttering toward the edge of the dock. I trotted over and snatched it up moments before the wind carried it into the lake.

I inspected it closely. It was a traditional design, with a hint of bohemia. A floral pattern. But funky. *This was Erin's scarf.* And she would probably want it back. Maybe it was a gift. A family heirloom. It looked expensive. I swallowed hard and looked toward the departing ferry.

Without much thought, I took off running toward the boat as it instigated a lazy pivot out of the harbor. I mean *the woman left her scarf.* The guys turned and watched as I sprinted past. "Wait! I have a scarf!"

Franklin was peering out the porthole, baffled, his head twisted sideways. "A scarf? What scarf?"

I waved it over my head. "This one! It belongs to Erin, the cello player. Stop the boat!"

"The jello … prayer?" he called back. "What's a *jello prayer?"*

It was far too late for detailed explanations. I hit the dock running. If I could get my right foot square on the two-foot rim around the hull, I could pull myself up on deck and return the precious heirloom. I remember glancing toward the upper deck. She leaned on the railing and watched me, but I didn't have time to interpret her expression. I took a breath and leaped, clutching the purple scarf and channeling—to the best of my abilities—Jessie Owens in the 1936 Olympics.

The guys told me later that I was ten to twelve feet short. To describe it as "not even close" would be far too generous.

The lake was frigid. I splashed down, nuts first, and plunged four feet under the water, the mysterious gurgle of lake water instantly muffled the shocked laughter of the boys. I broke the surface, gasping, the frigid shock causing me to cough and hitch reflexively like a panicked old horse. It was not a healthy sound.

I looked up toward the ferry. There she was. Her expression didn't render appreciation. Just deep concern. The kind of concern that causes one to call 9-1-1. "Holy hell! What are you doing?" she yelled down.

"I have your scarf!" I held up the dripping, purple rag in my right hand, paddling to stay afloat with my left. She squinted at me, the sun's reflection on the water causing chaos with her line of sight. She raised her hand to block it.

I gasped, "Since you're leaving for good, I thought you should have it."

"Thanks, Jack," she called down. "But it's not my scarf!"

The guys were gathered at the edge of the dock, erupting in hysterics. Smitty collapsed, holding his stomach and letting out a piercing guffaw. The others were supporting each other like soldiers after a battle, gasping with laughter. Cap Riley cut the engine and emerged from the pilothouse. He scrambled to the rear of the vessel and saw me floating.

"These props'll tenderize you in no time flat! Get away from the damn vessel!"

"Sorry, Cap. I was … *I have a scarf.*"

"A *scarf?*" Cap Riley wasn't going to waste a moment of his day trying to decipher what *that* meant. "I gotta schedule to keep!"

From the dock, I heard a booming voice. "Stop the boat!" There, dry as a bone and looking like a hero on the cover of a shitty romance novel, was Gordon. His blond hair was windblown, and he was dressed in a sporty blue windbreaker and khaki shorts, looking like he just returned from the America's Cup. He was holding a bouquet of red roses.

"Erin! Come back! We have to talk!" I followed his gaze toward Erin. Her face was red with anger.

I can only remember thinking one thing:

What-the-ever-loving-fuck?

"I told you!" she yelled down. "I'm leaving!"

"Baby! We need to talk!"

I bobbed like a drowned rat in the space between the dock and the ferry. *Baby?*

"Were you just gonna leave?" Gordon called up.

"That is the plan!" she yelled back.

"Let me explain! I got you your job back!"

"Aww, that's sweet," she said in a mocking tone. She

took a deep breath and bellowed: "Since you're the reason I lost it, *you fascist pig!*"

Gordon yelled up again, this time to Cap Riley. "Captain. Sir! I need you to bring the ferry back." He turned toward Erin and opened his arms in supplication. "Erin," he hollered, "let's get dinner at the Grand so we can work this out!"

Erin looked away from him, but it was all becoming a bit of a scene. She was clearly mortified to be the center of so much childish drama.

The good news was, the utter failure of my idiotic leap was no longer the lead story.

"Fine!" she yelled. "The only reason I'm coming back is that I have no other choice! I'm broke!"

Well, not completely broke, I thought, bobbing like a spectator in the cheap seats at a water polo match. She did have the cello cash. *Thanks to me.*

Cap Riley jammed the ferry into reverse.

"Just come back. It was all a *huge* misunderstanding! I'm so sorry," Gordon said. If he was lying, it was an impressive performance.

Resigned, I turned away and dog-paddled from the lovers' spat, slowed by the wet, heavy burden of my oversized shorts. My tip roll and wallet were drenched. My imitation Ray-Bans were at the bottom of Lake Huron with seaweed-covered hotel keys, bicycle parts, and various souvenir tchotchkes accidentally dropped in the lake over the last century or so.

And she was with Gordon.

I looked back as the *Straits II* eased back to the ramp. Franklin quickly dropped the gangplank and helped Erin, her cello, and her luggage from the boat. Resigned,

I scrambled up the wooden pilings, still holding that stupid, worthless purple scarf. Smitty and AJ helped me out of the lake while the other guys stifled hysterics.

"You missed the boat," Smitty said as he pulled me up by my arm.

"So much for not *diving* into a relationship," tossed out AJ as he grabbed a handful of my soaked golf shirt. Another shriek of laughter.

Foster joined in. "There's other fish in the sea, Jack. In fact, there's one right by your left foot."

The damn broke. *"Cod almighty ... that was fin-tastic ... you're hooked ... gill-ty as charged!"* It was *endless*, the abuse. It went on and on as I pulled myself out of the frigid lake and planted myself at the edge of the dock, shivering. I watched glumly as Gordon pleaded with Erin in the distance. AJ looked over at them.

"You know, Jack," said AJ. "You're entitled to ten percent of the cash your friend Lucky Charms made playing the cello. You were, in effect, acting as her agent."

"And?" I asked.

"They're having dinner at the Grand tonight. Go collect."

"Lucky Charms?" asked Smitty.

AJ nodded. "The perfect nickname for her."

Smitty nodded. "I get it. Like the cereal. Plus she's magically delicious."

I examined the soaked, purple scarf that likely belonged to a retiree from Southgate, Michigan named Thelma. AJ was right. I needed to collect.

"Smitty. Do you own a jacket and tie?"

"No. But I know somebody who does."

"Get it. Tonight we're going to the Grand."

CHAPTER SEVEN

Grand Hotel
   July 21, 1989

"Let's just rewind the tape," I could hear Gordon say, his voice quivering with desperation. "Let's go back to before all of this happened."

Then it was Erin's turn to respond, and the Irish came out. She was not holding back.

"Swingin' *Jaysus!* Okay fine. I'm *rewinding the tape* to the part when you told your little frat buddies you were 'hitting the talent,'" Erin said, contempt dripping like the butter on her lobster. A livid woman dropping Dublin slang in the Grand dining room was highly unusual. I was enjoying every minute of it.

"*Mitch* said that!" Gordon responded.

"And did you point out to *Mitch* that describing our relationship in that way was offensive? Disrespectful? Or as you Americans like to say: *A DICK MOVE!*" She was hissing the words. Gordon responded, voice low and adult.

"Erin, please. Let's not cause a scene. You're still technically an employee here."

"Oh, am I still *technically an employee?* And here I thought I was shit-canned. Don't act like you're doing me a favor just because you pulled some strings and got me rehired. Right now, I'm just a stupid bird on a bad date, and I can get as loud … *AS I WANT.* I'm only here because you *BEGGED* me to get off the *FERRY!*" It wasn't quite a yell, but it was inching closer.

I glanced over at Smitty. He arched one eyebrow and, with a playful grin, mouthed "wow." He was nursing a beer and held it up. "It's crazy, Jack. This beer. It's twice as much as Horn's. But it tastes *exactly* the same." I shushed him.

A large pillar separated Smitty and me from Gordon and Erin, who sat a couple of tables beyond. I could hear, as Gramps was fond of saying, "dribs and drabs" of their conversation.

We had been spying on them for ten minutes now, deftly avoiding ordering food. We wore jackets and ties, doing our best to blend in with the upscale crowd as they enjoyed their Grand Hotel meals. Grand Hotel waiters in white gloves and red jackets rushed in and out of the massive Grand Hotel dining room with Grand Hotel pewter trays full of incredible Grand Hotel food.

I refocused my audio binoculars on Erin's lilting, smoldering voice.

"The answer is *no.* You didn't point it out to Mitch. So instead, *I* pointed it out. And then I find out I'm fired from my job on an island in northern Michigan. A place *you* brought me. No work visa. Nothing. *Stranded.*"

"Pointed it out? Erin, respectfully, you smashed a pint glass over my head."

"Respectfully, I pointed it out by smashing a pint glass over your head." Her tone shifted. "Leave it. It was a cheap glass. I knew it would shatter easily. It barely left a mark. If we'd been in a pub in Dublin? You'd have spent the evening in the E.R. getting stitched up like an old holiday sweater. In Ireland, we use sturdy drink ware. It leaves a mark."

There was a long pause. I leaned in, straining to hear more. She softened. "Listen. You took me away from a bad situation. I'll never forget that. But …"

The clinking of plates and silverware drowned out their conversation. Without warning, she emerged from behind the pillar. I lowered my head and shielded my face with a menu as she passed by our table. Smitty didn't bother to hide; he just smiled broadly at her. She did a quick double take, unable to place him, but thankfully continued on her way.

"Real stealthy there, James Bond," I whispered.

He shrugged. "You didn't say *I* was supposed to hide. You said *you* were supposed to hide. I was being polite. Plus, she's beautiful! I literally could not, not look. It was like a tractor beam. *Beeeeeeeeyaaaaawwww* …" I could only assume this was Smitty's take on a tractor beam.

I dropped the menu. "I love you, Smitty. But sometimes you're a moron."

"Says the guy who jumped in the lake today with all his clothes on." He flapped his arms wildly. "*Stop the boat! I have a pretty purple scarf!*" He took a sip of beer and smiled, playing the memory back in his mind. Then he exploded in laughter and discharged a fine spray of beer all over the linen tablecloth. Across the dining room, I could see the maître d' fixing us with a cold stare. It was time to go. I brushed the beer spatters off my necktie and got up from the table, trailing Erin from a safe distance.

Smitty grabbed both our beers and dutifully trailed me. "Damned if I'm leaving these behind. Most expensive beer I've had in my life … Coulda had four shots of tequila at the Mustang for what we paid for these … I'm framing these fuckers when I get home." On and on he rambled as we left the dining room, discharging a cloud of economic gripes that likely still hangs over the Grand dining room to this very day.

We wandered around the tastefully decorated lobby for a few minutes, not exactly sure where she might reappear or what I would do if I saw her. Smitty inspected his surroundings.

"What's on your mind?" I asked him.

"It just hit me. I've lived on this island my entire life, and this is the first time I've ever been in the Grand lobby." He became uncharacteristically philosophical. "I mean, my old man and I spent a month a few winters back doing some plumbing repairs on the pool house toilet. But I've never been here in the lobby, with an actual tie around my neck."

"What do you think?"

Smitty inspected the scene wide-eyed, like an immigrant arriving at Ellis Island. "It's nice." He looked down at the intricately designed carpeting, and then up at a chandelier that probably cost more than his two-room shack in the middle of the island. "But you know, man, I don't think I ever need to be rich. I mean, I dunno … the upkeep alone."

He took another long look at the museum-like lobby. We both knew it had nothing to do with *upkeep* or what he *needed*. And just like that, the cloud passed.

He looked over, then ducked behind a pillar and hissed, "Lucky Charms, three o'clock and bearing down fast!"

I turned around to see Erin walking toward us. She stopped in her tracks when she saw me. "Hi! What a surprise!" I said. Another horrible opening line.

Smitty emerged from behind the pillar. "Surprise? Wait, Jack," he said. "You told me we were coming up here to see her." Somehow, in the last ten seconds, he had utterly lost the script.

"I never said that," I shot back, fumbling.

"What? You asked me if I had a suit. I said I'd check. Then we ... we talked about this!" He turned to Erin and made devil horns with his fingers. *"Free Bird!"*

Erin smiled at Smitty. "Can I borrow your man for a moment?"

"Borrow? Please. You can *have* him."

Erin took my arm and pulled me away to a small corridor next to the elevator. "I'm sorry about today. I like you. But I gave you the wrong idea. It's not me. It's that bleedin' cello."

"No," I replied. "It's you."

She looked over her shoulder. "I shouldn't even be here."

"You're right! You shouldn't be here."

"I mean *here*. With you. I'm on a date. Well. Sort of," she said.

"Well, I mean here. With *him!*" I leaned in. "I know about your date. I grew up with that guy. Don't be fooled by the lobster and the champagne and the Yale business degree and the good looks and the philanthropy and the—do you think that Gordon even *appreciates* the cello?"

Erin rolled her eyes. "Oh, stop the *fooking* lights. Nobody appreciates the cello. I'm not sure *I* even appreciate the cello."

"Well. *I* appreciate the cello."

"Right. You didn't even know what it was. You called it a 'big fiddle,' if memory serves me. I think you might appreciate cello players." She ruminated. "*Female* cello players."

"See, now you're getting hung up on details."

She sighed and broke away, walking toward the restaurant. I followed. To my right, the Terrace Room, the hotel's ballroom, was coming alive with the brassy sounds of a big band. It was one of the many undeniable charms of the Grand. They knew their clientele, and had since the Roaring Twenties. I lightly touched Erin's arm and rerouted her into the sprawling space, which was filling up with dancing couples.

A few summers before my mom passed away, she and dad had taken ballroom dance lessons at the Terrace. Dad lost interest, too preoccupied with work to keep up with the practice, but Mom wasn't going to quit. She quickly slotted me in as his replacement, much to my utter humiliation. That summer I learned a few steps—the foxtrot, quickstep, even a little cha-cha—but I kept the lessons my dirty little secret.

I remember two-stepping morosely with my mom as she chuckled. "You may hate this moment now, Jacky, but someday, trust me, some beautiful woman will be wildly impressed with your dancing skills, and you'll have your crazy mom to thank." I grunted and carried on with my steps, counting them off silently.

It wasn't the first time, or the last, that my mom's predictions would prove prophetic.

Erin looked at me closely, at the very least intrigued. I took her elegant hand in mine and guided her around the floor as the band played. Between the twists and spins, we managed to wedge in a conversation.

"You don't know the whole story," she said, after a turn.

"Yes. I do. Goes like this: There once was a beautiful woman from Ireland who, apparently, had lousy taste in men. The end."

Her eyes went dark, but she continued to stay in time. "Well, you're just the world's leading expert, aren't you? One little moment on the docks doesn't give you the right to judge me."

"One? We've now had *four* of what you call 'little moments.' I'll spare you the details of the last one, other than to say I pulled a whitefish out of my shorts this afternoon."

Despite herself, she laughed. It was a hearty sound, pure and full of unrestrained joy. I spun her around gently.

"Okay. I'll give you credit. You do leap. You don't leap far, but *you do leap.*"

The brassy tune wound up with applause from the dancers on the floor. Erin executed a sweet curtsy straight out of a fruity Elizabethan-era movie and immediately headed out of the ballroom. I followed behind.

"I'm due back to my date," she called over her

shoulder. "I'm not done with him, the arrogant bastard."

"Come on. Forget him!" But she kept moving. "You know, you're trouble," I continued. "You think *I'm* trouble, but *you're* trouble. You're like one of those women from Greek mythology." I was nearly shouting as she walked off. "You lure sailors to their death with your sweet music. What are they called again?"

"Sirens," Smitty stated matter-of-factly. He had been standing outside the ballroom, continuing to nurse his beer. I looked back at him, momentarily thrown.

"Yes. Sirens. No offense, but how do you even know that?" Smitty shrugged. Took a sip.

Erin stopped, looked back at me. I caught up. "Maybe I don't trust you, Jack."

"Why not?"

"You forget. I've seen you work. Scamming tips, dumping luggage."

Smitty appeared between us, joining the conversation. "Come on, Erin. He almost drowned for you today. *Take a chance.*"

I moved closer. "Let me take you to an island spot." She looked furtively toward the dining room. I reached into the inside pocket of my blazer and removed the purple scarf. It was still a little damp. "Even if this wasn't yours, you might as well have it." I handed it to her. I noted a reluctant grin as she unfolded it and inspected the pattern closely.

"This is an old lady scarf. I should be insulted you thought this was mine. It's really not my style."

"So hold on to it. We all get old eventually."

She looked up. "Okay. Show me an *island spot*. But no romantic gestures. I'm semi-involved." She looked over her shoulder. "And I'm starting to feel like a harlot."

"Absolutely no romantic gestures," I said.

"What's a harlot?" asked Smitty, genuinely interested.

Erin gestured to the dining room. "Let me finish up my shaming session. It shouldn't take more than ten minutes. He's on the ropes. *And don't follow me.*" She turned away. Smitty and I watched her head off.

"Well, done, buddy," said Smitty. He put a friendly hand on my shoulder. "Now. Tell me more about this dump."

———

How we ended up sitting at a makeshift dinner table in a secluded cove in the woods called Anne's Tablet, complete with candles and a bottle of red wine, escapes me. I assumed that Smitty placed an urgent call to AJ from the Grand lobby and told him to whip something up quick. AJ lived for that stuff. Regardless, the trappings of our situation screamed *romantic gesture.* There was even a small, polished silver bell placed on the table. Erin was looking at it, smiling. She rolled her eyes. "Oh, hell, just ring the damn thing. You went this far." I rang the bell.

From behind a tree emerged AJ, wearing a full Italian waiter get-up, hair slicked back, a small mustache penciled in on his upper lip and a towel wrapped over his forearm. He looked slightly more Cuban than Italian. He hustled over and quickly poured us a refill of the wine.

"Dinner will be here in … how you say? Pretty

soon?" He was overworking his Italian accent, but even at his most over-the-top, the guy still oozed charm. He disappeared behind a nearby rock, and we could pick up on some whispering. A woman's voice. Erin and I shared a look. AJ wasn't alone. The woman seemed to be coaching him in a frantic whisper.

"You're pushing. Acting is *re*-acting. *Be in the moment,*" the voice chastised.

"Yes!" AJ whispered back. "I read that in an acting book. *An Actor Prepares,* by Constantin Stanaloski? *Stansloski?* Or is it … Stan—something. Anyway, he's a Russian guy."

"And the accent's not working," the woman's voice added.

"Really? I can do German."

"German? No. You're already down the Italian road. And you're serving goddamn pasta! A little late to go German. It's fine. *Go!"*

AJ re-emerged, smoothing back his hair and smiling broadly. He was holding two steaming plates of pasta, which he carefully placed on the candlelit table. Erin grabbed her fork and attacked the food. How she had extracted herself from her previous dinner with Gordon was a question for another time, but she sure was hungry.

Not looking up, and with a mouth full of food, she said, "So tell me. Did you crash your bike on purpose to get my attention?"

AJ stopped short, eavesdropping on the conversation.

"Of course," I said.

AJ turned to Erin, raising his hand. "On thissa point, I musta call bulla-shit. There issa just no way dees guy, dees ... *Jack person* ... would ever dump on purpose." He smiled innocently. "More vino? No? I let you be. Ciao for now!" AJ disappeared again behind the rock.

I looked back to Erin. "I don't know that guy."

"Right."

"And for the record, you've now told my dump story twice. That was supposed to be a secret."

Erin shrugged, a twinkle in her eye. "Oops."

"Yeah, yeah," I said. "I can tell you think this whole dockporter thing is stupid. But I'm telling you, it's not. It's serious business. And by the time this summer is over, I'll prove it to you."

She smiled back. "Fine. But tell me about your *real* baggage. The kind you don't put in the basket of your bike."

"What are you, a shrink?"

"I have my issues. But I want to know about you. A man's only as interesting as his problems."

"You don't find me interesting?" I asked, genuinely curious.

"I'm deciding. Seems like a pretty safe gig. Riding luggage on a bike? Something's not adding up here."

"You sound a lot like my dad. But you got it all backward. Gordon is *safe*. College is *safe*. The real world is *safe*. Riding luggage? It's anything but safe. It's *dangerous*," I said. I noticed she darkened a little when I said the word "safe," but it passed.

"You just haven't found *it* yet," she said.

"It?"

"*It*. That thing that makes you get up in the morning."

"Listen. I get up in the morning and catch the early

boat. It doesn't matter how late I was out the night before. I'm always there. And I haul the bags. I load 'em up, and I ride 'em. All day. Every day. So, don't lecture me about getting up in the morning."

"If you say so. I'm sorry I questioned your life's work. It obviously has deep personal meaning for you." The sarcasm was visceral. And sexy as hell.

"Well. I do have one crazy dream," I offered. "You'll think it's absurd, but it's real."

"Wouldn't be sporting of me to call a crazy dream absurd. That's redundant. So, let me hear it," she replied.

"This summer, I'm going to ride twenty-one bags in the basket of my bike. We call it *blackjack*. It hasn't been done since 1975, when High-Rise Jimmy Oliver pulled it off, and most everyone, myself included, thinks it's impossible."

She nodded, processing. "It's measurable, it's a reach, and there's a time lock. If you're set on being a dockporter, you might as well be the best." She raised her glass. "Brilliant. Here's to twenty-one suitcases. To blackjack."

I raised mine. "You're up."

She took a breath, formulating her words carefully.

"I adore the cello. I was kidding earlier when I said I didn't. It may be the instrument I was born to play. It's radiant. It's physical. You have to hug it like a lover. And if it's good enough for Vivaldi, it's good enough for Erin O' Malley." She took a sip and shook her head. "But Christ Almighty, Jack. It's so *sad*. Just one time, I want to play music that isn't the soundtrack to the worst day of your entire life. I think the legendary philosopher Dee Snider of Twisted Sister summed up my dream best." She locked eyes with me and leaned forward.

"I wanna *rock.*"

I looked at her, waiting for more.

"You wanna rock?"

"That's it. I wanna *rock.*" Her eyes lit up, imagining the scene as if it were unfolding right in front of her. "On a stage, in a pub, in front of an off-their-face crowd. Not a cello—a fiddle! I wanna play the kind of music you *feel*, deep down in those places you don't always mention. I want to get 'em on their feet, dancing, sweating. going wild. *Rock and roll.* Then, when they're absolutely knackered, when they can't take any more …" She leaned in close. "I want to play three encores."

It wasn't hard to imagine her on a stage. We sat together in the glow of the candlelight, both caught up in our own thoughts.

Finally, I raised a glass. "To crazy dreams."

She raised hers. "May they both come true."

We toasted and sipped. She leaned back and looked me right in the eye. "Your dream's stupid. Mine's better."

Then, more whispering from behind the rock: "This is really going well. *She's hot!*" I heard AJ say.

"Kiss me, you no-talent hack!" the woman responded. Next, we heard the sound of mad kissing, light moaning, and clothing being rustled. Moments later, AJ reappeared with the wine bottle, hair a mess, adjusting his black clip-on tie. He poured us another glass and looked down like a proud Renaissance painter at the little scene he'd help create. It was obviously time for a monologue.

"Thissa young man here, he's a very generous,

caring man with a big heart and an even bigger house on the East Bluff. That someday he will inherit." There was a long pause. He blasted ahead. "He's hardworking, funny, brilliant …"

I caught his eye and signaled. *Too much.* He frowned, then readjusted his schtick. "… Yet, he's also, how you say, *confused?* Very stuck in his ways. Hates change. Doesn't want to move on. Can be greedy, a little misguided …"

He looked at me, his raised eyes seeking my approval. I glared at him. He frowned and adjusted again. "Yet still, a very, how you say, good catch? *Reasonable catch?* Whatever kind of catch." He stood awkwardly. "You decide. I'm, how you say, *outta here.*"

AJ then bowed theatrically and headed out of the thicket, mumbling to himself as he walked off, his accent dropping away.

"Tough crowd."

Erin and I continued the evening on the front porch of Wildcliffe. It was a quick walk from our dinner spot, and she was surprisingly game. We walked gingerly up the creaky front porch steps. Big Jack was in town for the weekend, and it was two in the morning. He needed sleep after the long drive from Detroit, and I wasn't ready to introduce a new 'friend' quite yet.

She stopped halfway up the steps. "This is your place?" she asked.

"Yup. We call it Wildcliffe."

"It's fantastic," she said, looking over the aged wicker and the sloping roof. She walked toward the railing and looked out at the moon reflecting off the Straits below, breathing in the night air.

We had a small, ancient refrigerator on the porch that traditionally housed several ice-cold rows of Stroh's beer, my dad's favorite. I opened the fridge door and pulled two from the rack. As I did, I glanced through the window into the family room. A fire burned in the fireplace, bathing the knotty pine walls in warm light. I heard a scratchy recording of the *Singin' in the Rain* soundtrack playing on the turntable.

Then Gramps emerged into the frame, spinning, from another room. He was dancing. He took a few steps and looked up as Gene Kelly hit the right notes. He kicked at a few imaginary puddles of water and took a few more steps. Erin joined me.

Watching the thin old man dance was mesmerizing. He wasn't exceptionally agile, but he possessed a practical grace. And he obviously loved it. Spying on his performance was inappropriate, and for a quick moment I recalled the times I had stood in front of the mirror in my underwear practicing spastic Mick Jagger moves to *Start Me Up*, and how mortified I'd have been if I found out I was being watched. The thought passed, and I kept watching.

"He's got some moves," Erin whispered. I passed her one of the cold beers, and she cracked it open without looking down.

The old man stopped in mid-spin, frozen like a dog sensing a squirrel. He pulled down the eyeglasses he had perched on his head and squinted through the window.

"That you, boy?" His voice was muffled through the glass, but it was clear enough. I knocked on the window and called to him. "Carry on! You look smooth!"

He waved his hands. "Nah. I need a break." He pulled the window open a crack and bent down, calling through the gap. "I was practicing for the Teamster's Ball. But I don't need new steps. I need a new wife." He looked closer through the glass. "You got a lady with you?"

"Yeah, Gramps. This is the girl I was telling you about."

He leaned even closer, pressing his face against the glass to get a better look. "Veronica?"

"No, Gramps." I looked over at Erin to make sure she understood this was a standard Gramps' routine.

"Sara? Was it Edna? Thelma? No, wait, it was *Jenny!*"

"No, Gramps. Her name's Erin."

"Right!" he said. Erin stepped up to the glass and waved at him. His eyes widened when he saw her. "Wow! Where ya been all my life, honey?"

Erin crouched down a bit, calling to him through the gap. "For most of it, I wasn't born."

He laughed. "Great line!" He gestured to us. "Bring your cocktails inside, rascals. Creaky ol' Gene Kelly here needs some company."

———

Erin perused framed photos on the living room wall. McGuinn family moments going back decades. Gramps pointed out a couple of handsome, straw-hatted men in front of the Chinese Theater in Hollywood. "That's me with my running buddy Billy Stanford. Old vaudevillian. Wanted in eight states for mail fraud, but a *great* guy."

He indicated a framed black and white of a cocky

young man in a fighter pilot's uniform. "That's me in my Helldiver, right before the Battle of Leyte Gulf. Boy, was *that* a lousy week. Shot down, pulled out of the drink, then the damn rescue boat sunk!"

He gestured to a faded color photograph in a homemade birch bark frame. "There's little Jacky on his Sting-Ray. Best paperboy this rock has ever known."

He looked at Erin. "You should know, I taught this scalawag everything he knows." He walked over to an overstuffed armchair and plopped down. He took some deep breaths, suddenly winded.

"Unless, of course, this little interlude ends with a slap in the kisser, in which case I take no responsibility for him." He smiled. "How old is your mother?"

"You're incorrigible, Mr. McGuinn!"

"God bless you for saying so. That is some accent you got there. Cork?"

"Originally. But I was raised in Dublin."

"Been there. Ever been to Limerick?" he asked.

"Of course," she responded. "I have relatives in Limerick."

I rolled my eyes. I knew exactly where this was headed.

"Great! Then you must know this one—"

"Gramps," I interjected. "Maybe we can hold off on the limericks tonight—"

But it was too late to stop the man. He stood in front of us and paused dramatically, as if awaiting quiet. His eyes twinkled. When he spoke again, it was in a mangled Irish brogue.

"*There was an old girl of Kilkenny, whose usual charge was a penny. For half of that sum—* " Erin joined in, and together they finished. " —*you might fondle her bum. The source of amusement to many.*"

Gramps' grin widened and he gave Erin a light hug. "You're something else, my dear. Not many young ladies know that little gem." He made a *shooing* motion. "Now, get out of here. I'm practicing. It's only 2:30 in the morning. You got three and a half hours until the sun comes up."

He signaled for me to come closer and pulled me out of earshot of Erin. She politely wandered back to the wall of photos to give us our moment. I turned to meet his gaze. He was no longer the same sweet codger who'd been kicking imaginary puddles to *Singing' in the Rain* ten minutes earlier.

"Listen, boy," he said, speaking in a low tone. "You're youngish, and you think you own the damn island. And don't get me wrong. I like that about you. You work your tail off and you celebrate accordingly at the end of each day." He looked over at Erin, who was pretending to be absorbed by a family portrait taken on the front porch sometime in the 70s.

"I had friends who claimed I have instincts about people. So I'll just say it." He nodded toward Erin. "You can't order a woman like *that* out of a goddamn vending machine on the Arnold Line dock. Don't let the summer sun fry your brain into thinking this is all a mirage. It's *not*. This is your life."

He patted me lovingly on the cheek.

"Now go have an adventure."

Erin was settled comfortably in my bike basket, which was now lined with a folded flowered bedspread to soften the wire edges. She was sipping a beer and telling me the story of how she met Gordon.

"We met in Dublin. At a pub, shockingly enough. He was looking at some land for a hotel. I was going through a rough patch. What can I say? We hit it off."

"A rough patch?"

She was silent and I didn't push her, focusing instead on Lake Huron rhythmically lapping against the rocky beach as the chain of my bike kept time. There was no rush. I could hear her take a deep breath. It all came out as an exhale.

"Our family pretty much lost everything. I'll spare you the details but it wasn't pretty. I dropped out of music school and got a job as a bar back in a pub to make ends meet. Gordon came in one night and we got to talking. He told me about this amazing island in Michigan, far away from Dublin. He pulled some strings and got me a gig playing music. So I just up and legged it."

We rode in silence for a bit.

"Legged it?"

"Left. Came here."

"Got it."

I couldn't help but notice she said nothing about her feelings for him. Then again, did I really want to know? We were having such a nice time.

"I don't see it. You two. He's a safe choice for someone like you."

"Well. Jack. It might not be yours to *see*." I passed under a streetlight illuminating her wild mane of black curls. "Obviously, Gordon and I are hitting some shit.

But before you go slagging him off, let me give you a tip. Every girl deserves to feel like Cinderella once in a while. And when the light's right, the guy makes a helluva Prince Charming."

She craned her neck and looked back at me, perhaps checking to see if her words had left a mark. Truth was, I did feel a sting of jealousy, but I wasn't going to mess up a perfect night by sulking. "What happened between the two of you?" she asked.

"He changed. The money. The schemes. This island is small. Eight-point-two miles around. It can only take so many new ideas. Shit, Erin. I dunno. Maybe I'm just a vindictive asshole. I mean, he's got everything. He's good looking. He's rich. He's got—"

"Stop right now, ya dingwop," she interrupted. "If you say he's got *me*, I'll smash your bullocks with a cello bow. Nobody's *got* me."

"I was going to say he's got perfect hair."

She giggled. "Oops."

"And … *dingwop?*"

"Sorry. It's a Dublin thing."

"Great word. Listen, I don't wanna ruin your image of Gordon," I said. "But it's common knowledge he'd make a deal at a wake."

"Fair play," she said. We rode on. "You *are* a bit of a vindictive arsehole. But I kinda like it."

"Can I show you something?" I asked.

It was 3 a.m. We rolled up in a foggy mist to Mister B's Ice Cream Shoppe on a quiet Main Street. I put down the kickstand and motioned for Erin to follow. On the left of the shop, there was a wooden door. I pulled out a key and jiggered it open, then pulled the string on a bare hanging lightbulb. We walked down a flight of stairs. It was my darkroom, a moldy lair piled high with old jars of rusty bolts, crumbling boxes, and random bike parts.

"The owner, Mr. B, lets me use it. I take care of his cone deliveries free of charge. Saves him a ton. He's not using it anyway."

"Well," she said, wandering in, "it's got a unique odor." She inhaled. "What is that?"

"It's a mix of photo developing chemicals and chocolate chip ice cream."

She smiled. "That's what I thought."

Fifty or so photos hung on wires, attached with clothespins. Wordlessly she began to inspect. She moved from one to another, taking her time. "What do you think?" I asked.

"You're good at working the angles." The "compliment" hung in the air. There it was. *Working the angles.* Was that like being a *tip man.*

"But ... ?"

She looked closely at a black-and-white shot of the empty dock. Stark, sure, but I thought it was pretty cool. She touched the border and turned it to let the light catch it. "Everything in its place, just like you told me when you described why you loved riding luggage." She looked at me. "You've got this amazing canvas of an island. But isn't it the *people* that give the island its life?"

Her eyes were alive. I felt exposed and foolish. Like a magician who had his magic hat turned inside out in front of the crowd, all pockets and secret hiding places revealed. She turned away, wandering past the other photos lightly swinging in our generated breeze. She stopped at a picture of a porter bike leaning against the green and red stripes of the Arnold Line freight shack.

"You're good. You just need to fill it all up with life. Go a little deeper." She looked closer at the photo and nodded, utterly sure of herself. "Yes. There's more you can do."

I started to regret ever showing her the photos. Truth be told, I was expecting to impress her with my secret talents. Be all artsy and shit. It was supposed to be a lay-up. The last thing I wanted was to be challenged.

Yuck.

"*Go deeper?* I don't understand."

A sad smile. "I know you don't. But the first step in fixing any problem is admitting you have one." She checked her watch, then leaned in and kissed me lightly on the lips. It was a quick peck that felt far friendlier than I cared to acknowledge. "Take me home, Ansel Adams. I'm knackered and I need my beauty sleep."

"No you don't." The moment I said it, I recognized it for what it was: high-density cheese.

"Brilliant line, Jack."

And with that, she trotted off toward the stairs.

CHAPTER EIGHT

Going Deeper
July 22, 1989

T he next day between boats, I attempted to read Mitch Albom's write-up on the current Detroit Tigers' debacle, one of my life's masochistic pastimes. The boys of summer had their feline asses handed to them by the California Angels and it was looking like a sweep. My Tigers fandom was a chronic condition passed down from Big Jack, who'd taken me to see Al Kaline get his 3,000 Hit Club award at Tiger Stadium. I'd been hooked ever since. I perused the *Free Press* sports page as a seagull greedily dug into an abandoned box of popcorn, but nothing in Mitch's sublime baseball prose was pulling me in.

I couldn't stop thinking about Erin O'Malley. It was irritating and a little exciting. Her rock-solid rebuke had struck a chord. *Go deeper.* What did that even mean? And who was she to judge me? I was *plenty* deep. I read books and stuff.

As I was folding up my *Free Press* to stow it under a bungee cord in my bike basket, Foster came skidding to a halt.

"Foster. Did you know Trina's having money troubles?" I said. "She might actually lose the WibHo."

"Did you know I have hemorrhoids?" He pointed at his butt. "I might actually lose my anus. But by all means, continue."

"I want to help her out. I want to … I don't know … *do something.*"

Foster leaned his bike up against the freight shack, chuckling and shaking his head like Cool Hand Luke. "Let me guess: The sexy cellist called you shallow."

How the hell did he know that? "No! I just want to help."

Foster hit me with a knowing grin. "Okay, Robin Hood, you know me. I love a good cause. Especially if it's hopeless. Trina's a good old gal. I lived at the WibHo my first summer. What's the issue?"

"Her taxes are past due, and it looks like Gordon, Inc. is harassing her into selling."

Foster smiled. "I knew it. All roads lead to Ireland. So, what do you want to do? Pass the hat?" he asked.

"I'm not sure, but it's a good start."

The dockporters never had a cause, but it turned out we were pretty damn good at raising cash. I had met with Trina and looked over her papers. An accountant I was not, but as I sat in the tiny WibHo kitchen between boats, she outlined a pretty compelling case for being flat busted. Taxes on the island were no joke, and she was a simple island woman who rented rooms, not some new-money bed-and-breakfast type with deep pockets. She plowed all her spare cash back into the hotel or into what she called her "knock-me-out scotch fund." She worked her ass off and suffered from swollen ankles and spiking arthritis.

And who was I to tell a seventy-five-year-old woman that she shouldn't enjoy her after-hours cocktails, although I did suggest that wearing three-inch high-heeled pumps from the '50s wasn't ideal for her ortho-pedic issues.

We still pocketed as much as we could for ourselves, but Trina was a new rallying cry. Something bigger than all of us. The WibHo was an *island thing,* and damn if we would let Gordon turn it into another pastel-painted, upscale, fake-authentic *inn.* There were plenty of those. This was for the future offspring of the Wheelers, the honeymooning couple who stayed at the WibHo earlier that summer.

We worked like dogs, covering each other's shifts with a hyper-charged spirit of camaraderie. All our extra cash went straight into a locked suitcase hidden under a forgotten stack of rotting life preservers in the freight shack. And day by day, the suitcase was filling up with sweaty bills, peeled off our fat tip rolls. Some contributed more, some less, but it all came out in the wash. It was a rhythmic quest, cash hitting palms on the beat and money piling up in the suitcase. *Bam-bam-bam,* it built to a crescendo like a jazz drummer's solo.

But would it be enough to pay off the WibHo's tax bill? We had no idea. We were dockporters, not hedge fund managers. When we finally got around to counting the money, July was almost over, and Trina's tax bill was nearly due.

We sat around on luggage carts as the sun cast long, bike-shaped shadows. We were sweaty from another tough day, sipping cold beers out of brown paper bags, noses sun-fried and spirits high. Since the mad caper was my scheme, I counted the cash. Spengler sat next to me, checking my math, and Fly sat next to him, checking his. I organized bills in neat little piles. The scene had a distinctly *On the Waterfront* vibe.

I finished the count and looked up at the boys, letting out a sigh. "Not even close."

There was an audible groan. Smitty quickly hopped to his feet. "Well. That's it, then. There's only one option I can see."

We fell silent, awaiting his idea. He took a deep breath and slowly surveyed the group and raised his eyebrows. "We buy jet skis."

The guys erupted in friendly boos and tossed a few empties at him, which he deftly ducked and dodged. "What? Jet skis are a blast!"

"We're not gonna spend the money on jet skis!" I said. "But there might be another way."

If you wanted to raise money on the island, like *real* money, you threw a party. I'd seen it my entire life growing up. The adults were always throwing parties for various causes. Big Jack said it best: Fundraisers give

people an excuse to "get loaded and feel good about it."
Ours wouldn't be some high society gala auctioning off
a gourmet dinner at the Grand or a wine and cheese hot
air balloon ride over the Mackinac Bridge. No, this was
a *Wildcliffe* bash. Antics for money.

We posted flyers all over Main Street. We called it a
fun-raiser—Spengler's clever wordsmithing—and the
good word blasted across the dockporter telegraph.
There was going to be a party at Wildcliffe to raise
money for one of our own. Five-dollar beers, seven-
dollar burgers, hot off the grill. Silent auction? Hardly.
If all went according to plan, it was going to get very,
very loud.

Fun-raising
   August 1, 1989

And it did get very, very loud.

The crowd was solidly island stock. The guys had
constructed a beer tent on the front lawn, and music
blasted classic rock from a set of old Yamaha speakers
we borrowed from the Chamber of Commerce. Foster
was operating the grill next to five coolers full of
donated meat from Doud's Grocery and the smell of
beef, hotdogs and corn on the cob wafted over the Wildcliffe lawn. He wore a white chef's hat, a rare menthol
cigarette dangling from his lips. Guess he figured if
you're going to suck in smoke for two hours, it may as
well taste like a breath mint. The locals were chatting it
up, holding red plastic cups, and children shrieked like
untamed monkeys.

On the porch, we had a full-on palm reading set-up. Madame Fantastico, with her thick black hair, gypsy scarves, and sparkling, jangling jewelry, held Fat Billy Brigg's palm. She was looking deep into his puffy eyes. She was known around town as June Hebbing and ran a souvenir shop on Main Street that sold rubber Indian spears and switchblade combs to tourist kids. But June had an alter ego and loved nothing more than to show up for parties and weddings in her full *Fantastico* garb. She agreed to donate all her profits to the cause, and there was already a line. I moved a bit closer to eavesdrop.

"You will meet a *beauuuutiful* woman," she said in her best faux Hungarian. Billy looked around nervously. He spotted his matronly wife, her hair done up in a beehive twenty years out of style and downing her second hamburger. He shifted in his chair and leaned close to Fantastico.

"*When?*" he asked.

I choked back a laugh and moved away, then caught my reflection in the porch window. I was wearing a blue blazer, clean jeans, and a red bowtie. It was a look. I figured if I was hosting a "fun-raiser," I would have to step up my game. Respectable but funky. Looking at the pictures from that night now, I cringe. I didn't look funky. I looked like a half-drunk weatherman.

Later, after a spectacular sunset, the crowd swelled and the music got louder. On the front porch swing, chatting with Gramps, was the woman of the hour, Trina LaFromme. I was worried that she might feel self-conscious—or worse, embarrassed—that her tax follies were exposed like a rash for all the island folks to see. But if it bothered her, she wasn't showing it. Gramps probably had something to do with that, as he laughed uproariously with her, sharing some outrageous island yarn. As I said, I was reasonably sure that some summer in the vintage past, the two of them had had their own amorous adventures.

Smitty wandered up to me holding a cup of beer, wearing the same ill-fitting jacket he had been sporting the night of our spy mission at the Grand. He inhaled his beer like a man emerging from the desert, following up with an insanely loud belch.

"*Bwwwwwaaaaaa* …" It kept going, so he deftly switched to spelling out the vowels. "AAA-eee-iiiiii-oooo-uuuu …" With one last reserve of gas, he rushed out the big finish. "*… and sometimes WHYYYY.*" It was disgusting. Yet brilliant. An older, raven-haired woman shot him a disapproving scowl.

"You're a pig, Smitty. A complete *pig.*"

Smitty lowered his head, chastened. "Sorry, Aunt Betty."

She resumed her conversation without missing a beat. Smitty stifled a giggle and whispered to me. "My Aunt Betty hates me."

"That's because you're gross," I said.

"I know. You're right. I need to change. And I *will* change." Smitty hit me with a thoughtful, level gaze. "Just probably not tonight."

He surveyed the party. His mouth dropped open. He elbowed me and leaned close. "*Holy shit!* That girl! The one with AJ. Over there." I followed his look. "She looks *exactly* like that movie actress. What's her name again? Corrine … Chemmie … something. She was in that movie with the door! You know! Where the door opens and sucks everyone in, and they're forced to see their own death ... *dammit, what's her name?"*

He was now punching himself on the temple, trying to bash her name into his brain. I looked over. The woman in question was chatting intently with AJ, wearing a rumpled Budweiser fishing hat, Ray-Bans, and jean cutoffs. She looked every bit the Michigan college girl. A lovely Michigan college girl. But still, a Michigan college girl. I squinted doubtfully.

"Nah, that's ..." I looked over. "Actually, I don't know who that is but she's not *famous*. I think she's a waiter at the Huron Street Café. Right?"

Smitty shook his head. "I'm tellin' ya, man! She looks like that actress." He took a deep breath and became oddly zen. He looked upwards, willing himself to remember her name. He clicked his fingers. *"Candace Layne!* That's her name! See, I knew I could remember if I just calmed the hell down and thought for a sec."

I looked at her again, squinting. "I don't see that at all."

But of course, once again Smitty was correct. It didn't look like Candace Layne. It *was* Candace Layne. But none of us knew that yet. Except, of course, AJ.

I snatched a crappy microphone we had connected to the speakers. It was time to play emcee and make some money. "I'd like to raise a glass to my dad for allowing us to trash Wildcliffe tonight." Big Jack, standing with friends, smiled sheepishly. "And, of course, a toast to my grandfather. Hizzoner, the mayor! To you, Gramps. On it goes!"

The crowd, now gathered on the porch, echoed the sentiment. *"On it goes!"*

To appreciative applause, Gramps bowed theatri-cally, sweeping his Michigan ball cap with a flourish. I plowed ahead. "Now in 1922, legend has it the dock-porters took on the local island polo team in a game we now call 'porter polo.' Bikes versus horses. But after dockporter Kirby Kotter had his tenders crushed by a Clydesdale in 1953, the game stopped."

I paused, letting the boys add some of their own flourish to the story. In unison, they held up their cups in a toast. "To Kirby."

I continued. "But once a summer, the porters divide up and play each other for charity. Nowadays, it's bikes versus bikes. This year, we're playing for our guest of honor, Trina. The boys here raised six-hundred bucks for her little tax issue. We got another three-hundred here tonight, thank you very much. But we need to double it. So, rather than a typical auction-type thing—"

Smitty grabbed the mic from me. "—which is *LAME!*"

I grabbed it back. "Yes, thanks, Smitty, for that insightful comment." I turned around to the crowd. "We challenge anyone here to three-on-three porter polo. Rules are simple. You score on us? You keep the money. We score on you? You match the funds."

The theme from *The Blues Brothers* kicked in from the speakers. Fly strolled up behind me wearing dark sunglasses and a black suit, his right wrist handcuffed to the red suitcase full of cash, like Jake Blues. In a matching black suit, Spengler trailed, crossing his hands in front of him like Elwood Blues, standing guard, dead serious. The crowd roared, loving it.

It was a lock that some flush islander would step up

and take the bet. Knock around a ball a few times, get skunked by the boys. A charade and a joke, but a charade and a joke for a noble cause. We double our money. We send Trina home happy, safe from the taxman for the rest of the summer.

I looked around, waiting for a volunteer.

I heard a voice from the back. "You're on!" Moving through the crowd with a pearly white, shit-eating grin, was Gordon.

I choked out a laugh. It came out sounding a little forced. "Gordon Whittaker? I have to say. I'm … impressed." I wasn't impressed. I was highly suspicious. Since I knew it was Gordon who was plotting to take the WibHo away from Trina not three weeks ago, I could only assume this was some sort of face-saving gesture.

"Where's your team?" I asked.

"Right down there." Gordon smiled and pointed. The lawn crowd parted as three electric luggage carts whined their way up the side driveway of Wildcliffe, each driven by a beer-wielding frat boy, each holding a mallet. My heart was now pounding.

This scene wasn't in the script.

Foster sauntered up to me, trying to go unnoticed, and whispered, "Let it go."

"Jack. I understand if you're not up for it," Gordon called over. "You can't beat golf carts on one-speed bikes. That's just stupid. Oh, but wait—didn't you once say a golf cart can never replace a dockporter?"

The crowd murmured and laughed. Things were heating up, and hell, who didn't love a little competition at a party? Nobody understood the big picture, and why would they? In the corner of my eye, I could catch side bets going down and money changing hands.

"Let's get it on!" someone called out.

I studied the crowd, my eyes finally landing on Erin leaning against the porch railing with a glass of red wine. She looked vaguely uncomfortable, perhaps the only other person at the party that understood the subtext behind the showdown. She also looked stunning. Casual, in jeans and a denim shirt, long dark hair in a loose ponytail. I locked eyes with her for an instant.

"You're on," I said. The crowd roared. "Tonight we drink, tomorrow we ride!" I added for good measure, gamely attempting to appear in control of my own funraiser.

The truth was, I was shitting bricks.

Looking back, the scene seems absurd. Three half-drunk guys in their early twenties lined up, side-by-side, straddling their bikes and looking across a poorly lit field on the East Bluff at three other half-drunk guys sitting in golf carts. All holding polo mallets.

You couldn't have created a more ridiculous, juvenile face-off if you had a week to brainstorm and a bag of weed. There was no doubt that Gordon had set this entire situation up to make us look like complete fools. A *screw you* to me and the boys to punish us for our *screw you* to him and his family.

It was an epic island *screw you*-off.

Makeshift goals were rigged up at either end of the field—tiny kid's soccer goals we had stored in the Wildcliffe cellar. The sun was setting, and long shadows of birch trees strafed the ground. Foster and Smitty were smacking a ball back and forth between them. I signaled for them to huddle up. It was time to get this over with.

"We'll get to the ball first and run a Kirby Double Dribble. *Boom*. Two passes and a crossover. It'll be over like that. Trust me, they're freaking," I reassured the guys as they looked across the field at the electric golf carts dubiously.

Gordon and his two cronies were lounging in their carts, chatting, sipping from red plastic cups full of Stroh's beer, and chuckling at some inside joke. *My Stroh's beer.* They looked calm as yogis, if yogis happened to be in college fraternities.

While the rest of the island was enjoying the show-down as another quirky island duel between two old pals, I knew Gordon's motivation better than anyone. Yes, he wanted Trina's place. But he also wanted to make his own statement by demonstrating how outdated the dockporter concept was. A quaint but obsolete relic of an older time.

Put to music, Gordon's metaphor went like this: Sleek luggage carts were The Beatles, and we were nothing but a crew of irrelevant fat Elvises in Rhine-stone jumpsuits. In his mind, it was time to exile all of us back to Graceland to croak on the toilet.

———

Rick the shit sweeper strolled out on the field with a whistle and a lit Pall Mall in his mouth, a wooden croquet ball in his grizzled right hand. He was wearing his ever-present government-issue green jumpsuit. His expression was droll, as if he wasn't exactly sure why he was even there. Gordon goosed the accelerator, and his cart skidded to a halt two feet away from Rick, the electrical engine whining in little spurts as he moved into position. I rolled my bike up to him.

"Alright, then. Let's do this thing!" Gordon said exuberantly.

Rick could barely contain an eye roll. The front-porch crowd had gathered on the edge of the field, most of them well-lubricated and whooping it up. Gramps stepped out and turned to the crowd, quieting them.

"Since we all have cocktails to tend to, this match is going to be quick. The first team to score …" He paused dramatically. "What's the word I'm looking for?" He looked up, as if awaiting enlightenment from the heavens. "Oh yes. I remember now. The first team to score … *wins!*" Rowdy applause.

Gramps turned back to the field and gave Rick a nod. Rick leaned over like a ref at a hockey game, his cigarette dangling. He glanced left, then right, making sure all players were in position.

"Is everybody ready?" yelled Gramps. The crowd cheered. We nodded gravely.

"Then … PLAY BALL!"

Rick dropped the ball, stood up, and grimly walked to the sidelines without looking back. I got the vague sense he thought the whole spectacle was ridiculous.

In hindsight, it seems like the match lasted about eighteen seconds, but it was probably less. One of the unique features of porter polo was that it was famously difficult to score. Matches often went on for hours and ended in a tie because the sun went down.

Not this time.

Gordon buzzed over the instant Rick backed away, drew his mallet toward the heavens, and smacked the ball dead center. The hollow *crack* echoed through the pine trees that surrounded the field, and the crowd cheered.

The ball skipped, unencumbered, toward Gordon's grinning buddy, who accelerated his cart in a short electric burst, effortlessly catching up to the pass. Foster and Smitty pedaled furiously toward the ball while I rode my bike toward Gordon, feeling that I should "cover him" like some sort of half-assed streetball player. He hit the pedal and moved past me like I was standing still, the rear tires of his cart kicking up a rooster tail of loose dirt into my face.

The way I remember it, the ball was passed twice, and back to Gordon, who by now had left me in the dust. Literally. He smacked the ball hard, and we all watched in wonder as it flew through the air, framed by the glorious backdrop of Lake Huron, and hit the back of the tiny child's net with a soft, ropey thud.

We lost so quickly that even the crowd didn't know what happened. Gordon and his pals hopped out of their carts and executed a well-choreographed victory routine, which, of course, charmed everyone. Their dance quickly disintegrated, and they jumped around and hooted like vicious hyenas after a kill. The first thing I did was shoot a glance toward the sidelines, scanning the crowd for Erin.

There she was.

Doubled over in hysterics.

———

Gordon stood on the Wildcliffe porch, holding the red suitcase full of money. While I never honestly expected him to keep it, I also knew that by losing, we had blown any chance of doubling the cash and likely doomed Trina's financial bailout in the process. Gordon took the microphone. Trina was now scowling at him from the steps. He regarded the suitcase and spoke.

"As Jack said, this is a bet. And a bet is a bet. And …" he looked over the assembled revelers, his chin raised high. "… we won!"

He dropped the microphone, turned, and walked off with the case. The crowd groaned. A few light boos. Suddenly he stopped, did a dramatic about-face, and skipped back, picking up the microphone, his eyes mirthful.

"Oh, *come on.*" He held the suitcase aloft. "Do you think I could possibly keep this? The WibHo is a legend!" He continued. "You provide a service. The thing is, not everyone can afford to stay at the fancy hotels." His eyes sought me out, then landed. A glint. "Seriously, I bet a generation got their start in those creaky old beds." I stepped in closer. It all sounded sickly familiar. "In fact, I bet a *couple* of generations got their start there!" The crowd laughed with him, appreciating the sexy-time undertones.

He continued, "They'll bring *their* kids to this island." I could feel my sweaty scalp and ears heating up. *He was delivering my speech.* It was the identical spiel I'd given that afternoon early in the summer to Trina after dropping off the Wheelers' bags.

But what could I do? Tell him to shut up? How would that go over? And I had to admit it: He delivered my speech better. I chomped down on my tongue.

He continued, "That's the way we do things here. We take care of our own. *On it goes!*"

The porch crowd responded with a low *awwwww.*
Gramps tipped his hat toward Gordon. *Shameless!* He
even had the gall to pinch the line that I'd pinched from
my Gramps.

With a budding showman's gift for PR, he withdrew
a check from the pocket of his khaki Dockers and held it
up. "This check is written out to you, Trina, on behalf
of my mom and dad and the entire Whittaker family. It
covers your back taxes in full ..." He paused dramatically. "... *for a year.*" The crowd erupted in cheers.
"Thank you for everything you do for this island."

Trina, stunned, tears in her eyes, walked straight to
Gordon and gave him a heartfelt hug.

Gordon wasn't upstaging me. He was kicking my ass
all over the Wildcliffe porch. He'd pulled off the impossible, transforming himself, his gang, and even his stupid
little golf carts into the cavalry, arriving to rescue the
aging damsel and her fading hotel. The whole scene
reminded me of one of Bull's cheap-ass bungee cords
stretched too far. Shit, I practically teared up myself.

The flushing sensation was creeping down my neck
and heading toward my ass. I reflexively joined in the
clapping. The sound of my own claps and the unfiltered
relief on the face of Trina brought me back.

We did it. Not exactly how I imagined doing it. But
we did it.

Then, the cheap, metaphorical bungee cord
snapped. From the back of the porch, I heard a
panicked woman's voice crying out: "Call a doctor!"

I barely remember pushing through the tightly clus-
tered crowd, but what I saw next will stay with me
forever. It was Gramps, stretched out on the wicker
swing. His skin was pallid, blue, his mouth contorted.

Big Jack ripped open Gramps' plaid shirt with both hands. His buttons flew off and one of them hit me straight in the eye. The oddest things stay with you. Gramps' eyes were closed. He wasn't breathing.

I spotted his University of Michigan baseball cap on the ground. Faded blue—almost brown—with a block letter M. He had once told me he'd worn that hat to 138 Michigan football games. He *had* to be bullshitting, but maybe not. It was a pretty precise number to make up. The old man was a superfan if there ever was one. I picked it up and brushed it off as dad pressed rhythmic hands down on the old man's chest, trying to restart his shattered heart. Then the crowd parted, giving him space as an island medic rushed in and began proper CPR.

But I already knew.

The light had gone out.

Funeral
  August 7, 1989

Gramps' funeral was one of the most well-attended and non-depressing funerals the island had ever known. His respect level cut like a Ginzu knife across all strata of the island. The well-to-do business owners and wealthy cottagers were there because, in many ways, he was one of them. A hard-driving, successful entrepreneur in his day, he was a man who had created businesses and knew how to talk finance with the best of them. He was, as his obituary accurately stated, "a business leader."

I may have been the only person attending the

funeral that day who knew how he felt about that monied scene. He'd labeled it all as "phony baloney" to me many times. "Jacky, you can be whatever you want in this world, but for Chrissake, stay away from the phony-baloney bullshit." He didn't golf, and he'd never joined a country club or owned a sailboat. But he played the game, pressed the right flesh, and was beloved by that crowd.

The islanders had their own reason for loving him. It was more straightforward: He spent time with them. Whenever we couldn't find Gramps for dinner, the first place to look was either the Mustang Lounge or the pool hall above Horn's Bar, where he'd be racking it up with the locals. He was a legendary pool shark and loved nothing more than to listen to island stories from the old-timers, many of whom had the strong Chippewa bloodline that guaranteed a fiery tale. While my ancestors may have fled Ireland for a better life in America, these islanders had never fled anything. Their ancestors had paddled beaver pelts in canoes through these very Mackinac waters long before the word "tourist" had been invented. Gramps worshipped that reality.

We had the service at Ste. Anne's church. As Father Pete finished up his sermon, a light round of laughter echoed through the large, airy space. I craned my neck, glancing first at my sister Beth, who had come up for the service from her job downstate, then to my dad. He leaned over and whispered to me. "Get your hankie ready, kid."

From the back of the church, two members of the University of Michigan marching band, in full uniform and holding trumpets, strode in time to the pew. Father Pete stepped back to give them space. I shared a look with Beth. She shook her head and hit me with a look that said *don't ask me.*

The trumpeters stood for a moment, silently counting off a start. They raised their instruments in unison.

It was the most beautiful version of *The Victors*—the University of Michigan fight song—I had ever heard. Slow and solemn.

The congregation erupted in a spontaneous laugh-sob as the musicians played their respects. My dad looked down at his feet. I could hear teardrops slowly drop-drop-dropping on the paper program in his hand. The song finished up. He raised his head and wiped away a few tears.

He looked over at me, breaking into a wide grin, and began to laugh. He looked skyward, and, almost to himself, he whispered, "... *on it goes.*"

———

Gramps was gone, but the wake at Wildcliffe was a party, just the way he would want it. The Kingston Trio, his favorite band of all time, blasted on the stereo, a rousing version of *Tijuana Jail.* Laughter and stories echoed across the porch. I stood with a few of the boys and took it all in.

"The old guy did a lot," Foster said, observing the crowd. "Look at all these people. We should be so lucky when we kick."

I noticed Gordon and his father, silver-haired and heavy-set, chatting in a quiet corner. Bill Whittaker had the glowing jowls of a wealthy sailor and always smelled like expensive aftershave. Erin stood with them, looking pleasantly bored. We connected with a glance. She excused herself and walked over to me, putting her hand lightly on my shoulder. It wasn't the moment to notice such things, but it was obvious she'd never shared our dinner escapade with Gordon the night she abandoned him at the Grand. So I guess she wasn't even considering me a credible threat. *Wonderful.*

"I'm sorry, Jack. It was a true honor to meet your grandfather. I'll never forget that night. Watching him dance."

"I'm glad you got that chance," I said. "He liked you." I thought back to Gramps' speech to me that night on the porch and smiled to myself. *He liked you a lot.*

She noted the brown leather camera case strapped around my shoulder. "Capturing some life with that thing, I hope."

"Today?" I said. "No. Actually today our featured subject is—wait for it—*death!*"

"Jesus, Mary, and Joseph, Jack. You're terrible." She smacked me, but it was obvious she appreciated a little taste of dark humor.

"Ah. He'd be fine with it. And yes, I've been taking a ton of photos lately. Your mysterious little lecture that night? *Go deeper?* Turns out it wasn't complete gibberish."

"Good. You never know. You just might be talented."

I started to protest, but she cut me off. "Just take the compliment, McGuinn. I don't hand many out."

I nodded. Fair enough. Truth was, I was embarrassed and could feel my face flushing. *Talented* was a word nobody on planet Earth had ever used to describe me.

I turned away and noticed Gordon, wearing a

tailored dark suit with the tie undone, speaking with my dad. He leaned in, nodding thoughtfully and gesturing as Big Jack listened closely. Bill Whittaker was standing a few steps away, keenly observing the exchange. I felt my stomach tighten. Something didn't feel right. Erin followed my gaze to the conversation.

"It looks like you were right about him, Jack."

"Which part?"

"You said he would make a deal at a wake." She shook her head. "Looks like that's exactly what he's doing."

CHAPTER NINE

Moving Out
August 9, 1989

T he next time I was alone with Big Jack was on
a rocky stretch of beach at the tip of the island
called *Pointe Aux Pins*, miles from town. We'd
often ride there when I was a kid to skip stones, and he'd
casually interrogate me about my life, doing his best to
catch up on the lost summer days we had spent apart.

I tossed a flat rock sidearm across the glassy lake. It
danced beautifully for about five skips but caught the
edge of a minuscule wave and flipped and tumbled like
one of those hydroplane speedboats I used to see on
Wide World of Sports. Instant destruction.

"Kerplunk," Big Jack said, watching with arms
folded. "I'll never forget the summer you won the stone-
skipping contest. What were you, twelve?"

"Eleven," I said, kicking at the rocky beach, hunting

for another flat stone that would fit between my index finger and the base of my thumb. I was particular about the shape and weight of my skipping stones. Selection was everything, I'd come to understand. I stopped and looked at him. "But I don't think that's what we're here to talk about."

"No. I guess that's not today's subject, kid." He walked to the edge of the water, looking out at the horizon at a distant ore boat cutting across the straits. He shaded his eyes. "What's the name of that freighter?"

Ever since I was old enough to read, I'd been tracking ore ships—"freighters"—as they moved taconite pellets through the Great Lakes. I had a telescope from Sears mounted on Wildcliffe's front porch along with a copy of *Know Your Ships*, a yearly periodical that listed every Great Lakes freighter.

Over time, I had learned to recognize any ship instantly, merely by sizing up the telltale markings on the smokestack. Their names had become familiar as friends. I squinted. "Looks like the *Roger Blough*."

"That's what I was thinking. How long is she?"

"858 feet, I think."

"She's a biggie." It occurred to me that many Great Lakes ore boats had male names. The *Roger Blough* is a *she?* The things you learn from ship-watching. We shared the moment, watching the ship push through the Lake Huron waters. Her payload of iron ore would eventually be unloaded on trains downstate, delivered to refineries, shoveled into a blast furnace, and spat out as a midsize family sedan. Which, in a perfect world, would be sold by McGuinn Oldsmobile.

"What happened?" I asked.

The day after the wake, Big Jack broke the news to my sister and me that he sold Wildcliffe. Done deal. He delivered the announcement at a sit-down on the front porch. After nearly vomiting, my reaction was to get up and walk away. What a selfish jerk I was. But that front porch had been my world from the time I could crawl. Was it Neil Young in *Helpless* who sang *all my changes were there?* It was a bone-deep ache.

He looked away from the freighter and walked a few steps down the beach. I'd never seen him look that lonely. "The cars aren't moving the way they used to. We held on as long as we could."

I threw another flat rock toward the water, which also *kerplunked*.

He continued, "Your grandfather was a business-man, too. He wouldn't let this family sink under the weight of memories." Then he tossed a rock. "I won't either."

"When did this all go down?" I asked.

"Talks have been going on for the last month or two. The Whittakers brokered it. Mainly the kid. Your old pal Gordon. They have a client who might want to convert it over to a bed-and-breakfast, but they weren't definite, and I didn't push." He kicked at some rocks. "It's a good deal. It'll give us some runway, and right now, we need it."

Gordon. *Again.*

"Why didn't you ask me for help?" The moment I spoke the words, I regretted it. Big Jack didn't look back at me. He focused on the ship, now shrinking from view.

"I'm pretty sure I did."

Straight to the gut this time. And he was right. For years he had practically begged me to join the family business. Help. Learn the ropes. *McGuinn and Son.* And for years, I had been acting as if the moments I had carefully crafted for myself would last forever.

"Jack. Don't think about this as losing Wildcliffe."

"How should I think about it, Dad?" I turned toward him, now desperate for fatherly insight. He was looking out at the lake. He seemed to be giving the question it's due consideration. A smile slowly lit up his face, as if he'd stumbled upon a magnificent discovery.

"Think about how lucky we were to ever have it in the first place. It's not a normal thing to have a summer cottage on Mackinac Island. Let's choose to be grateful." He hurled a flat stone hard across the water. It sailed and picked up speed, pattering at least fifteen times before sinking.

"Holy shit, dad. That was impressive."

"Might be my best ever." He smiled and added softly, "On it goes, kid."

The line had made so much more sense when I had pictured myself standing on that porch as a crusty old man, surrounded by my old, crusty pals. Maybe our wild-eyed grandchildren now ran the streets, just as we had.

I had assumed "on it goes" simply meant *congrats, you undeserving knucklehead. You inherited a sweet-ass pad with a view.* I was embarrassed at my hubris.

"Does it, Dad? Does it *go on?*"

He looked straight at me and said, without hesitation: "That's up to you now."

The next week was a blur as we moved our belongings out of Wildcliffe for the last time. Aside from the dusty, physical work, what I remember now is the crappy television set my dad always kept on in the kitchen. On the news, President Bush was signing a bill bailing out something called *the savings and loan industry* from paying back their massive debts. That's fine for them, I thought, but for reasons beyond my feeble grasp of economics, I had to clear out my underwear drawer by noon.

It wasn't Big Jack's fault that Oldsmobile crapped out both the Delta 88 *and* the Cutlass Supreme with lousy diesels, or that the Omega was a hyped-up disaster that barely got him to the island on Friday nights. Hell, if you're handing out government money, write a fat check to Carroll Shelby and get Olds back in the game. I *liked* my summers on the island.

But nothing was fair that week.

I helped pack up box after box of McGuinn family treasures. Because of some arcane regulation that must have passed side-by-side with the "no cars" law, Mackinac Island homes *included* the original furniture, probably to avoid turning the island into an insane, chaotic double episode of *Antique Hunters*. So, logistically speaking, the move out was not difficult. But emotionally, it was brutal.

As I filled up a large cardboard box with odd crap from the pantry drawer, I discovered the old game of *Clue* that we had played so many times growing up. For years we all crowded around a card table in the downstairs family room, which had windows looking out over a panoramic vista of the Straits of Mackinac, and played *Clue*. Rain or shine.

There was something about the game that aligned

perfectly with Wildcliffe's fading wood vibe. I never saw a ghost but if Gramps had told me someone named Colonel Mustard had murdered someone called Professor Plum with a candlestick in the pantry, I'd have believed it.

Upon reflection, *Clue* is a pretty twisted game. Marketed to kids, it implied that murder with blunt objects was legitimate family entertainment. *That's horrifying.* I opened up the box. The cards were worn, and the board itself had split at the folding seams. It was an over-the-hill game, easily replaced with one quick drive to a mainland K-Mart. But we never upgraded. And I'd be damned if I'd toss it in a dumpster after this long. Maybe I hadn't played in ten years, but it sure as hell wasn't garbage.

And this is why packing took five full days.

That week, Wildcliffe was pulsing with electric, eclectic McGuinn history. Even the *dust* felt significant. In other rooms, my dad and sister were mining memories of their own, dislodging moments and inspecting them for their emotional significance. It was painful, time-consuming work.

As I lugged a plastic garbage bag loaded with emotions to the curb, I passed by the storage shed. The door was open, revealing a line of rusty bikes. We always had a few clunkers around for guests to borrow. They were nothing to shout about, but they added to the vibe.

Wildcliffe had always been a place where friends were encouraged to grab a bike and take a spin. My dad now was donating the bikes to the island fire department for their yearly charity drive, including my old Schwinn Sting-Ray—the paperboy steed. The sparkly orange banana seat was rotted, and both tires were cracked and flat.

In the corner, behind a shelving unit stacked with boxes of shingles, was another old Schwinn. This model was called a Hollywood. It had been my mom's bike. It was green and had two rusty side pannier baskets. A few summers before she passed, she had swapped the old classic out for a more functional, sporty mountain bike. I had lobbied her hard to stick with the Hollywood and avoid what I dismissively called "chasing trends." But she brushed me off with a smile. She wanted gears. And why did I care if she bought a new bike? I couldn't explain it then or now.

"You just hate change," she laughed. "How did your zany mother spawn such a little *purist?*"

I tossed the bag into the dumpster and wheeled the Hollywood out of the condemned line, stashing it behind the house. It was salvageable.

And I had plans for it.

I stood with my dad and sister on the dock. I was still in my porter garb but had taken the afternoon off to make sure the six full luggage carts made it onboard. A McGuinn Oldsmobile truck waited in Mackinaw City to transport the remnants of Wildcliffe Cottage to some nondescript Southeast Michigan storage unit.

I had a contract with Trina at the WibHo and, frankly, there was no other place to go anyway. I wasn't going to spend the summer in the sweltering humidity of southeast Michigan. And more importantly, I had a bet to win.

Dad had made a deal on my behalf. I could remain in the tiny apartment above the dilapidated barn behind the cottage. It galled me that I would essentially be a guest of the Whittaker family. That said, my self-right-eous indignation didn't stop me from taking the deal. I still needed a place to sleep.

A bed beats pride.

Dad pulled me aside and looked me straight in the eye. "Kid, listen to me. Whatever it is you're looking for might be on this island. It might not be. But since you're staying. *Find it.*"

It occurred to me, the McGuinn family men were absolute geysers of vague, cryptic wisdom. *On it goes.* Now, *find it?* All this deep, imparted circumspection, yet I could barely balance a checkbook. Even so, I was grateful for any plan, even one as opaque as *find it.*

"I'll try. I promise. I love you, Dad."

He pulled a handkerchief from his back pocket and unabashedly wiped away a tear.

"I love ya too, kid." He took one last look at the house on the East Bluff. From this distance, it still looked like ours. It was hard to fathom we'd just cleared it out. He turned back as if he had remembered something important.

"One other thing." He looked toward the vending machine. "Do us all a big favor."

"What is it?"

"The McGuinn family paid its dues. I'd like to believe the island will remember us. But you never know. So, for me, your grandfather, your mom, your sister, all of us …" He pointed at the list carved on the wall by the vending machine. I wasn't aware he even knew about it. "For God's sake, kid, *ride blackjack.*"

He broke into a wide grin and hugged me close. My sister finally broke and sauntered away to have her cry in private. In the corner of my eye, I could see Cap Riley leaning on the railing of the ferry. He knew the score. Always did. He'd watched our family come and go for most of his thirty years on the dock. Cap Riley and I locked eyes for a moment as Dad squeezed me tighter. The captain gave me a discreet salute and turned away, heading into the pilothouse to fire up the engines.

Ten minutes later, the *Straits of Mackinac II* picked up power, diesel engines ramping up, roiling the Lake Huron water. I reached in my pocket, pulled out the Instamatic, and brought it up to my eye. It was a blur. One tear. Maybe two. *Tops.* Regardless of my impaired vision, I snapped four pictures in succession.

I bought a can of Mountain Dew from the vending machine and walked to the end of the dock. I sat down, my feet dangling six feet over the water. For the next half-hour, I watched the ferry motor toward the mainland until it was just a speck against the blue horizon sparkling with sunlight.

And then it was gone.

I set my bags down on the floor of the dusty barn apartment and looked around. It was a tiny two-room space that smelled like manure. While we hadn't had horses for years, the smell was a legacy and would likely never dissipate. The boys followed me in and wandered around the place in silent awe of my shocking fall from grace.

Fly glanced doubtfully through the smudged glass window and looked toward the main house. "So, who exactly was it that stole your future nest egg, Jack?"

"No idea." It was true. The whole thing had come together so fast. "The buyers wanted to remain private. But Gordon brokered it."

"Of course he did," Smitty said. "Guy's got no queems."

"*Queems?*" Spengler said, inspecting the aged, brownish bedspread thoughtfully, like a scientist. "Do you mean *qualms?*"

"Probably," Smitty responded without a trace of shame. "Yeah. *Qualms*. That sounds better."

Foster was deep into another letter, now lounging on the creaky couch. "*Eres espectacular*. I'm spectacular, she says! But *what's* spectacular? This shit is driving me *nuts!* Dammit. I should've studied abroad."

Smitty looked over. "What? You studied lots of broads, Foster."

"*A*-broad, Smitty. It's when you go to another country and—never mind." He resumed his laborious decrypting.

I joined Fly at the window, looking out across the weed-covered backyard at the main house. "Weird," I said. "That cottage there is a part of me." I looked around the apartment. "So, this dump is like a small, grosser part of me."

"Like, sort of, living in your own waxy eardrum?" AJ asked hopefully. The guys joined, game to help me through the puzzling metaphor.

Foster looked up. "Or like living in your own mucus-infected nostril?" he asked.

"Or in your own ass, in a way," Smitty concluded. "I

mean, it does smell like shit in here. So it's kinda like …" He trailed off. "Ass-y? I dunno."

All the guys nodded. While the conversation had devolved into scatological gibberish, I remember feeling grateful to have such supportive pals.

Smitty continued. "Naw. You know what? This place is *great*. Seriously. Little caulk. Some paint." As he finished, his foot broke through a rotted board, and his leg disappeared up to his knee.

"Shit!" he yelled, reaching for help.

"—Some major structural work," Spengler added.

We yanked him out of the fresh hole in the floor, and Fly dropped a grimy red carpet over the rotted cavity. "Don't step here," he warned me. "Ever."

My philosophical waxing session was not over. "There was a time when you could make an argument that Gordon and I were equals," I said. "We both had family cottages. He has class. I have a tan. But now?" I looked around. "I would *never* bring Erin here."

"Erin? *Here?*" Foster laughed. "You couldn't convince that woman to visit this shitbox if you scored her a gig with the Boston Pops. She's got standards."

"You're wrong, Foster. She likes me. I can feel it."

"I think Jack might be right," AJ piped in. "See, now he's *wounded*." He turned to me. "You're like a sad little deer with a broken hoof." AJ was now, apparently, a zoologist. He continued. "You've been banished from the forest and you're limping across a busy freeway. No Wildcliffe Cottage. No front porch with a view. No fridge full of free brewskies. You're pathetic." He looked at Foster. "Tellin' ya, Foster, some women love that stuff."

Fly spoke up. He was over it. "Listen, if you're still

stressin' about Lucky Charms, *crawl out of your own ass* and do something. And forget trying to impress her with luggage. That woman is an *artist*. That's your ticket. You got any talents you've been keeping a secret? Time to bust 'em out. And you better move fast. Gordon? He's *rich*, and he's *pretty*." Fly glanced toward the bathroom. "And I'm guessing his shitter's functional." He looked out the window, craning his neck. "Looks like the four o'clock is rounding the break wall, boys. Can't miss the boat."

The guys nodded and shuffled toward the door. I joined them. They had passed down the verdict, and my pity party was over. It was time to crawl out of my own ass.

Wonderful.

Now *that* was stuck in my head.

The family was gone. Wildcliffe Cottage was gone. I made a bet I probably couldn't win. So I decided to restore a bike.

Mom's old Schwinn Hollywood had potential. Foster had a decent workshop attached to his apartment up in the woods, so on my next day off, I began sanding, painting, and cleaning up the old rig. I stayed with a deep shade of emerald green. It was the only decent-looking spray paint I could find at the hardware store. I thought Erin might appreciate a green bike, being Irish and all. A stereotypical assumption, but I was not well-traveled.

After I finished the renovation, I rolled the bike to the dock and locked it up tight with a chain and padlock. I walked over to the payphone mounted on the freight shack and dropped a quarter in the slot. I hadn't used a phone in three months, and it felt strange in my sweaty hand. I heard a voice fumble and pick up.

"Erin?" I asked.

"Who wants to know?" *Unmistakable.*

"This is Jack."

"Oh. Hi, Jack." She sounded receptive. *This was good.* "How are the photographs coming?"

"Better. Thanks to you. But listen, that's not why I called." I paused, now exceptionally self-conscious. Why *did* I call?

"Erin. Listen. I've been thinking." I charged headlong into a monologue I really should have rehearsed a few times. "The pity party is over. Fly's right. It's time to crawl out of my own ass. *Wait!* That didn't come out right." I trailed off.

There was a long, brutal pause on the other end of the line.

"Have you been drinking?"

"No," I fumbled. "Not drinking. *Thinking.* I've been thinking about what you said. The photos. No people. Not going deep. And it's not just the photos. It's everything. I'm all surface. I'm a tip man!" *Rambling! Blowing it!*

"I'm just in it to … sssssssssss—" I could hear myself trailing off into an awkward hiss, like warm air seeping out of a rubber tire. A seagull landed on the dock piling and settled in, staring at me with piercing eyes. Judging me.

"Shit. Forget all that. I mean, what I'm trying to say is—"

"Stop talking," she said. "Allow me to save you from yourself."

"Thank you," I replied, truly grateful.

"You were right all along about Gordon. He *would* try and make a deal at a wake. In fact, he did. Your grandpa's wake, to be exact. It was pretty disgusting. The more I thought about it, the more it opened up my mind about some things." I heard a bed creak, as if she wanted to be sitting down for this next part of the conversation.

There was a long pause, and then she spoke: "So. You want to give this a shot?"

After my earlier stammering, this was the last thing I expected to hear. I blurted out an answer: "Hell yeah!"

I was immediately embarrassed by my exuberance but felt better when I heard a chuckle on the other end. We finished up the call with a plan to meet up the next day.

I hung up the phone and hopped around the dock like Rocky at the top of the Philadelphia Museum of Art steps, arms raised high, throwing air-punches. A few wary tourists passed by, giving me a wide berth.

Then I lowered my arms and took a deep breath as reality settled in. Being the underdog was much more manageable. I knew how to play that role like a champ. And Cap Riley's assessment early in the summer was accurate:

Erin was *way* out of my league.

———————

Two days later, I found myself plopped down in the stern seat of a borrowed canoe, camera strapped around my neck, paddling Erin across Haldimand Bay. Other than her guest room at the WibHo, it was the first time she'd experienced the island from a vantage point other than the privileged heights of the Grand porch or Gordon's stately family cottage on the West Bluff. As she took in the crystal blue water and gazed at the island, it was clear that slumming it with a dockporter was okay by her.

"Today, I'm taking you from the bottom of this island to the top. We'll traverse the entire socioeconomic stratosphere. You'll see how it's just like the real world, only smaller." I paddled a few strokes. She smiled, the cool island breeze blowing through her unkempt, jet-black hair. "We start at sea level. Where we all began, emerging from the slime. Hungry for tips."

She leaned back. "Darwinism. Sexy."

"Smile." I snapped a shot of her. I knew instinctively it was a good moment.

Meanwhile, about forty-five yards away, the boys were lounging on hay bales and tossing around a football, waiting for the next ferry. I wasn't there, but much like my imagined dialogue between AJ and Candace Layne, I'm reasonably sure it went something like this:

"You can't compare Louis Vuitton to Hartmann. There's no parallel. Louis has *class.* The gold standard." AJ prattles on.

"What do you know about class?" asks Fly. "Until very recently, you were bustin' a mullet and a gold chain. Louis is tacky."

"Nah, man. Louis is love. Never steered me wrong."

"That's exactly why you're going to make it in Hollywood," counters Foster. "You're a Louis Vuitton man. Style over substance. All gold labels and shit-brown fabric but no heft. No durability."

AJ is cool as always. "Maybe. But someday, you'll be visiting me in my Beverly Hills mansion designed by Louis Vuitton himself, floating in my gold-labeled Louis pool and eating sushi off 'shit-brown' Louis plates, and you'll understand!

One Louis to rule them all!" he yells.

Somewhere during this absurd exchange, I'm assuming Foster spots Erin and me paddling the canoe in the distance. He breaks into a winning grin and turns to the team, a devious idea visibly blooming. He says something like this: "Boys, let's take a moment to reflect on the suddenness of young love. It hits you. You never see it coming. Total surprise. Take our boy—"

The guys see where this is going and smile at each other. Foster continues. "He's in love? Perhaps. But has it *hit* him? Has he been smashed in the face with love?"

Foster tosses Smitty the football. "You're right, Foster," nods Smitty. "He never has. I've known him since we were kids." Foster gives Bull a nod. Nothing more needs to be said. Everyone moves into position. Bull stretches his kicking leg, tests the wind, squints.

Again, I'm guessing.

Bull says something like, "Looks like about thirty-seven yards." His face hardens. "Tee that shit up."

Smitty holds the ball in place. Bull readies himself in his kicker's stance. He executes a quick Lord's Prayer, takes a deep breath, and boots it. The moment of contact with the half-dead football is breathtaking.

POW! The kid has serious skills. The ball leaves the atmosphere, end-over-end, and arcs left. Foster shields his eyes as they track with the ball, now beginning a lazy drop downward.

Toward the canoe.

"Oh, baby, it's so good," says Smitty.

I let the canoe drift and snapped a few shots, mostly to impress Erin. The young artist shtick. My words were spilling out like a rookie carriage tour driver. "I've always loved this angle. It reminds me of the rowboat scene in *Somewhere in Time.* You know, they filmed that movie right here on Mackinac Island."

"I know. I love that movie," Erin replied.

"Really? I love that movie too!" *Wow,* I thought to myself. *Shameless.* While I appreciate it now, back then I thought it was one of the cheesiest movies I'd ever seen. I was flat-out lying to her.

"I wouldn't have guessed that," she said. "You strike me as more of the *Rambo* type. Maybe *Rocky.*"

"Rocky? Rocky is cheesy. It's okay for low forehead types. But come on. *Somewhere in Time* is a classic. So romantic. Like when Superman finds the new penny in his pocket and goes back in time? *'Richaaaaard!'* It's devastating."

Devastating? Lord. Who the hell was I trying to be? Nevertheless, I continued. I was eleven the summer they filmed the movie, and I had a few worthy anecdotes for just such an occasion.

"My mom worked as a wardrobe assistant on the movie. My dad was convinced she was having a fling with Christopher Reeve. Caused a huge blowout, but they worked it out."

I was making this part up. It was serious drama that summer. For a few months, Hollywood invaded the island, and it seemed everyone, including my parents, lost their minds.

"Your mum? Where is she?" she asked.

"She passed a few years ago. Cancer."

"I'm sorry."

I just nodded. She didn't push it and I was grateful. It wasn't the moment to indulge in melancholy about Mom. Besides, that was something I could handle just fine on my own.

Recalling that summer made me feel good. My mind wandered back to a moment in 1979. Jane Seymour and Christopher Reeve riding bikes past Wildcliffe as if it were the most normal thing in the world. I was standing in the front yard with the hose, pretending to irrigate the geraniums, but, in reality, waterboarding a garter snake that had poked through the wall alongside the driveway. I heard a female British accent and looked up. It was stunning, the cumulative beauty of those two specimens together. Seymour was a vision in khaki shorts, her hair in a ponytail. Reeve was in white tennis shorts and a ragged yellow T-shirt. He noticed me watering the grass. He smiled and they rode on.

I had a thought, profane and clear as a bell: *That was fucking Superman.*

As I steered the canoe toward the Round Island lighthouse, I began rethinking my opinion of *Somewhere in Time*. Maybe it wasn't so bad after all. There was something to be said for a good old-fashioned romantic film. They just don't make—

—WHAM!

The football careened in from outer space like a sputnik satellite and smashed me square in the face. I was knocked instantly into the lake. Say what you want about Bull and his popsicle stick arms; that skinny shit could kick the hell out of a football. Erin shrieked, delighted at the spectacle of me grasping at the canoe, which rocked too steeply to the left and then to the right.

Yep. She fell in.

Our *Somewhere in Time* moment transformed into a double feature of *The Poseidon Adventure* and *Gus* the Disney movie about a field goal-kicking mule. In the distance, I could hear the familiar howls of laughter from the boys as we floated like drowning rats, scrambling to pull ourselves back into the unsteady canoe.

Erin and I climbed the creaky stairs of the barn apartment to dry off. We were still in mild hysterics, and my ears were still ringing from the football's impact. I handed her a dry towel.

"If you think I'm going to dry off in front of you, you've lost your mind," she said, looking at me with a faint smile.

"I have nothing but honorable intentions," I smiled.

"Good God, you're full of shite." She walked over to me, towel around her neck, leaned in, and kissed me. This time, it was not a friendly peck.

This time, it went on. And on.

And that's all I'm going to say about that.

At that moment, the biker broke in.

"Really? That's all I'm gettin'?"

"Really," said Jack. "It's not that kinda story."

"Fine. But for the record: You pretty much suck. *Proceed.*"

CHAPTER TEN

The Crazy Dream
Mid-August, 1989

The next week was something out of a ridiculous rom-com I would never, ever pay to see. After years of gleefully mocking *Somewhere in Time*, I found myself starring in a junior varsity sequel of that very same movie. Only this time it had no time travel, period clothes, or a bad penny.

I presented Erin with the restored Schwinn Hollywood. We rode, exploring every square inch of the island. Her riding skills were impressive for a Dublin city girl, and even with the occasional death wobble, she looked fantastic on the bike. I couldn't help but think my mom would be happy to see her old rig back in action, even if she had given it up for the lazy comfort of gears. Mom was right. *I was a purist.*

The island is small, and it didn't take long for me to rediscover all the secret hiding places I loved as a kid, snapping hundreds of pictures along the way. My interest in the art of photography had always felt like a dirty secret, packed away in a weird artsy Pandora's box along with The Smiths, Warhol, Annie Leibovitz, and Truman Capote. Erin had pried open the lid. For the first time, I strapped on the leather camera case with pride.

We scrambled up a hidden chunk of limestone above the island's shore road past the boardwalk and shared a 40-ounce bottle of Mickey's Malt Liquor. Erin had complained about the "weak as piss" nature of Stroh's beer, a staple of any well-rounded Michigan diet, so I found another option. We sat and looked out at the water as waves broke on the beach in uneven white lines. I noticed she'd become reticent. "Is everything okay?" I asked.

"I want to explain something. It's been on my mind." She paused to make sure I was paying attention. "You once mocked me a bit. You said Gordon was a 'safe choice.'"

"He is."

She nodded, but it was the look of a patient teacher, not a lover. "My father is one of the most charming, interesting men I've ever known. When he walks into a room, everybody turns their head. And it's not because he's my father that I say this. Everyone who knows him agrees. He makes people feel like they are the only person on earth. The man literally vibrates with life." She took a sip, then set the bottle down, carefully balancing it on an outcropping of rock.

"He's also a liar, a thief, and, as of two years and six

months ago, a convicted felon. He destroyed our family for the most stupid, unforgivable reasons."

She scooted closer to me, looking me straight in the eye. "Houses that are safe don't get washed away during hurricanes, Jack. Safe cars have seatbelts and airbags. And people pay extra for it. Only when describing *people* does the word 'safe' become an insult. I'm not with Gordon. Okay? I'm here. With you. And I like you very, *very* much. I'm also not expecting safe. *Yet.* But unless you drive four hours to Cloverhill Prison to spend forty-five minutes with your interesting, charming father—who is now dressed in an orange jumpsuit—you can't begin to know how wonderful 'safe' can sound."

Her eyes didn't leave mine.

I felt foolish and exposed. Schooled even. *I loved it.* The best lessons are taught in the most unusual places. This one took place on a limestone rock partially obscured by cedar trees a few miles past the boardwalk. She picked up the Mickey's bottle and poured a little out on the rock in front of her, gangster-style, smiling as she watched the beer foam and spread out.

"Let's go see your grandfather," she said.

We spent some quiet time at Gramps' headstone at St. Ann's Cemetery, located deep in the interior of the island. I placed his Michigan cap on the rock along with some lilacs we picked on the way, tied together with some stray luggage tags I found stuck to the base of my basket. It was a crude arrangement but wound tight with love.

That night, we ended up on a blanket on a wooden

stockade called Fort Holmes, the island's highest point. The harbor stretched out below us, the reflections from the yacht docks and bobbing buoys shimmering across the dark, calm water in oranges and blues. Directly across the water was Round Island, illuminated in a wash of moonlight. We were pleasantly buzzed off cheap red wine. We had passed it back and forth, and now we were enjoying the warm, red glow of bargain bin Merlot.

Erin leaned back and looked to the sky, letting out a slow sigh. The Milky Way looked close enough to touch.

"My God. The stars sure shine bright when you get away from town."

"That's exactly why I wanted to bring you here."

She scoffed. "Right. To see the stars. And I'm sure you've never used *that* line before. 'Hey girl. Wanna see the stars? I know a spot!'" She smacked me playfully.

"I never claimed it was an original line. But it's never not been true," I countered.

She stretched out on the blanket and propped her head on her elbow. "It's August. What's next for you, Jack McGuinn?"

I paused, not sure how much I wanted to share. "Depends on some things."

"Things like?"

"Just some things I have … pending." I realized how ridiculous it sounded. *Pending?* I was thinking about Gordon. About the bet. I might have been there with Erin, but Gordon still had me by the tenders. Riding twenty-one bags was physically impossible, and deep down I knew it. But it wasn't a situation I wanted to share with her, particularly at that moment. She settled back, returning her eyes to the stars.

"Don't take this the wrong way, but you don't strike me as a fella that has things *pending.*"

"I had a feeling you'd say that. Dumb word. *Pending.*" Now it was my turn to sit up straight. I began babbling like a man on truth serum. "The thought of wearing a jacket and tie, chained by my ankle to a desk is like *death.*"

"Chained to a desk? What'ya going on about? You don't have to sell cars, Jack. You can be whatever you want. Take pictures for a living."

I continued on my train of thought. "What if I can't ride twenty-one? What if I *am* a 'tip man.' All charm, no balance."

She looked at me, perplexed. "You need to get out of the sun. Your brain's turning into oatmeal."

"Forget about it, Erin. Let's talk about you. Where are *you* going after the summer? Because I don't want this to end."

"You don't want what to end?"

"This. Us. I don't know. All of it. This summer. My long-gone cottage. The cello. The luggage. These ..." I indicated her tan, exposed knee. "... these ... *jeans* with the perfectly ripped holes in the knees."

Her Irish eyes smiled back, amused and a little devious. "Why you poor little boy. I think you're in love!" She broke out laughing and took my head with both hands, pulling me close for a deep kiss. I felt a combination of invigoration and total humiliation.

It was fantastic.

———

"Shit! It's eleven o'clock. *Get up!*"

"Wow. Mr. Romantic." But she was laughing when she said it. "You had your tumble; now it's time to split? I see how ya are."

We were covered by a blanket and bathed in the moonlight. Our Fort Holmes date had evolved into something more sensual and energetic. I had inadvertently rolled over on a sharp pinecone, which jammed hard into my right butt cheek. I awoke with a jolt of pain and realized we were running late.

I hopped up and took her hand. "I have a surprise for you. Let's go!"

We raced our bikes down the miles-long slope that led from Fort Holmes to Main Street. I'd taken this madcap late-night cruise since I was eight years old, but Erin was having some difficulty keeping up.

"I'm scared! It's too dark!" she shrieked, her voice muffled by the rush of the wind.

"The road's up there!" I shouted, pointing to the sky.

She caught up, following my lead, and slowly looked skyward, terrified but willing. Above, the star-lit canopy between the tall pines on either side of the road created a perfect celestial pathway, easy to follow if you had the guts. To island types, it was all second nature. Riding a bike on a darkened road demanded you simply look up, even after a bottle of red wine.

"Trust the stars!" I yelled.

"Trust the stars? What the *fook* does that even mean?!"

"There's that word again!" I yelled back. "It means … the stars. *Trust 'em!*"

Her eyes adjusted, then widened with wonder. The pathway of stars revealed itself above her. As the wind blasted through my eardrums, I could barely hear her repeating it to herself like a mantra.

"Trust the stars … trust the stars …"

Once Erin got the hang of inverse cosmic navigation, she let loose. We both whooped like kids, and the route of stars led us to town. We whipped past the Grand Hotel.

Erin screamed out, "Hellll-ooo, cellll-ooo! I hope you're safe, luv!" Down the final decline with the dogleg left, we went and ended up gliding down Main Street with our feet up on the frames of our bikes. We rolled up to Horn's Bar, winded and exhilarated. Erin's hair was a wild, tangled, dark mess, and her eyes glistened with tears of wind and speed. We coasted to a stop in front of the bar.

"Ah, home sweet home," I said. "You trust me now?"

"You or the stars?" she said.

"Me," I said.

"The verdict is still out," she responded. "But you are full of surprises, Mr. McGuinn. A highway of stars? That's worth an entry in the diary."

"I'll take it," I said. I removed a red bandana out of my back pocket. "Now, trust me a little more."

She shot me a suspicious look. "Okay, I think I've seen this movie, and it doesn't end well for the girl." She shrugged. "But hell, you got me to race down a hill at night half snockered without ever looking at the road, so sure. I'm game."

She stood up ramrod straight as I approached. "I'm ready, executioner. I only wish I was a smoker, so I could have one last cigarette before I die."

I tied the bandana lightly around her head, covering her eyes, and took her hand.

"Walk slow. I'll guide you."

"So we're clear: You're telling me I'm about to walk into Horn's Bar blindfolded?"

"That is precisely what I'm telling you." I opened the creaky door and walked inside, guiding her with a hand around her waist. Two hundred or so rowdy islanders packed tightly on the dance floor all quieted themselves as we entered. Everything was on a ferry boat-like schedule.

"One step up," I said, as I led Erin to the stage. Her hands reached out helplessly. Victor "Buckshot" Repasky, the singer and guitar player, gently took her hand. Buckshot smiled broadly, toothy, like a pirate, loving the moment. "There we go, sweetie. Be careful now."

I joined her on the small stage, turned her toward the crowd, and slid off her blindfold. She squinted and took in the scene as the crowd murmured in anticipation. AJ approached the stage and handed her a bow.

"M' lady, your bow," he said in his best awful Shakespearean dialect, then backed away like a subservient courtier.

"This isn't my bow," she said, staring at it blankly.

"It is tonight," I said. "Erin, this is Buckshot. This is his band. The Buckshot Band. Tonight, you're playing with them."

Buckshot was the leader of the sloppiest, most

crowd-pleasing four-piece jam band on the island. They could cover anything, from the Beatles, to folk, to R.E.M. Buckshot grinned, a twinkle in his eye. "Nice to meet you, Erin. Got something for you." He reached behind the battered drum set and produced a fiddle case. He opened it up and presented it like a waiter serving up fine dining.

"Been scoutin' for a fiddle player for years. We know all the Irish standards."

She removed the fiddle from the case and looked at me. Her eyes lit up, her mouth opened in a moment of uninhibited joy. She looked out over a revved-up crowd, hooting and hollering for music.

"The crazy dream," she said. I'll never forget the look of wonder on her face. It may have been the highlight of my life.

———

Horn's Bar was utterly out of control that night. Summer was racing toward autumn and there was no time to waste. The cold witch was on her way down from parts north and the energy of island nights ramped up, night by night. By mid-August, the merriment was audible on the streets long after closing time. By Labor Day, it was chaos.

The establishment was divided between the stage and bar section but when things got volcanic, the division magically vanished and Horn's was awash in that unique thumping vibration that can only come from good live music and free-flowing drinks.

Tonight, the worn wood floor was literally bouncing,

an unearthly eleven on some rock-and-roll Richter scale. Erin found her place in the universe, and we were all witnesses. It was *her night,* and damned if she was going to let it go to waste.

I arranged it, tossing a few hammies to the band earlier in the week. They'd learned a few standard Irish tunes like "*Whiskey in the Jar*" and "*The Irish Rover.*" But it was clear the moment she hit the first note, she needed no help. She knew every song in the band's setlist and exactly how to make the music sound better with her fiddle. It was as if the only thing Buckshot had been missing was a beautiful, talented fiddle player to lead the greatest bar band in the known universe.

She moved with the chord changes, flinging her wild hair, slamming her Doc Marten boots to the beat, connecting with the boys in that magical, unspoken way only real musicians understand. She sweated and she laughed, her wild, flashing blue eyes focused and charged. The crowd hooted and screamed, energized and insane, even for Horn's Bar in the late 80s, which was a very high standard indeed.

At one point, while the dance floor bounced, shaking the foundations, AJ hopped up on the stage and broke out in an impromptu *Riverdance* simulation, arms crossed, legs flailing, sweat flying off his jet-black hair like a wet rag. It was ridiculous, and the crowd loved it. While Erin was giving Charlie Daniels a run for his money, AJ's spastic dance moves channeled something closer to Jerry Lewis.

I wandered over to the bar to grab a round. As I reached for my wallet, I heard a voice.

"I got Jack's drink. Whatever it is." I looked up to see

Gordon. The man in black sat silently next to him, looking bored and entirely sober.

"She sounds amazing," Gordon called out over the music. "Never knew she could play like that." He was calm, and it was vaguely disturbing. He had to know Erin and I had been spending time together, although I never asked her for any specific break-up details, figuring that was her business.

"There's probably a ton of things you don't know about her," I shot back over the din of the crowd.

"Having a good night tonight?" he asked, looking me over.

"If you're buyin', I am. Make 'em all doubles, Snake."

Snake, the skinny, tattooed bartender, smiled, on to the scam.

"The good stuff, right, Jack?" he called back.

"Yup. Anyone named Glen," I said.

"I know a dude named Glen. Last name Fiddick"

"That's the guy!" I called back.

Gordon remained calm and took a sip of his drink. He was looking straight ahead. I could see him in the mirror behind the bar. His face was weirdly distorted by the old, warped glass. "I have your cubicle all picked out, Jack. The staff of the luggage team will be wearing matching cornflower blue jackets and kelly green pants. It's all *very* tasteful."

"Sounds cute," I replied.

"What size do you wear?" Without taking his eyes off me, he produced a ballpoint pen from the pocket of his red Patagonia jacket and clicked it, then grabbed a napkin from the bar. He sized me up like a tailor. "Let's start with the jacket. Forty-four regular, I'm guessing? You're going to have to supply your own dress shoes, though. Plain black is fine. You okay with that?"

"You're going to lose," I shot back.

I honestly had every intention of grabbing my drinks from Snake and resuming the critical business of having the night of my life. But, of course, I couldn't stop myself. I wheeled around to him, inches away now.

"You stole the only thing that ever mattered to my family."

"*Stole?* Jack. Your dad *sold* it to us." He leaned in closer to be heard over the music. "Besides, you're as much to blame for losing Wildcliffe as anyone, and you know it. If you hadn't gone all Sir Galahad with Trina at the WibHo, we never would've even *considered* Wildcliffe. We were looking for property. Period. That's what we do."

He pointed his finger at me. "Maybe if you'd joined your old man at the dealership, you'd have held on to the place. Maybe you'd be entertaining Erin on the front porch instead of rolling around in the barn with all the horse shit."

He looked toward the stage. "You know what? Here's a fun idea. Later, you can request a song. But what song?" He looked up as if hunting for the right idea. "I know! How about *If I Were a Rich Man.*" He leaned in even closer. "I heard she can fiddle the hell out of that one."

The man in black turned away, choking back a laugh. I could feel my ears getting hot. "Snake!" I gestured to the drinks. "Put it all on my tab instead."

Gordon spun his barstool to face me. "Don't you

think I would rather do your job? Ride around the island all day on a bike full of luggage, hustling tips? But I can't. I have responsibilities."

"You couldn't ride luggage if you wanted to, Gordo. You have no balance. You never did. Even when we were kids, you were a wobbly piece of shit."

He smiled back, unfazed. "I think *you're* the one with no balance, Jack. Check your bank account to see if I'm right."

I pointed toward the stage. "I'd like to stay here and chit-chat, but I'm gonna go kiss your ex-girlfriend in front of you, and everyone in this entire bar."

I took the drinks from Snake and headed off. I didn't want him to see it, but he'd gotten to me.

Moments later, I hopped up on the stage with two drinks. Erin was finishing a song and the crowd was going mad. She set the fiddle on a music stand, accepted the cocktail, and to rousing cheers, took a deep sip. I grabbed her by the waist and pulled her close, planting a deep kiss for all the island to see. Over her shoulder, I stole a furtive glance toward Gordon's barstool. *Sonofabitch was gone.* Ah well. It was still a kiss for the ages.

Spengler strode over to the stage. I handed him a tambourine as the band broke into a fiddle-fueled Beatles cover. He looked at it like it was a dinosaur bone. "You shake it!" I called down. Spengler did. But he didn't look too happy about it. "What's wrong with you? This is a party!"

"I got a story, Jack!" he called over the music.

"That's great! You're on your way, man! What is it? You uncover a cocktail waitress witch coven at Arch Rock? Huron Inn maid strike? Next stop, *The Washington Post!* Spengler Woodstein! *I can feel it!*"

"No, Jack. This is quite bad."

I stopped short. "*Quite* bad? That sounds worse than just bad."

"It is."

I hopped off the stage and pulled him away from the blaring speakers. "What's this about?"

"I need to show you something."

I'll never know how Spengler got his hands on the plans. In the sick reality of the moment, I forgot to ask. The resulting string of events it set off made it a minor footnote, but there was no denying this was an impressive scoop. The boys and I had left the party at Horn's and were staring down wordlessly at Spengler's handiwork. Spread out on the flower-patterned bedspread of my crappy apartment were plans and blueprints that indicated the end of Mackinac Island as we all knew it.

I finally broke the silence. *"Casinos?"*

"Yep," Spengler replied. "Pure bargain basement. It's that guy in black we always see with Gordon. His name is Carter Eagan and he's been working with the Whittaker family behind the scenes for the last year. He buys property through a company called Bluewater, LLC. Wherever he goes, the town instantly turns into a total cesspool. Although financially speaking, a wildly successful cesspool."

Foster inspected the plans. "Where did these come from?"

Spengler looked away. "I can't say. I'm, you know …"

"—You're a *journalist*," Foster said. Spengler smiled grimly, appreciating the compliment if not the circumstances.

For the next few minutes, we inspected the sketched renderings of the island like dumb monkeys. It was a weird parody of the island we loved. Completely reimagined. Vast plots of land behind the bluff were lined with massive, modern hotels and casinos. Hand-sketched tourists were entering and leaving a multitude of new establishments. It was tacky and disgusting. Spengler finally spoke up.

"The guy's got a financial interest in a casino chain called Drunky Pete's and a club he calls Cheaters. And you know that chain of strip bars called Nude World?"

Smitty perked up. "Hell yeah! Of course! The place is *great!* There's one in Houghton. And Marquette. I think there might be one in—"

I cut him off. "This is a disaster. How did it happen?"

Eighty percent of the island was a state park, protected from situations like this, but something had gone horribly wrong. Spengler inspected his notes.

"It's complicated. Gordon and Carter Eagan took advantage of a loophole. The holding company has about $300 million they're willing to invest in the island. The only way you can develop state land is if it falls under 'recreation.' It's very vague."

AJ piped in. "Some people golf for recreation. Some people hit the roulette table."

"Exactly. Because the state economy is in a slump, they approved it without a vote. I guess they assumed that it would be done right with the Whittaker's involved. *Island people* and all. The state saw an adrenaline shot. They made the same deal on five different island lots. The first development is right where we're standing. This is going to be the main casino."

"Wildcliffe," I said, looking out the smudged window toward the house.

Spengler nodded. "It gets worse, Jack. They're actually *calling* it Wildcliffe Casinos." My jaw tightened with rage. I thought about Gramps. How he had discovered a quaint but run-down old cottage for sale in the 1950s, bought it cheap, rechristened the place Wildcliffe. He had transformed the cottage through sheer force of will and personality into a gathering place for our family and our friends. The notion of a casino defiling that legacy, quite simply, made me want to puke.

Smitty was oddly silent, staring at the renderings without expression. Finally, he turned to Spengler, speaking slowly. "Are you saying that Mackinac Island— my ancestral home for hundreds of years—might become a casino town, complete with gambling and strip bars?"

Spengler exhaled. "That is the way it looks."

"That ... is ..." Smitty looked up and away, scanning the barn ceiling for the appropriate word to express himself.

"... *awesome!*"

He looked at us. "I mean aw-*ful!* Did I say awe-*some*? No. This is *bad*. We should *definitely* do something." He nodded assertively, apparently satisfied with his plan.

I sat on the bed, shaking my head, my butt crumpling the blueprints. Here I was, making small-time bets while Gordon was planning the biggest steal in island history.

"He played me like a … like a …"

"—cello?" Smitty piped in.

"I was gonna say *fiddle*, but yeah, sure. He played me like a cello."

CHAPTER ELEVEN

My Downward Spiral
August 15, 1989

I avoided joining the family dealership as a badge of honor, and it caused a boatload of tension between myself and Big Jack. I didn't dig that "new car smell," didn't want to be an "and son," and preferred an old Schwinn to a new Oldsmobile.

But for all my griping, I did learn a thing or two working during school breaks in the parts department of McGuinn Oldsmobile. For instance, how to hot-wire everything and anything, from an '84 Oldsmobile Toronado to, say, a golf cart. It was a nifty trick passed down to me from one of my dad's more ethics-challenged mechanics. If he only knew how useless I really was to his future at the dealership, he wouldn't have wasted his time trying to win me over. Regardless, it stuck.

So, at 3 a.m. the night I learned of the plans for the island, I found myself at the end of the Arnold Line dock where Gordon stored his small but growing fleet of gleaming electric luggage carts, attempting to get one started. I vaguely recall a half-consumed bottle of Mad Dog 20/20 nearby. Perhaps I was mumbling to myself.

"Fast, efficient? Hauls forty bags? Never tries to sleep with the guests? *A-ha!* But does it *float*, Gordo? Shouldn't that be a key feature? I mean, we live on an island after all!"

"Three encores, Jack! It was brilliant! *Better* than the dream!"

I looked up from my work, wrench in hand. Erin was riding toward me on her bike, her figure barely illuminated by the dock's halogen backlights. The moment she got close, her face darkened. With me hunched over and the bottle nearby, she knew I was into something bad.

"*Jaysus.* What the hell are you doing?"

"Leave me alone!" I called back. "You don't want to be a witness to this! I'm being … *illegal.*" I stood up. "Did you know about the Big Plan? Your old squeeze is taking over half the island! It's not just these stupid luggage carts." I kicked the cart hard. Pain shot up from my big toe. "It's the whole fucking island!"

She put down the kickstand and walked toward me cautiously, still lightly perspiring from the jam session. Her face sparkled in the strange late-night light. She gazed at the bottle. "Don't eat the head offa me, Jack. I have no *idea* what you're going on about," she said.

"You sure? After all, wasn't he the one that *took you away from it all?* He must've whispered something about this little operation during your pillow talks." I looked back down at the wires of the cart with a hot flash of sobriety and shame. I had just crossed a line.

"*Asshole!*" she snapped. "I was open with you."

"Right. And I'm asking if he was *open* with you, Erin."

"I didn't discuss real estate with him, if that's really what you're asking." Her face lost all expression. A wall of disdain grew. Another brick with each word. If I could just refrain from talking, maybe I could salvage … *nope.*

"Well, that's too bad. Here's a tip, though. Maybe if you're nice, Gordon'll hire you to play the fiddle at the island *titty bar!*"

She knew nothing about the casino plan. It was obvious. But for reasons I can't explain, I didn't care. My brain was a mashed-potatoes-and-gravy blend of resentfulness and despair. I hopped in the golf cart and pushed the start button. The electric motor kicked in with a whine.

"Ha-ha! *It's alive!*" I yelled.

She turned away and walked to her bike. "You're thick as a plank. Have a nice swim."

"*Swim?* You think I don't have a plan?" I called back.

"You never have a plan, Jack."

"Well, this time I do! I have a great plan! And it's not … what's the word? *Pending!*"

She mounted her bike and silently pedaled away. I watched her go. I remember catching the wavering orange lights of the yacht docks reflecting off the water. A living canvas of color that would never grow old. I took it in. My sanity flooded back in a warm rush.

Then it passed.

I stepped on the accelerator and steered the cart

directly toward the end of the dock. If I remember correctly, the idea was to leap out, à la James Dean in *Rebel Without a Cause* or Kevin Bacon in *Footloose*, at the exact moment it jettisoned off the dock in a slow-motion tumble into the lake. I would thus prove to the world— or at least to the island community—how committed I was to preserving Mackinac Island's rich heritage. Lauded for my act of subversive bravery. *A hero!* Shit, man. It was almost Greenpeace-y.

It didn't quite go down that way.

As the edge of the dock approached, I turned to my left to jump out and smashed my knee hard on the fiber-glass dashboard with a sickening crunch. It was excruciating. I grabbed my knee in agony rather than continuing my planned cinematic tuck-and-roll exit from the cart. It sailed over the edge of the dock like the final scene in *Thelma & Louise* and splashed loudly into the cold, dark water.

With me in it.

⸻

The boys passed the hat and sprung me from jail around noon the next day. They hadn't known I was fished from the lake and arrested until they showed up for the first boat in the morning and I was nowhere to be found. Trina stopped by the docks to let Foster know I was sleeping off a bender in the clink after driving a golf cart into the lake. It was serious. This time, I imagined, the boys didn't cackle.

Much.

The chief of police had known me since I was nine and allowed me to sleep off the previous night's debacle without interruption. Big Jack had donated the only car on the island—an emergency police vehicle—and of course Gramps knew everyone from the beginning of time. The McGuinn family still had some leftover good-will chips on the table for me to squander. I had all the advantages a cottage boy could expect. Except, of course, getting away with it.

I survived, but the golf cart was now resting on the bottom of Haldimand Bay. Gordon didn't press charges, according to the deputy working behind the desk, a sleepy-eyed officer in his sixties we all called Barney Fife. He counted out the bail money, had me sign some paperwork, and let me out, all while fixing me with a stern look that said *you little shits have no idea how good you have it. Yet every summer, you still manage to screw it all up.*

Island cops had that look down pat.

I limped out of the holding cell on Market Street and squinted at the blazing sun. The boys showed up with the money, but they stood across the street, hanging back, letting me adjust to civilian life in my own way. My temples were pounding like dual sledge-hammers, my right knee and toe were screaming, and I had a raspy cough from the drafty jail cell. I wasn't thinking much about Gordon or casinos. At that moment, I mostly wanted to find a discreet bush behind which to expunge the previous night's Mad Dog.

I gazed at the whitewashed houses lining Market Street. I had ridden my Sting-Ray past them since I was a kid; permanent, immutable island fixtures. I counted on Market Street the way you depend on an old friend. This time it all looked doomed.

I was at a point where I desperately needed to start

making some good decisions. Instead, all I could muster was another terrible one: I needed a drink.

———————————

Now that I was a free man, I rode straight to the Pink Pony, my *second* favorite bar on the island. The Pony was part of the Chippewa Hotel and always had its share of tourists. When I was a kid, the place was an infamously rowdy spot, much like Horn's Bar was for my generation. My parents often took the entire Wildcliffe guest roster down to the Pony to carouse and sing along with the piano player.

Back then, it was legal to take kids into bars, so I retained a fondness for the joint, having snoozed in their pink, Naugahyde-covered booths on multiple rowdy occasions before my tenth birthday. I'd fade to sleep to the uproarious but oddly soothing peals of laughter from my parents and their downstate friends. The Pink Pony was now cleaned up, tasteful, and absolutely *not* where I should have been. That said, I wasn't well-known there. If I wanted to sit and drown my sorrows for, say, *hours and hours*, I could do it without being recognized.

So that's what I did.

Jimmy Buffett was playing on the stereo as I saddled up. I ordered a Stroh's and a shot of Jameson, a favorite of Gramps. He was a man who could handle his liquor, and when he said, "I'll have a shot and a beer," it sounded like poetry. I convinced myself that I was honoring the old guy. Bukowski, on the other hand, might've called it *crawling into a bottle*.

The day went on. More Buffett songs. Soon it was

Bob Marley's *Rastaman Vibration*. As the place slowly filled up and the sun went down, a singer took the stage with a banged-up acoustic guitar and began belting out all the tourist favorites. It was lovely. Time gently eased into irrelevance in that hazy way so unique to a day-drinking kickoff. I don't remember when I noticed Foster sitting next to me. It was almost startling.

"Whoa! Hey! What are you doing here?" I said.

He signaled for me to quiet down. "You're yelling, Jack. And I've been here for a half-hour."

I grabbed a shot that was waiting in front of me and held it up. "This one's for you, Foster. The old dog. *The master.* The best dockporter on the island!"

Foster toasted back with his bottle of beer. "I agree with the sentiments, grasshopper, but why do I get the honor?"

I leaned in, sentimental. "Because you get it. Everyone's always thinking about movin' on and what's next, and I say screw what's next! And so do you!" A thought occurred to me, wildly profound at the moment. "You know what's great about you? You *don't* put your money where your mouth is. That's the sign of a real rebel, man. You *stay!*"

He smiled, sizing me up. "Guess what? I passed Spanish. Got my degree. Did it all by mail."

I stopped short and noticed the first woozy spin. Just a brief moment of fun-house imbalance. I shook it off and straightened. "Wow. That's ... *why?* I thought you hated Spanish."

There was always some sort of twisted honor in Foster's ten-year rebellion against earning a college degree. He was absolutely bright enough to pass college Spanish. And if the legend was accurate, a degree for

Foster meant an inheritance. Potentially a big inheritance, a windfall that could keep him in designer sheets for a long time to come.

Foster leaned in close, eyes blazing. "It was those sex letters from the señorita, man. The more I could understand, the more I *wanted* to understand."

I nodded back. *Sex sells,* as the advertising types always said. Foster shook his head, correcting himself on the spot. "No. Wait. *They weren't sex letters."* His eyes focused forward, concentrating on some revelation that was directly in his line of sight.

"What were they?" I asked.

"They were *love* letters."

"I don't know what you're talking about." *But of course I did.*

"I'm talking about a few things. One: Technically, I'm rich. So, yes, the rumors are all true. Two: I'm going to Vera Cruz to track her down, and I'm going to talk to her. *In Spanish."* He sipped his beer. "I wanna make a change."

He turned to me. "I know what happened. The island. The casinos. Gordon. The whole operation. It's sick, man. I know this summer you think of yourself as some goddamn crusader. But listen to me. *This is not your fault.* You should scoop up that fine lass of yours and go. Make your own change."

I gestured to my glass. "I made a change. I switched to gin and tonic."

He didn't laugh. "I'm serious. Do you want to be doing this when you're forty-five? Shlepping other people's suitcases?"

He looked at me as if he wanted the truth, so I gave it to him. "Yeah, Foster. I kinda do."

He broke out in a broad, warm smile. He grabbed me in a headlock and pulled me close. "Jesus! You don't get it. She might be the love of your life."

"Well, guess what? The love of my life hates my guts." I took another sip. "I'll just ride blackjack. Show her that I do have some balance." I looked at Foster. "*A load man!*"

Foster looked straight ahead, studying the guitar player. "Jack, about that. There's another thing you need to know."

"Please," I said, "continue the hit parade, Casey Kasem. You're leaving. I went to jail. Mackinac's gonna be the next Reno. Bring it on!"

Foster exhaled. "You're off the docks. Your antics last night didn't go unnoticed by the ferry line big shots. They can't have a hot-wiring maniac meeting hotel guests."

I looked at him closely, trying to decipher whether or not this was a joke. It was the kind of thing he would say to mess with my head. Foster was known to let pranks play out for months. But he looked away, signaling to the bartender for another beer. This time, he spoke without looking at me.

"What did you expect to happen? You're lucky they even let you out of jail."

So, there it was. It was the final nail in the coffin. *Fired.* There would be no blackjack ride and, therefore, no more dockporters. Not that that mattered, as blue-haired old ladies looking to score big on the nickel slots don't tip. And I'd be *managing* this shit show. In a suit. And kelly green pants. Yup. The bet was settled. The war was over without a shot fired.

I needed to make a getaway. Foster was morphing in

front of my eyes into something that eerily resembled an adult. His intense eyes, lined at the corners from years in the sun, were now looking straight through me. He appeared almost wise, and it was freaking me out profoundly. I downed my shot, then his. I grabbed his face and kissed him hard on the cheek.

"You're my hero, Foster. You're the reason I became a dockporter. Don't you grow up on me!"

He looked at me, concerned.

"You okay, buddy?"

"Nope!" I pulled out my wallet, fished out a twenty, dropped it on the bar, and stumbled away. I knocked into a heavyset tourist couple, spilling their cocktails.

"Watch it!" the bartender called over. He shot me that cold, hard look that only bartenders know. It's a look that says *one more time and you're out.*

"I'm watching it!" I stammered.

Lord, I wasn't speaking too well either. My tongue was thick, and the place was starting to spin. I stumbled out the door, almost running over ... who? Someone I knew. *Wait.* It was Vicky with a group of giggling friends.

"Hi, Jack the dockporter!" She looked at me closely and immediately downshifted to low concern.

"Oh, boy. We should probably get you some fresh air."

"I was going to get some fresh air! That's so weird!" I must have been shouting because she shushed me and yanked me out onto the street, gesturing for her friends to go on ahead. I think she also signaled to them that I was a stumbling idiot by making crazy circles around her temple, but I can't prove it.

"Listen," she said. "I was going to grab some food with my friends, but instead, let's hang out. We can have a burger down on the beach, you and me. There's a party at the boardwalk."

"Yes! You and me hanging out sounds *great.*"

I did have a hazy image of seeing Gordon as I rode Vicky in my basket toward the boardwalk bonfire party. He was lingering at the head of the dock with some of his lackeys. I remember the green Izod shirt and khaki pants and a bemused expression when we passed. I looked straight ahead. But out of the corner of my eye, I could sense a grin from Gordon as he followed us with his eyes. Oddly enough, I rode perfectly straight, and Vicky didn't appear nearly as terrified as she should've. With summer upon summer of practice, I was always able to still my spinning melon when I was on my bike.

We sat on a log surrounded by the buzz of an island beach party, illuminated by firelight. I glanced around at glowing faces. The silliness of small moments shared. But all I felt was lousy. I needed to get away from it. I took Vicky's hand.

"Let's sit by the water." It came out sounding like *less sippa thwater.* "All this *joy* is giving me a headache."

She chuckled and rolled her eyes. "Yeah. *Joy* ... and a shit-ton of cocktails."

We stumbled toward the dark water's edge and sat down on the rocks, listening as waves lapped against the shore.

"Vicky. I have a girlfriend. Well. Had one."

She was unfazed, even happy. "Aw. Deep down, you're a good guy. I'm proud of you." She paused, thoughtful. "Well. I *would have* been proud of you. I guess." She shrugged. "Actually, I'm not too sure what the right response is to that one."

"Yeah. Me either." I was on autopilot now. "Her name is Erin. Erin from Dublin. She plays one of those massive violins."

Vicky nodded. "You mean, like, a cello?"

"That's it! A cello! I can never remember that."

"Aw. That's so cool."

"Yeah, but now she hates me."

She broke out in her now-legendary cackle and raised her cup. "Well, Jack McGuinn, the dockporter who has a house on the East Bluff but hauls other people's bags—here's to that."

I raised my cup and toasted her glumly. "By the way, not one thing you just said is true. I'm none of those things. I'm not a dockporter, I don't have a house on the East Bluff, and I don't haul other people's bags. But … *but* … the last time I checked, my last name was still McGuinn, so … cheers to that!" I slammed it down like cold Gatorade after a hot day on the docks.

And that's the last thing I remember.

The pain shot out from my temple, followed by a sharp kick in the gut. I howled. It was the very definition of the term *rude awakening.* I looked up into the star-filled sky, trying to get my bearings. Vicky was lying next to me; her sweater pulled up, exposing a tan midriff and a hint of a pink bra. She was sleeping deeply, like a happy little baby. *Wham.* Another hit came hard to my butt. I covered up.

"Ya *gobshite!* What the hell is *wrong* with you!?"

There was no mistaking that accent. What sounded so lovely in our tender moments was now frightening, like an angry female pirate. And I could only assume *gobshite* wasn't a compliment. I scrambled to escape, stumbling to my feet, the loose beach rocks shifting under my tennis shoes.

She was brandishing her cello bow like a broadsword and advanced on me slowly, her rage heightened by the faint orange glow of the dying bonfire.

"I asked you a question, Jack. What … is … wrong … with … *you?*"

I was now holding my head in pain. Everything was muddled and unclear. I had no memory of getting cozy with Vicky. I wasn't even sure where I was at the moment. The party was long over, and all that remained were sparking embers from the bonfire and a soft line of sunlight easing up over the horizon. *Four a.m. light.*

"Answer me!" Erin demanded.

I stumbled back, then regained my bearings. "What's wrong? Hm. Let me think. Aside from being clobbered with a cello bow, everything! I lost my house, my family, my job, my island …"

"—Me!" Erin shot back.

"We never, like, did anything!" Vicky broke in. Erin and I both looked over. She was pulling herself together, equally confused, yanking her shirt down and smoothing her dark hair.

I lit up. "We didn't? That's great!"

Erin squinted doubtfully and watched Vicky put herself together and stand.

"Are you certain?" Erin asked.

Vicky chewed on her lower lip for a moment and

pondered the question. She had no interest in lying. She looked down, then over toward the remnants of the fire.

"Actually, no. I'm not that sure. I mean …" She said the next part softly. "… *maybe* something happened?"

Erin exploded at me again. *"I thought you were ready!"*

Although I had no concrete memory of the night's activities post-last gulp, I was straight-up busted and reverted to a new tactic. I took a deep breath and jumped right in.

"Ah, who cares? I mean, it's perfect, isn't it? Summer's over. Time to ditch the homeless jerk drifter and go back to safety. Back to the Gordons of the world. I get it. I have no problem providing you with your last big fling before you head off into Safe City. I've done it for lots of girls. Hell, I'm the *Last Fling King.* Don't think, even for a second, you're the first!"

Whack!

One more cello bow across the back of the head for the road, and she was gone, running across the rocky beach. I grabbed my noggin and dropped to my knees. I could hear the sounds of her maneuvering her bike, along with a wildly impressive string of profanity. *Peiceofshitloserfookincheatsonme?!*

Then she pedaled away.

It was over. Just the sound of waves breaking on the rocky beach. I stood there for what felt like an hour but was probably less than a minute.

"Are you, like, *okay?*" Vicky asked.

I stood perfectly still, pondering an answer.

"Ask me something else."

"Brother! What the hell were you thinking?"

Jack looked over at the biker, who was now glaring at him as the ferry crashed through the storm.

"She hit *me*! In the head! With a cello bow!"

"So what?" he snapped back. "You deserved it. You can't talk that way to Erin. She's an emotional person, sure, but she's also a wellspring of compassion. You're *blowing it*, man."

"No shit, Dr. Phil. The only reason you feel that way is because I'm doing such a good job telling you the story."

The biker pondered that for a moment.

"You make a valid point. Okay, fine. Go on."

———

It was a dark stretch of island road where this phase of the story comes to a crashing and ignominious end. After the brutal instrumental beatdown, I dropped Vicky off at her employee dorm. She was sweet but confused, now caught up in a blurry drama she didn't understand, and only wanted sleep. The morning had not yet broken, and I wasn't interested in pedaling through town. I needed to ride.

Hard.

———

I pushed the old bike with reckless abandon, standing on the pedals for more torque, every muscle in my body burning. Despite having hauled half a million pounds of tightly packed luggage during my dockporter career, my legs never worked harder than they did on this around-the-island sprint.

My eyes watered, which streaked across my cheeks, and morning bugs careened straight into my open mouth. The sound of breaking waves was the only guide at this pace, but I trusted my instincts. And even if I didn't, there was no slowing down. Like steam, it needed to escape. Fired, jailed, Gramps gone, kicked out, casinos in, Dad, Mom, the fumble of the only decent relationship I'd ever had—all of it converging in an intense flare of pain and speed.

The wind muffled in my ears and my mind raced. Why was I so cruel? She did nothing but show me the light. She shared her pain with me. She was open and honest about her relationship with Gordon. Hell, she practically slipped me a cheat sheet on how to love her. My only task was to memorize the damn thing. Instead, I tore it up into little pieces, tossed it in the air, and embarked on this historical binge.

I didn't see the yellow caution sign in the middle of the road until I clipped it with my front tire. Instinctively, I turned the wheel of my bike and veered left off the road into a patch of deep brush and small, scrappy beach trees. The instant my front tire hit the loose stones, I was launched like a supernova, barely able to tuck and roll before landing. It was a painful, NFL-caliber thud. My bike flipped and bounced behind me, finally clattering to a halt three feet from my head. I lay still, heaving in exhaustion.

The morning sun hit me square in the face. An interrogation lamp from a lousy cop show. I squinted, stirred, and inspected my surroundings, using only my eyes, not moving my prone body. Three feet away, small, gentle waves lapped on the shore. A few seagulls strolled up and down the empty beach, scavenging for scraps and squawking with constant complaints. *Seagulls are such malcontents.*

My head craned sideways. I wasn't wearing my watch, but I knew it was after 10 a.m. I rolled over and struggled to sit upright. I looked to my left. A small, tanned boy, probably seven, sat Indian-style about four feet away. He had dark, shaggy hair and looked out at the water as if awaiting a visit from a pirate ship. He glanced over at me as I struggled back to life, curious but unfazed.

"Are you alright, mister?" he asked.

"Yeah. I think." It was all I could muster.

"Okay. Good." He looked at my bent-up porter bike. "My dad's getting me some rocks over there." He gestured toward the bend in the beach. "He's going to teach me how to skip stones."

I struggled to my feet and limped to my battle-scarred bike. The front-wheel curved wildly like a Salvador Dali painting. The basket was a parallelogram. Unrideable. The kid watched me as I pulled the bike upright.

"You crash, mister?" he asked.

"How'd ya guess?" I responded, trying to sound like a playful big brother but knowing it came out grumpy.

He smiled when he saw the weirdly bent wheel. "Well, you can probably fix it. Or just get a new one."

I rolled the battered bike to the main road. "Have fun with your dad," I called.

"Thanks!" the boy called back.

He was now standing with his father, inspecting a handful of flat rocks. It was a lovely moment, and I wished for an instant I'd appreciated it more when I had it. I turned away and rolled the wounded bike back to town.

CHAPTER TWELVE

Keeping it Clean
August 17, 1989

The four-mile trek with my bad knee and thrashed bike seemed to take weeks. I was dirty and swimming in rivulets of grimy sweat. I also had some time to process. Jail. The binge. The beatdown. The crash. How did Erin know where to find Vicky and me? I half-remembered Gordon standing at the dock as we rode past. Was it possible that he tipped Erin off? Maybe followed us and found us passed out on the beach? Could he have repositioned us to look as though something sleazy went on?

No. It was all too much, even for Gordon. In my exhaustion, I was stumbling into the shady world of conspiracy theories. *Did Kubrick fake the moon landing? Is Paul dead? Who was on the grassy knoll?* What I needed right now was a warm shower and a workable bike, not a headful of paranoia.

But still …

As I hit town, I passed Bull riding an impressive load of luggage through frantic Main Street traffic. He didn't notice me, but if he did, I'm not sure he would have given me more than the obligatory nod, a quick upward jerk of the head that signaled *I see you and I'll buy you a cold one tonight, but right now I'm busy.* The kid was as focused as a surgeon, and he sure as hell would not forget everything he'd learned by getting all chatty during a ride. I felt a sharp sting of rejection as he blew past. To him, I was another irritating walker with a screwed-up bike blocking his path. Brotherhood only goes so far when you're chasing the big tip.

Stumbling into Doud's Market, I headed straight to the freezer section for a pack of frozen peas to soothe my head. Then it was off to Marquette Park for some shut-eye. It's safe to say I'd never looked worse. I settled on an unoccupied patch of fresh green grass near the street and lowered the wounded bike carefully. I stretched out and closed my eyes.

The irritating grind of a shovel scraping pavement could only mean one thing. I opened my eyes and sat up. It was Rick, with a sunbaked mound of horse dung piled in his oversized spatula. As if on cue, a long-haired, goateed retro-hippie strummed his guitar and began an off-key rendition of *Knockin' on Heaven's Door* to three enthralled—and demonstrably tone-deaf—retro-hippie girls. The sixties made a strong comeback in 1989. The Grateful Dead topped the charts, and tie-dyes and frisbees popped up on the island like dandelions. Now, the girls joined in. Sweet, awful singers.

Scrape went Rick's shovel.

There would be no nap today.

Rick whipped the shovelful of horse mash into his galvanized cart. He wheeled closer to me, absently sweeping an area near the curb that already appeared spotless. He spoke to me without looking up. "Heard your sweetie gave you quite the beatin'."

To the best of my recollection, Rick had never once uttered an unelicited word to me.

"Ex-sweetie," I said.

The island telegraph was functioning fine without me. Nobody was going to miss out on this yarn, and nothing ever slipped past Rick. I adjusted the bag of peas, which were blessedly doing the trick. Rick scratched his head.

"Fiddle bow or cello bow?"

"What?" I asked.

"She whack ya with a fiddle bow or a cello bow?"

I thought about it. "It was a fiddle bow. I think. I don't know. It was dark. All I know is that it hurt like hell."

He looked me over. "I'm guessin' you're right. Fiddle bow. A crack from a cello bow would probably give ya a permanent stammer. So she smack any sense into ya?"

"I dunno." I paused, contemplating the last forty-eight hours. "Probably not."

The pain thawed the peas to nearly eating temperature. It crossed my mind to rip the bag open and have at it, but I refrained. The only solace I could find was watching Rick do what he did best. He'd choreographed his shoveling technique, moving like a dancer in the Bolshoi Ballet with just a touch of a Canadian curler.

His practiced routine was oddly calming. *Sweep, sweep, scoop, plop.* Again. *Sweep, sweep, scoop, plop.*

"Why do you do it, Rick?" I didn't expect him to say much. He rarely did. But this time, he planted his shovel upright, leaned on it, and wiped his brow.

"Well it ain't the money. Plenty a decent gigs that don't involve wet stacks of shit. Ya know? And believe me, the ladies ain't clamorin' to spend quality time with a man in my line of work. So it's also pretty lonely."

He looked out at the bay. The riggings of the sail-boats in the harbor clanged gently. A ferry rounded the break wall. Despite the recent dramas—both large and small—life continued on the island.

He turned back to me. "I like knowing I'm keeping the place clean. Makin' it a little better." He pulled out a handkerchief from his back pocket and blew his nose, inspected his snot, folded it, and put it away. "I'll miss that part when it's all gone. Imagine there won't be much use for an old shit sweeper in a casino town."

I waited, wanting more from him. "Yeah. I heard that news too," he said. "Big development. Whatnot. Suppose shit happens. Nothin' lasts forever." He chuckled at some private joke. "Just ask them fur traders. Don't see too many a them no more." He looked up to the sky, choosing to change the subject. "Gonna rain tonight."

I followed his gaze. Not a cloud in the sky. He grabbed his shovel, threw it in the cart, and rolled on to the next pile. "Have a good one," he called back gruffly.

It was time to rehabilitate my warped front wheel and straighten out the disfigured basket. On the cool grass of the park, I flipped the bike on its side, and with a grunt I managed to successfully step on the bent end of the wheel and apply enough body weight to bring it back to roll-town.

The hippie called over, still strumming his guitar, which was covered with a patchwork of band stickers. "Brah, you need some help?"

"Ummm. Honestly. You could stop playing for five minutes. That would be a tremendous help." The second it came out, I regretted it. It was a rude comment. But then again, he did ask.

He grinned back, golden-retriever happy and not the least bit offended. "No problem. I kinda suck anyway." He laughed and turned to the girls, accepting the stuffed one-hitter they were passing his way. On to the next thing.

Once the wheel work was complete, I moved to the basket. After a few minutes of grunts and wheezes, I'd achieved work on par with any of the world's great sculptors, an example of pure dockporter impressionism.

I mounted up and rode. A basket of new proportions and a wheel with a gimp. I was proud of the work, despite the strange sensation in my lower extremity. The offset from the revolution created a wobbling, rhythmic movement. It felt like a masseuse was kneading my right ass cheek with a croquet ball. Odd but not altogether unpleasant. Between intermittent blasts from ferry horns, random clip-clops of horse hooves, and the rhythmic scrape of my wheel against the fender, I was starting to feel human.

It felt like eons since I'd slept in a proper bed, if the rusty, slinky-rigged contraption above the barn could be called a bed. But it had a mattress, the sheets were relatively clean, and at that moment, it was Shangri-la. I lay down gingerly, my body tender from the various thrashings, expecting an instant, blissful slumber. But it didn't come.

A thunderstorm was sweeping across the island, cracking the sky open with deafening lightning and thunder. Rick was right about the rain. *Of course he was.* The window by the bed was open a crack, and wisps of water were blowing in every forty-five seconds or so, covering my face with a spritz of cold mist. I sat up and jammed down hard on the sill, shutting it with a thump.

I sat up straight. The last week's images seemed to play on a video loop projected on every flat surface. On the far wall, I saw Erin playing her fiddle, eyes possessed with unmitigated joy. I could see her lips pressed on mine as we kissed on the stage, and could hear the roar of laughter, hoots, and applause. On the bathroom door, I saw a montage. Tiny green electrical wires of a golf cart. Bars of a jail cell. Erin riding into the night. The knowing look of a seven-year-old kid on a beach.

And, of course, the blueprints of Wildcliffe Casino.

I opened the window to feel the rain.

I pondered Rick's words. *Keeping the place clean.* It made perfect sense. But how could I scoop up this enormous pile of shit when it was likely backed by millions of dollars and dropped with a splat in the middle of the road by monied, connected hotshots that knew the game? And who was I? A vandal. A drunk. An unemployed vagrant with nothing but a wobbly Schwinn and a series of bow-shaped welts all over my body. I no longer had any influence over island events.

I squandered the last of my credibility with reckless, stupid behavior. Bad choices. Hot-wiring. Overconsumption. Cheating and debauchery. Time to face facts. I was no longer a shoveler. I was the shoveled. Steaming excrement, casually dropped from the unpuckered ass of a tired draft horse at the end of a long Mackinac Island day.

But we had to stop it. Could Spengler step up to the plate and knock out a journalistic home run? Maybe. Fighting power at this level would be a Herculean task for a skinny, wannabe writer from Warren, Michigan, whose biggest byline thus far was my Gramps' obituary. And there was no way a small-town newspaper that catered mostly to tourists would take on that kind of risk.

And would it even be enough?

Suddenly, the wind kicked up and howled. Tall pines brushed against the side of the barn. Torrents of rain pelted the glass. I was frozen, as if the most subtle movements would crack me like ice. My eyes darted to the beat-up dresser and the metallic edging of my Instamatic camera.

My heart was now hammering in my chest.

"Isn't it the people that give it life?"

Erin's critique from earlier in the summer rang through my head, and for a moment, I thought she might be in the room. The photos I'd taken after her casual rebuke were undoubtedly better. Full of life, just like she suggested. Carriage drivers, construction workers, waiters, friends, and tourists. Many of the photos hung neglected in the darkroom under the ice-cream shop. Another crack of lightning. A gust. The storm was directly overhead now.

"Isn't it the people that give it life?"

I hopped out of bed, tripping over myself as I pulled on jeans and a raincoat.

In the driving rain, I rode to the darkroom in a frenzy of inspiration. Now, soaked to the bone, I stared at the photos as if somebody else took them, breathing in the musty smell of old cardboard boxes and developing fluid.

Spengler stood next to me, equally rain-soaked and disheveled, but intrigued. I had yanked him out of bed thirty minutes earlier, and now he was gamely rolling with my deranged, ill-formed concept. The moment stretched out as he allowed the photos hanging on a clothesline to wash over him.

"What do you think?" I asked him, taking a breath. "Give it to me straight."

He continued to study the images, inscrutable and professorial. Then he nodded, slowly at first and then with vigor. "Yes. *Yes!*" He turned to me, adjusting his glasses. "If I can write an interesting story, and we add your photos, maybe we can stop this thing. *Public opinion.*" He tapped his temple twice. "That's our angle. An exposé … *with heart.*"

Mackinac Island was a beautiful woman with classic looks and style to burn. "A real looker," as Gramps would say. And she was about to be transformed into a garish whore with a wrinkled pink dress, beat-up heels, and clownish makeup. Like *Pretty Woman* in reverse.

We had to stop it. Or die trying.

"You better get writing," I said.

"You better take some more pictures," he shot back.

We stood there, looking at each other, both unsure of the next move.

"I'm going back to bed," Spengler finally said.

"Me too. Let's start tomorrow."

For a few musty, intense days, the center of dockporter life was the darkroom under Mister B's. More photos hung from a clothesline, covering the moldy walls. Spengler relocated his IBM Selectric to the dusty workbench and was pounding out typed pages, hunched over the machine like Beethoven writing a symphony. Smitty and Fly tacked the casino plans to the wall as a constant reminder of the importance of this insane caper.

The boys came and went, covering each other's boats and assisting with the intel, willing our home-grown exposé to life. We had a deadline to hit.

I heard footsteps on the wooden stairs. Two sets of feet—one heavy and male and another lighter and more balletic. AJ emerged into the swinging overhead light. Trailing behind him was the mystery woman I had seen him with at Trina's party. This time, she wasn't wearing a fishing cap. She followed AJ into the light, stopped, and looked around. Even in jean shorts and an oversized Ferris State sweatshirt (obviously borrowed), she looked like something from another universe. Deep blue eyes and tan from the summer sun, she radiated light, even deep in the bowels of our grimy, darkened headquarters. AJ put a protective arm around her waist and took in the gloomy room.

"Moody. Where are we keeping the serial killer?" AJ asked.

Fly looked over nonchalantly. *"Killers.* There's two. One's in the men's room. We feed him human intestines every Thursday. He's cool with it."

AJ nodded. "Great. I don't know if I can get human intestines, but the Mac Attack Double Burger might be close enough. Where's the other one?"

Fly shot back with a spooky "Who *knooooooows!"*

AJ turned his attention back to us. "Guys. I want you to meet somebody very special to me. We've been seeing a bit of each other this summer, but she told me if I didn't keep it a complete secret, her manager would have me sued. She even made me sign something." He looked at her sweetly. "What was that contract you made me sign?"

She smiled sweetly back. "That's an *NDA.* Stands for *non-disclosure agreement."*

"Right. *NDA.* Anyway. Meet the star of countless rom-coms, TV series, and Hollywood's newest recluse: Miss Candace Layne."

Smitty's jaw dropped and he let go of his end of a blueprint he was hanging. It dropped to the floor as he broke into a twitchy celebration dance, bouncing around the room, kicking over boxes to the music playing on a boom box.

"I knew it! I knew it, I knew it, and I *told you, Jack!"* He turned to Candace. "You were at the fun-raising party! I knew it was you, and nobody believed me because they all think I'm an idiot, which is sometimes true. But this time *I was right!"*

Candace smiled, charmed. We crowded around her, introducing ourselves and basking in her stardust. After days of creeping around in a dungeon breathing developing chemicals and ink, this was exactly what we needed. She wandered around the basement, inspecting the photos and schematics like an actor preparing for the opening shot of an important film.

"AJ here told me all about this disgusting casino development." She continued her tour as she spoke. "I've fallen in love with the island, and I'd like to help." She turned and looked at us. "So what can I do?" Her directness was disarming. We fell silent.

"I know!" Smitty blurted. "You could pretend to be …" He exhaled and trailed off slowly, a pained expression on his face. "… I dunno."

Fly spoke up. "What if you … you …" He also faded out in mid-sentence.

AJ turned to me. "What do you think, Jack? Is there a part for Candace in this production? She's starting to get bored with the rock, and I don't want her to leave." Candace shot AJ an *aw, you're such a sweetie* look, and he smiled back.

The room got quiet. For the life of me, I couldn't figure out how to work her into the plan. Likely because there *was* no plan, other than writing the exposé, figuring out how to get it printed, ginning up righteous indignation, and blowing up the Death Star.

She spoke up. "Come on guys! I'm offering my entertainment services for the low, low price of … *free*. I can sing, act, and dance. There must be a part for me." We watched as she transformed into a desperate

Southern belle, falling back a few steps, her arm draping across her forehead.

"Why, ah just don't know what I would do if ah missed out on such a theatrical experience!" She stumbled against some boxes, fake-fanning herself. "Ah might just … collapse in anguish."

She was *good*. We broke out in applause, and she executed a hammy bow.

"She's also double-jointed!" AJ piped in. Candace cuffed him on the side of the head. She broke into an upper crust English accent. "That was supposed to be our little secret, you disgusting cad!"

She checked her watch and whispered something to AJ. "Well, lads, ta-ta for now. Off to polish off a half-pound of pistachio fudge. I'm prepping for a possible role in the sequel to *Willy Wonka and the Chocolate Factory*. I'm playing Violet, the blueberry girl. Must plump up!"

"Really?" asked Smitty.

"Nope!" she responded, cheerily. "I just like making up excuses to eat fudge."

AJ turned to her. "Violet! You're turning violet!" They giggled and headed off in a flurry of fake accents and obscure film references, thumping back up the wooden stairs.

There was a moment of quiet as we all shared looks. "Actors," said Fly. "They're all nuts."

Spengler was deep in thought. "Smitty, was she in a movie called *Death's Door*?"

Smitty looked over. "She was. People said it sucked, but I saw it in Cheboygan and thought it was awesome! Crazy, man." He embarked on a rambling synopsis of the film. "The door like, sucks you in—and you see your own death—but it's all backward and in the final scene, she and her boyfriend sort of ... eh, it's tough to explain. Like it sort of reverses time through the door and she's, like, *nooooo!*"

He was done. "But yeah. She was in that."

"Hmm." Spengler was stroking his chin.

"What's up?" I asked.

"We just may have a position for her in our organization." With that, he sat back on his stool and continued tapping out the story.

If our little exposé was going to work, it was going to need photos. It was time to stretch. And as much as I wanted Erin by my side, I was at least wise enough to know that would never happen. I hurt her and didn't deserve her guidance. I would need to seek this vision on my own. The Smiths' lyrics bounced and echoed through my brain.

"You just haven't earned it yet, baby ... you must suffer and cry for a longer time."

I set out on my bike with my camera in a leather case, strapped on to my back. No fancy lenses. No tripod. No proper technique. No formal training. All those useless tricks would come later in life, and none of them would improve a bit on the work I did that day.

My first stop was the WibHo and Trina. Her dark eyes projected a thousand stories, tales that mattered to those who understood the island best. When I rolled up, she was sitting on the porch wearing a purple, floral dress and sharing a bottle of cheap scotch with her maintenance man, Big Pete Brodeur, and one of the hotel guests, an affable-looking man in a grey sweatshirt emblazoned with UP NORTH. They were deep into it, gossiping about the latest island scandals. Trina took sips from her faded "I Love Paris" coffee mug that she favored for her porch sessions and occasionally threw her head back in unfiltered laughter when the moments were right.

I asked permission to capture the revelry, and they obliged, only vaguely curious why. I couldn't help but wonder if Erin was up there in her room, and I glanced toward her window. I shook it off. Focus was vital. In every way.

I got my shots and thanked Trina for her time. We never discussed me being 86'd from the docks or exactly how that might impact her business. I was her only dockporter. But none of it mattered. She lived on island time, and if there were hard discussions to be had about my employment, they would come in due time. At that moment, I was a photographer on assignment. She sensed a larger mission, and I was grateful not to be asked what it was. Looking back, that was probably the moment I turned pro.

Next, I pedaled to Ryba's Fudge Shop, where we'd wasted so many hours watching loaf after loaf of fudge formed and cooled on marble slabs. I snapped close-ups of the next generation of fudge-junkies watching in wide-eyed amazement, just as we had.

The compositions created themselves as I found inspiration in the small moments. I was moving like water. Fast. No time to think, just make. Would there be a place for such uncut sweetness in a casino town? It was unlikely. A casino town's lifeblood is fast, easy money. Next-level vice. Darkness. All the more reason to get the shot. *Snap* and reposition. Then *snap* again.

Find the life.

I glided down to the Arnold Line dock next. While technically I was banned, nobody would gripe as long as I wasn't working. Just a civilian with a cheap camera. I moved in, capturing the energy and movement of the arrival. This was my world. I knew the angles.

Bull, Foster, Fly, and Smitty were doing what they did best. Connecting, directing, charming, moving the bags. A smile here. A wink there. Checking the watches. Loading up.

When things calmed down between boats, I found new angles as the boys pitched quarters and grilled up whitefish they pulled from the bay. Toward the end of the dock, I spied an exposed, shiny wheel of one of Gordon's golf carts peeking out from under a green weather tarp. I walked over and yanked it back to reveal the electric machine.

"Don't even think about it!" Foster was wagging a finger at me and smiling.

"Don't worry, old man. I've learned my lesson. Crime doesn't pay."

Foster shrugged. "Eh. I don't know if I'd go *that* far." He nodded toward a stack of bags. "It pays a little."

I stepped back and took three quick shots of the golf cart fleet. After the kinetic action of the boys at work, the carts radiated mechanical lifelessness.

I moved on to see Rick. I located him on a stretch of the Grand Hotel hill. *Sweep, sweep, scoop, plop.* He had just what Trina had. A story in his eyes. He allowed me to take a few photos for the very reasonable price of a thirty-pack of Stroh's and a promise that he didn't have to pose, stop working, look at the camera, or smile.

There was more. I moved fast. Limestone formations

at Arch Rock. A waiter scarfing down a French dip sandwich in the Fort Mackinac commissary. The checkout lady at Doud's Market. The banjo player at Horn's. Capturing. Composing. Crafting. It was a mad sprint. And it was exhilarating. I felt like an athlete.

The island was life. I needed to show it.

After I finished shooting, I inhaled a Snickers and a Mountain Dew and hopped on my bike to ride back to the darkroom, eager to get the photos developed. As I passed through town, Spengler swerved his porter bike and joined me. He was smiling like the bird that ate the canary and working to control a melting chocolate ice cream cone in his left hand.

"You get the shots?" he asked, mouth half-full.

"Sure as shit tried. What's the latest?"

"Remember how I told you the hardest part of this idea would be actually getting the story *printed?*"

"Yup. And I told you we'd figure that out later," I replied.

"Yup. You did," he said. "Which was just about the most useless advice ever. Thing is, I'm friendly with the guy that runs the presses for the *Island Gazette* in St. Ignace. His name is Kent. He's from Alabama. He's grumpy but he likes me, ever since I ghostwrote an anniversary card for his wife. She loved it."

We swerved to avoid a carriage full of tourists. He continued. "It got him laid for the first time in a long time. Like *years.* Anyway. He's the gatekeeper. He knows how to run the presses, and he's got the keys to get in. Everything we need to print the story."

"Great! So, how do we get to him?"

Spengler smiled. Borderline cocky. "Well, funny you'd ask. Guess what his very favorite movie is."

"Gone with the Wind?"

"Nope."

"Breakin' 2: Electric Boogaloo?"

"Nope."

"Caddyshack?"

"Nope."

"Citizen Kane?"

"Nope."

I rolled it around in my head. Then it snapped into place. "Oh. Duh. He works at a newspaper. The one with Robert Redford and … what's his name. Dustin Hoffman."

"—*All the President's Men?* Nope. You won't guess it." He looked over with a satisfied smile, milking the moment. *"Death's Door."*

"Death's Door?" I said. "What's—*oh! Death's Door!* The Candace Layne movie! Holy crap!"

I was waiting for the next part. "Great! So … what do we do now?"

"No idea." Spengler looked straight ahead. "But I'm sure you'll figure it out. You always do."

CHAPTER THIRTEEN

Swingin' Iggie
August 21, 1989

L ake Huron was smooth as glass as the ferry
churned from the island toward St. Ignace. The
sun was setting a brilliant orange, and the boys
were gathered around the bow, leaning on the railing,
sipping cold beers and trading stories from the day.
You'd never guess there was petty larceny on the docket.
On the other side of the pilothouse, AJ and Candace
engaged in what appeared to be intense dialogue. I
watched them through the pilothouse window, where I
steered the ferry as Cap Riley read the paper. I knew
what was going on. Fly had summed it up best: "Actors.
They're all nuts."

St. Ignace was the Southernmost town in the upper
peninsula, located at the northern end of the Mackinac
Bridge's five-mile span. It was less touristy than Mack-

inaw City, which some considered a budding Branson, Missouri, in both style and substance. St. Ignace, on the other hand, was more working class, and many of the residents made their living in construction and maintenance work on the island. In an old, rambling warehouse a few blocks from the shore road was the printing press for the *Island Gazette*.

Cap Riley absently scanned the box scores, grateful for a break after a long day of ferrying tourists to and from the island. It was like old times, I thought. Many nautical miles had passed under the rumbling hull of the ferry since my first piloting stint as a kid, probably fifteen years back. The island was on the brink of massive change, and none of it was good. But through it all, the steady hum of the *Straits of Mackinac II* diesel engine remained consistent.

Cap Riley spoke up as he read. "Headin' over to Iggie for a rowdy night at the Driftwood?" St. Ignace, to the locals, was affectionately called *Iggie*, or on a wilder night, *swingin' Iggie*. He was quizzing me without wanting to pry. Not his place. I hesitated for a moment, then plunged ahead with yet another semi-lie.

"Yeah. I figured a night off the island might be good for the gang. Nothing like the Driftwood on a Friday night, right? We'll grab the first boat back in the morning."

There was no way I'd implicate Cap Riley in another one of my schemes. What was about to happen at the printing press building later that night would need to remain a private affair. Cap Riley nodded and went back to reading. He fell quiet for a bit.

"I was sorry to hear about your grandfather. And about selling your place up there on the bluff. I met a lot of interesting characters at Wildcliffe cottage. Your dad and mom, rest her soul, always treated me like family."

"Yeah, well, they didn't know you like I do, old man," I shot back, not wanting to get too sentimental. Cap Riley stayed quiet, probably feeling the same way. He then folded up the paper and stood up. "Step aside, boy. I need to earn my union wage."

I moved away as he deftly took ahold of the wheel, scanning the horizon.

Riley's eyes landed on AJ and Candace. "Looks like AJ's got himself a live wire. Good for him. A talented kid like that needs a challenge." He watched silently for a bit, intrigued. He pursed his lips, concerned. "They fightin'?"

"Nah," I said. "She's an actress from Los Angeles. They're, well … they're practicing a scene." I knew it sounded ridiculous, but it also happened to be the truth. Cap Riley hit me with a sideways glance. Apparently, *practicing a scene* was not something he was interested in exploring further. We both watched as they stalked each other like two feral cats, gesticulating wildly.

Cap Riley's eyes thinned, his face transforming with recognition. "Wait a minute. *I know her.* Was she in a horror movie called *Death's Door*? She goes through this door, and she can see her death, and in the end—well, it's damn hard to explain, but it scared the hell out my wife. And *me*, truth be told."

Incredible, I thought. What was it about this flick? For a box office bomb, it sure had a lot of fans in the Straits of Mackinac region.

And there we were. Snow White and her seven sunburned dwarves, all striding down a dark St. Ignace alley with just enough moonlight to navigate. The mission was clear, and there was no turning back. If the moment were a movie scene, we'd undoubtedly be walking in super-slow motion.

We approached a nondescript steel door with a riveted frame. Spengler, lugging a massive binder of typed pages and photos, stepped up. He knocked three times on the door, counted a few beats silently to himself and knocked another three. Nothing happened. We shared looks.

"Is this the right place?" I whispered.

"No, Jack," Spengler whispered back. "This is the *wrong* place. That's why I'm knocking in code." The gang stifled laughs and I shut the hell up.

The door opened a crack. A balding, frosted mutton-chopped face peered out, glanced up and down the street, and exchanged a look with Spengler. This was Kent, the printing press guy. He checked our crew skeptically.

"Weren't expectin' no hockey team, Spang." His accent was Southern but the tone was pure, no-bullshit *Iggy*.

"They're here to help, Kent. Work the presses. Bind the papers. Whatever you need. The best muscle in northern Michigan. Trust me."

Kent nodded, albeit skeptically. "These are the bellmen you told me about?"

"Well," said Spengler, doing his best to keep the temperature low. "We like to be referred to as dock-porters. We ride luggage on our bikes."

He looked us over. "You ladies haul suitcases to hotels?"

"Yes, sir," said Spengler.

"You take folks to their room? Show 'em how to work the TV remote?"

"Yes, sir."

"You're *bellmen*."

I shot AJ a look. It was time. He nodded back and then approached Kent. "We'd also like to introduce our guest of honor, and the star of *Death's Door*, straight from Hollywood, Ms. Candace Layne."

Candace emerged from the back of the group, her fantastic movie-star teeth illuminating the alley. She walked straight up to Kent and extended her well-moisturized hand. His grim mug miraculously transformed into a shy, little boy grin that revealed a few missing teeth. He stood up straighter, tucking in his ample gut, and took her hand.

"Wow. I am a huge fan, Miss Layne. I mean, I loved *Death's Door*."

"You …" She shot him a thousand-megawatt smile. "*And nobody else.*"

From the back, Smitty called out, "I loved it."

Kent rechecked the ally and motioned for us to get inside. We followed him in, and he latched the door behind us. With his blue-jean coveralls and Jackson Pollock-esque ink-stained running shoes, Kent was turning out to be the ideal eighth dwarf. He led us toward the back of the cavernous workspace. We maneuvered around shadows of tall tables and machinery. A strange aroma filled the air.

"That smell," Candace whispered.

"Ink, I think," Smitty whispered back. Then louder. "Hey. I made a rhyme!"

Candace threw back her head and laughed. "You're too funny."

"I think so too." He motioned toward the guys. "Would you mind telling these clowns?"

"Clowns?" Candace announced to us. We stopped and looked toward her. "Listen up: Smitty's funny. Deal with it."

Smitty grinned. More vindication.

Kent stopped and turned to the group, raising his right hand. "Listen up, y'all!" The banter ceased. Kent waited a moment, then continued, his Alabama drawl making him sound like a cop in a Burt Reynolds movie.

"First thing's first. I am now officially breaking the goddamn law. That may or may not matter to ya'll, but I want to make that point crystal clear. Spengler here made me aware of a dire situation on the island that seems worthy of some additional, albeit illicit, actions. In this case, we'll call what we're printing here a *Special Edition of the Island Gazette*." He enunciated the phrase *"Special Edition of the Island Gazette"* slowly and deliberately, as if to make a legal point. "Next, I have no authority to approve a *Special Edition of the Island Gazette.*" Again, with effect. "Therefore, as I said, I am breaking the goddamn law. And so are you."

He took a deep breath and glanced toward Candace. His tough-guy veneer melted away, and he shook his head in amazement at the idea of a movie star in his midst.

"Also, there were assurances given to me by Spangler here that there would be a special VIP ... what'd you call it?"

"Meet and greet."

"Meet and greet, that's it—of a certain talented actress who's here all the way from Hollywood. Miss Layne's presence during this print session is such a surprise, and … well, ya'll. I'm honored."

AJ broke in with a mock Shakespearian voice. "The honor is ours, good Sir Kent the Printer. We look forward to reaping the benefits of your time-honored skills."

Candace jabbed AJ with her elbow, shushing him. "Too much!" she hissed.

There was a long, awkward pause. Kent spoke again, slow and dry. "Whatthefuck-*ever.*" He continued. "Okay, then. Keep them overhead lights off. Let's get to type-settin'."

Spengler handed the pages from his binder to me. I quickly looked them over and handed them off to Kent, who spread them out on a standing table next to an old Linotype machine, inspecting the layouts. For a minute or two, Kent rubbed his greying chops with his hand. It was impossible to decipher his grunts and sighs.

"Spangler. Is this shit stew your handiwork?"

"Well," Spangler looked at me and shrugged. *"Ours.* We were in a rush."

Kent sighed and shook his head. "Next week, you and me are gonna have a session about proper gutter width and font size. This won't print standard how you got it here." He shook his head, stealing a moment to set his eyes on Candace, who responded with an endearing smile. It calmed him. He shook his head and rolled his eyes in a way that implied: *See what I gotta deal with?* I had to admire Candace's craft. She provided more direct motivation with an understanding smile than an army of Tony Robbins clones.

Kent turned back to the table. "Well, at least these pictures are kinda nice, and I'm assuming all this copy says somethin' worth readin'. I know you got a way with words, Spang. At least my wife thinks so."

As he absorbed the layout, his brow furrowed. "Jesus. *Casinos?* On Mackinac Island? That ain't right." He was suddenly energized, and began reworking blocks of copy and photos quickly. Spengler and I shared a look, both thinking the same thing: *At least Kent likes the story.*

"Yeah, I can probably swap these two elements here. We should lead with this copy block and shrink these down to fit here …" He trailed off, mumbling to himself, warmed up and done with his curmudgeonly throat-clearing.

He moved over to the machine and began typing out Spengler's copy. The contraption whirred and clicked, and lead slugs dropped into a bin. We crowded around to watch him tap down on the keys, fascinated. There was no denying the good ol' boy was a pro. At one point, he looked up and noticed us standing around him like tourists. He stopped working and shot us a wary look that said *back the hell off* in no uncertain terms.

With nothing to do, the boys plugged in Foster's CD player and pushed play. The English Beat kicked in with their frantic, fantastic ska. We jumped around like fleshy, sunburned pogo sticks, slamming into one another with loving, brute force. Kent looked over with disgust for a moment but didn't absorb the distraction.

Hours later, Kent stood in front of the group, covered with ink and holding up the proof of a still-wet front page. "Here it is. Nine revisions later. A *Special Edition of the Island Gazette*."

We erupted in a cheer and crowded around, clapping Kent on the back. He signaled for us to quiet down lest we get busted, but there was no hiding the joy he felt. Capers, when done right, can be infectious.

"Alright, gang. Give it one last look, and we can set the presses. There's still time for a limited run if you dipshits don't get all nitpicky."

He set it down on the table and cracked open a can of Milwaukee's Best while Spengler and I gave it one last scan. No ads, no gossip, no birthdays, no death notices. Just hard, painful facts about the casino plans accompanied by my "human interest" photos of life on the island.

Now that our exposé was hardening into cement, I was able to look at it objectively. And it was powerful. After ten minutes poring over the pages, Spengler and I nodded to each other. There were a few typos, some awkward spacings, and three photos that got flipped, but the clock was ticking and this wasn't *The New York Times*.

"*Print it*," Spengler said.

"Wait!" AJ strode up to Kent holding a folding chair, which he placed next to him with a flourish. He was speaking in his weird Shakespearian accent again.

"Here-ye!" AJ said. Kent rolled his eyes but smiled. "We realize time is of the essence, Sir Kent the Printer. Before we commence to all that newspaper-ing, we would ask that you join us for an exclusive, one-night-only ... *performance of a lifetime!*"

On cue, Fly, Bull, and Smitty flicked on two hand-held work lights and swung them around to find Candace, who appeared from behind an old press. She was wearing the same wardrobe she wore during the final scene of *Death's Door.* Fake blood matted her blond hair, and her face transformed into a twitching mask of terror. She took a few steps toward Kent and paused. His jaw dropped. He instantly recognized the scene she was reenacting.

AJ gestured for Kent to sit. *The VIP.* Foster appeared out of nowhere and produced a red-and-white-striped container of popcorn and a Coke with a straw. Kent, shocked but pleased, accepted the snacks and sat. He secured the Coke between his knees and scooped a handful of popcorn into his ink-stained hands.

For the next ten minutes, Candace Layne and her co-star for the night, AJ, acted out the final scene, line-for-line, of Kent's favorite movie, *Death's Door.*

It.

Was.

Amazing.

Full disclosure: I hadn't seen *Death's Door*. But I'd bet the house the live version we saw that night was much better. Candace was flawless. Her movie screams were multilayered, chilling, and freakishly high-pitched. Her near-death flailing was wildly convincing. Even with minimal dialogue, AJ *crushed* the soon-to-be-dead boyfriend's role as if he were born to play it. When he puked up the death-geyser of blood, courtesy of Faygo Red Pop, we all cringed. Even the makeshift mood lighting was on point, as Smitty, Fly, and Bull darted in and out of the action with their hand-held lights, never disrupting the flow of the acting.

Through it all, I kept glancing at Kent. His eyes

sparkled and danced in wonder. When not distorted by the munching of mouthfuls of popcorn, his face was set in a blissful grin. Finally, Candace froze, perfectly still, like a mannequin. She looked out into the darkened audience, paused, and uttered: "And ... *scene!*"

There was a stunned, silent beat followed by wild applause. Relative to the size of the audience, it was deafening. Candace smiled broadly, accepting AJ's warm hug as we crowded around, slapping backs and heaping praise. Bull appeared out of nowhere with a bouquet of carnations and handed it to her. She accepted it with hammy graciousness, mouthing, "Thank you, thank you! One and all, thank you!"

Kent stood with us, a scrap of paper and pen in his hand. He knew damn well nobody was going to believe this tale. At the very least, he was getting her autograph.

So maybe *Death's Door* didn't connect with audiences when it came out in theaters. Perhaps it was panned by critics. Maybe her performance was called "tedious" by some shit-bird reviewer who would never do anything nearly as impressive his entire life. But it sure as hell connected with us that magical night at the old printing press building in St. Ignace, Michigan.

Kent got his autograph, folded it up carefully, and slid it into his back pocket. He walked over to a metallic lever on the printing machine and yanked it down with a grind and a clang. The press roared to life.

The ferry docked on the island the next morning, and most of the guys hurried off to change for work. As for me, I had a shitload of *Special Editions of the Island Gazette* to deliver.

"How many you want?" Fly was hanging back to help me load up as I straddled my bike.

Earlier on the ferry ride back to the island, I staged a paper folding clinic for the team. "First, you fold just enough of the paper to tuck the right-hand section into the left, right here in the opening under the paper's main fold. You tighten the roll by holding the top section with your left hand, twisting the roll …" The team followed along intently. Candace picked it up faster than anyone. Soon enough, we had the papers prepped and ready for maximum fling.

Now it was time to deliver.

"Load it up," I replied. "I'm dropping one off to every house and business on the rock. I'll keep it up until there's nothing left."

"Full court press, my man. Make 'em cry," said Fly.

I kicked off and pedaled hard toward Main Street. The newspapers were stacked high, held in by the over-the-topper bungee usually reserved for luggage. In craning for a line of sight, I caught a quick peek at the headlines we'd hastily written back in the darkroom. The main header screamed in 24-point text: *PARADISE LOST! State Sells Off Island Land to Casino Operation.* It wasn't the most creative headline, but there wasn't a whole lot of time to fiddle with clever wordplay. Besides, it was probably better than the alternative we considered: *HOLY SHIT, WE GOTTA DO SOMETHING!*

Halfway down the page was another header: *AN ISLAND WORTH SAVING,* a photographic collage from that frantic day-long shoot, as well as images from earlier in the summer. I included a shot of a sweat-drenched Erin playing the fiddle at Horn's Bar as the patrons bounced on the dance floor. She'd probably administer another beat-down when she saw I used it without her permission, but I'd actually welcome that over the excruciating radio silence I'd been enduring since our blowout.

I rode past Marquette Park, tossing a copy to Lennie the Thief, who ran the Horse and Buggy Tours. I rode by the yacht club where Sailor Bart was holding court and tossed three or four copies. Then it was past the hotels and inns along the shore road and up the brutally steep hill to the East Bluff, tossing papers left and right. Some were underhand, some hook-shots. My paperboy aim, for the record, was still spot-on.

The *Special Edition of the Island Gazette* hit the streets like a summer storm, drenching everyone, from the most seasoned islander to the greenest summer worker. Heading into Labor Day weekend, there was a palpable energy in the air, fueled by our story. The state news wires picked up the exposé, and outlets as far south as Detroit ran their own segments. Stunned shop owners stood on the Main Street sidewalk in small groups of twos and threes, discussing the implications. *An island worth saving* was a tagline for a mini-movement, as businesses and hotels posted signs with the message in simple blue and green type.

I'd be lying if I said I didn't enjoy the attention. The city council pardoned us in advance for the *Island Gazette* break-in. It was, they said, a "noble cause," an opinion the police *didn't* hold when I drove Gordon's golf cart into the lake. In contrast, Emile Cranston, Jr., the *Gazette* owner, presented Spengler and me with an engraved bronze plaque. He also gave a shocked Kent a promotion. Not for nothing: Cranston also took full credit for running the story, but we were okay with that. It was a free lesson in smart, albeit crass, business. Cranston hadn't made the money to buy his cottage on the West Bluff by being a fool. Besides, we wanted results. His circulation tripled overnight, and we were hoisted up the flagpole as the island heroes of the moment.

To my surprise, the more prominent downstate news outlets picked up my photos for their stories, all credited, of course. The simple images struck a nerve. The faces and places resonated with a much larger audience. You didn't have to be an island type to recognize the passing of something precious.

More than a few business owners stopped me and asked if I'd shoot an ad for their shop or hotel. A *Detroit Free Press* reporter, on the island to file a follow-up story, even slipped me his card, telling me I had "an eye." I clipped all the articles with my photos and taped them in my scrapbook, figuring Big Jack might like proof his son wasn't a complete screwup. Okay, maybe the clippings were for me. While the attention would have been far sweeter if I had Erin by my side, this unexpected burst of success, technically speaking, didn't suck.

At this point, all we could do was wait.

That same week, the city council held meeting after meeting to figure out how to derail the approaching catastrophe. Spengler and I attended, expecting to explain precisely how we had come into possession of the incriminating plans. Spengler, who was now comfortable describing himself as a "journalist," simply declined, claiming his *first amendment rights.* I smiled to myself whenever he said it. Spengler, the bespectacled, dad sock-wearing dockporter, was now claiming *first amendment rights.* It was a far cry from writing product copy for Auntie Annie's Old Tyme Taffy Shoppe.

As for me, I didn't have much to offer in these informal interrogations. I merely co-masterminded the caper and snapped a few random—albeit highly moving —photographs, if I do say so myself.

Ultimately, they dismissed us. Leaving the council's conference room, I noticed a stranger. He was tall and thin, wearing a suit and surrounded by a coterie of other suits that looked like lawyers. He was staring grimly at a photo of Main Street from the turn of the century that hung on the wall. Council members spit-balled schemes, but he looked lost in his own world. Something about his suit screamed *good enough for government work.* There was no doubt in my mind this worried man was there to represent the State of Michigan.

Gordon and the entire Whittaker family fled the island the day the story broke. The casino scheme leak was not part of their master plan, and laying low on the mainland was not the worst idea in the world.

The hastily assembled press conference had to be one of the shortest in the history of press conferences. Standing in front of the tiny Town Hall building on Market Street was Emile Cranston, owner of the *Island Gazette* and a

City Council member. There was no microphone, so he called out loudly to the gathered island crowd and a handful of reporters and camera crews. I stood with Smitty and a few of the guys off to the side to listen to the verdict. I could see Spengler standing toward the front, holding a pen and pad, ready to take notes.

Cranston continued. "The council has completed days of discussions regarding the casino plan with a member of the House of the State of Michigan, who would like to share some, I guess you would say, some … *words*. This is Mr. Matthew Swain," Cranston said.

No applause. Just murmurs and apprehension. *Share some words?* I craned my neck to get a better look. Swain, the same thin man I'd seen during the meeting, stepped forward. He didn't look any happier. I hoped that was just the way he looked.

"Yes. I do have some … *words*." He took a deep breath. "Unfortunately, there's nothing the state can do. It was an embarrassing mistake, but it's also…" He paused, taking a deep breath, then continued. "… completely legal. Bluewater, LLC broke no laws, and while we recognize that the plans totally alter, perhaps even ruin, the island's rich character, it's a done deal." Then he removed a handkerchief from his jacket pocket and dabbed his eyes. "I'm sorry." With that, he turned away and walked inside the Town Hall, to the surprise of the stunned, silent crowd. *Some words*, I thought.

———

People love a sad human-interest story. And maybe that's all our little island story was. The exposé was a massive hit. It motivated the community precisely as we all hoped it would. Everybody, *and I mean everybody,* agreed that the plan must be stopped. It was a grotesque, obscene, predatory idea and would ruin everything.

The story also had no effect whatsoever.

Casinos and golf carts were coming to the island. No amount of handwringing, protest, or published stories could stop it.

I learned a lot of lessons that summer. I learned about love and how to lose it. I learned about change. I learned about life and death. I also learned this: Just because everyone hates something, that doesn't make it illegal.

We read about these situations all the time. The stories pop up sporadically on the inside pages of a newspaper or on the local nightly news. The headlines scream some version of the same thing: *Local Community Fights Developers over the Fate of Small-Town Way of Life.* It's usually an ugly condo development, a casino, Walmart, or some other aesthetically awful but economically sensible scenario. But the thing is, we hardly ever follow up on what happens after the story fades.

Who won?

I guess we're too busy to find out. Nine times out of ten, the small town loses the fight, and everyone works for last year's villain. When big changes come, they hit fast and hard, like a violent hurricane. The landscape transforms so quickly that nobody even remembers what it once looked like. When was the last time you overheard someone wax nostalgic about the quaint little town of Reno before it was an obscene, garish monument to bad bets? Besides never?

Anyway, we lost.

CHAPTER FOURTEEN

Reactivated
September 1, 1989

F riday was cool and sunny. *Nippy*, as Gramps would've put it. I was standing in front of the post office, observing as a formation of cotton-white clouds over the bluff slowly transformed from Abe Lincoln's profile into a baby T-Rex in a cowboy hat.

AJ skidded to a halt. He wore a pink blazer, a green bow tie, and white brogues. He also sported heavy-framed Buddy Holly-style glasses with no lenses. Somehow, he pulled it off. *Handsome sonofabitch*, I thought. He opened up his blazer a peek, posing like a Sears catalog model. "Whaddya think?" he said, holding the position. "Modern, but retro. Upscale but old school." He struck a new pose, this time reflective. "Country club vibe meets post-punk New Wave. Sharp as hell, right?"

I shot him a skeptical once-over. "You look like a

young Rodney Dangerfield. Or Ronald McDonald going golfing."

He thought about it, then nodded, pleased with the critique. "I love *both* those guys. I'm escorting star-power tonight, so I figure I need some style. Something that separates me from the pack. Something that says, 'Yes, these idiots are my pals, but no, I'm not one of them.' You should see Candace's dress, Jack. Seriously. She looks like a movie star."

"Seriously, AJ, she *is* a movie star."

"You make an excellent point, as always."

"Where are you taking her?" I asked.

He cocked his head. "Where am I taking … what are you talking about? Tonight's the Dockporter Ball! We're taking the freight boat over to Squeegie's Bar. It's catered, man! Bound to be an epic night!" He did another double-take. "Jack. You bought a ticket to this bash, like, two months ago!"

I completely forgot tonight was the biggest, most outrageous party of the year. The big end-of-summer bash. We called it the *Dockporter Ball,* but it was open to anyone who could spring for a ticket and had a titanium liver. It was not for the faint of heart. The previous year, Smitty and AJ boarded the boat back to the island at the end of the night buck naked, carrying the shuffleboard from the bar under their arms while their dates belly danced in tiaras to provide cover.

This *ball* was one-third formal affair and two-thirds Detroit Zoo.

AJ leaned in and put his hand on my shoulder. "We did everything we could to stop this casino shit. It's wrong. We all know that. But that's one more reason to make this year's ball a rager of historical—

hell, even *hysterical*—proportions. It may be the last one. *Ever.*"

Was this supposed to cheer me up?

"I won't be back next summer," AJ said. "I mean, what am I gonna do, be a crap-ee-ay?"

"A crap-ee-ay?" I asked.

"Yeah. The guy who runs the craps table. You know. '*No more bets!*'" He raised his hands as if warning some imaginary gambler to stop. "A crap-ee-ay."

"Jesus, you're turning into Smitty. It's pronounced *croop*-ee-ay."

"Ah, right. Croop-ee-ay. Well. I don't wanna be that either. I'm a showman. I'm Carlo Bolognia. I'm the boyfriend in *Death's Door*. These streets are my stage. I'll be damned if I'll—ah, never mind. I'm starting to depress myself." He lithely switched topics as he reattached a bungee cord to his basket.

"What's the issue?" he asked. "No date? No problem. Invite Vicky, the swimmer from State. I mean, at this point, you might as well." AJ squinted. "Wait—scratch that. She's going with Smitty. Anyway. The point is, just because you have no date, no life, you live in a barn, and technically, you're no longer a dockporter, doesn't mean you shouldn't …" He trailed off and patted me on the shoulder. "The boat leaves at six. It won't be the same without you."

He waited for me to respond. I didn't.

"That was my pep talk. Gotta run." He checked his Swatch watch and was off in an Italian pastel blur of pure *id.*

I thought to myself. *Maybe Erin would want to … no.*

I shook off the idea. I wouldn't even know how to ask her.

Checking the McGuinn family mail was pure routine, spawned as a chore when I was a kid, something that needed to get done every day. Like coffee or a morning poo. Without a family to speak of, the island mail flow trickled to mostly coupons and flyers, which would go straight into the trash. You didn't have to be a raging tree hugger to notice what a colossal waste of time and energy this cycle was.

> *Open mailbox.*
> *Take note of junk.*
> *Toss junk in the trashcan.*
> *Repeat.*

The metal box, number 103, was five rows up and three rows over. I unlocked it and pulled out a lone, clean, white letter. Something about it instantly screamed *official*. Not at all colorful and junky like the typical sales mail haul. And it was addressed to me: *Jack McGuinn, Wildcliffe Cottage.* This alone was jarring. I didn't receive a whole lot of mail back then. The most intriguing aspect of the letter was the return address. *Rhode Island School of Design.* I'd heard of it but only in passing. The sum total of my knowledge was that it was located in Rhode Island and it was a design school, all of which was indicated in its name. Also, that the cool kids called it "RISD."

I ripped it open and began to read. Understandably, the letter was exceedingly well-designed.

Dear Mr. McGuinn: On behalf of the admissions team at the Rhode Island School of Design, we want to acknowledge the receipt of your application. We were very impressed by your submitted portfolio and achievements and feel that you would make an excellent addition to our student body. We would like to set up an appointment at our campus in Providence at your earliest convenience to discuss your potential enrollment for the upcoming ...

It continued on with more college admission-sounding optimism but I stopped reading and held the letter away from my body as if it were radioactive. I gazed around the half-empty post office. The place smelled like old wood and the metal of rows of heavy-duty mailboxes embossed with floral embellishments. The service clerk behind the counter, a big friendly gal, laughed with a balding old-timer as she handed him a package.

"Jeez, whatcha got in here, Bennie? Looks *illegal!*" Her accent was pure Michigan *yooper*.

The old-timer wheezed back. "None your bee's wax, Janie!"

"Well, you have fun with it, whatever it is!"

"Oh, I will."

The old guy walked out with his package, a newfound skip in his step. Janie smiled to herself and turned back to her package sorting. I looked at the letter again. I was just about a thousand percent certain I'd never applied to the Rhode Island School of Design, or any other school for that matter. *It was an art school.* Pink Floyd, Annie Leibovitz, and Andy Warhol went to art school, not beer-chugging Michigan ex-dockporters.

I climbed the spotless, whitewashed steps of Grand
Hotel's massive front veranda two at a time. The sky was
overcast now. The rain was coming. On the roadway
outside the lobby, carriage drivers unrolled plastic cover-
ings to keep their passengers dry. Usually, guests strolled
across the porch at this hour and took in the expansive
view of the Straits of Mackinac with the bridge in the
distance. With the approaching rains, the guests moved
indoors to browse the lobby, which also served as a hotel
history museum. Others were likely nursing cocktails in
the Cupola Bar, situated like a fancy hat at the top and
center of the wide, spectacular structure. I walked to the
very end of the 600-foot-long porch to where I first
heard her play. There was nobody there.

A chair and table. A tasteful arrangement with a rose
bouquet in a Grand Hotel-branded vase. But no Erin. In
place of her cello was a shiny, gold harp. Did Erin also
play the harp? And why didn't I know the answer to that
question?

"Can I help you?" I turned around. A male staffer in
a sharp red uniform stood at attention, holding a tray of
five stemmed glasses filled with white wine. He looked
vaguely familiar but I couldn't place him.

"Where's Erin? The cello player," I asked.

He looked at me blankly. Then at the instrument.
"That's a harp."

"Yes, I know that. But where's Erin, the cello
player?"

He nodded back. "That's a harp," he repeated.

"I understand but I'm looking for the woman, Erin,

who plays the cello." I spoke slowly, as if to a small, not-so-bright child. "She's usually set up right here."

He continued to stare, then looked at the spot where Erin wasn't. He seemed to want to understand. Then he broke out in a wide, sunny grin.

"Oh! Yeah! Sorry, I just started a few days ago."

That's when it hit me. He was the stoner from the park. The loose, raspy patter was a dead giveaway.

"I thought *you* thought that was a cello, and I was like, 'bro, that's a harp.' Yeah. Anyway. Um … she quit."

He sensed my surprise but charged ahead. "No, but the harp player, Nancy, is awesome. I don't even like the harp at all, and even I think she's good. Super soothing. Sometimes I hang around this area and, like, chill out. Just listen. It's *really* nice." He was done selling the experience and took a few steps back. He gestured to the wines. "Take one, bro. They're free."

"Thanks." I grabbed one of the white wines and gulped it down like water. "When did she quit?"

"Lemme think. I overheard them talking at the front desk yesterday that someone named Erin left the island. Something about going back to … was it Amsterdam? Italy? Iceland? It started with a vowel, I think."

"Ireland?" I asked.

"*Ireland!* Of course! She was Irish. That's where they're, like … you know … *from.*"

I nearly knocked the poor guy over as I sprinted down the long porch to get to my bike before it rained. *Left the island?*

I hopped off my bike while it was still moving and brought down the kickstand. Trina was working the front desk, checking in a guest. She smiled at me as I passed. I waved and bounded up the stairs, took a left, and strode down the musty hall. I approached her room, recalling my exchange with the honeymoon couple across the hall earlier in the summer. It felt like another lifetime.

Her door was ajar. Music played from inside the room. The Cure. *Just Like Heaven*. I tapped on the door. It swung open, and I wandered in.

She emerged from the tiny kitchen carrying a cardboard box and let out a shriek. "You don't knock?! I nearly wet myself!"

I felt foolish. And creepy. "Sorry. I ... the door was open. Sort of. I heard you left."

"Did you use that excuse with the honeymoon couple way back when?" Her eyes now twinkled with the memory. "My God, weren't those two a couple of frisky rabbits. I didn't sleep for days, what with all the bedsprings creaking."

She set the box down on the bed and began placing folded clothes in a pile. The Cure continued to play. I softly sang along. *"I'll run away with you ..."*

"Did you say something?" she asked, not looking up as she sorted.

"The lyrics. *I'll run away with you.*"

"Right," she said. "Somehow, I doubt that." She finished her sorting and walked to the foot of the bed, standing right in front of me. She didn't look angry or sad, just curious. "What do you want, Jack?"

"I'm sorry, Erin. About what I said. *The last fling king.*

All of it. I didn't mean any of it. I was screwed up. I overindulged and became opinionated."

She nodded. "Meaning you got shitfaced and became an asshole."

"You could put it that way."

"Fine. I'm sorry about the crack upside your head. It had to hurt."

Unconsciously, I touched one of the healing-but-still-lingering contusions on the back of my noggin. She moved back to sealing a ziplock bag full of makeup.

"Cracks. With an *s*. Probably the most pain I've ever felt. But the wounds have almost healed."

I recalled hearing about Erin breaking a glass of beer over Gordon's head earlier in the summer and felt a vague sense of relief. At least there was another member of the beatdown club, even if he did happen to be my sworn enemy.

"I still don't know how I ended up with her. I mean, like that. It makes no sense. It ..." It was true. I *couldn't* remember.

She softened and smiled. She sealed a box. Moved another suitcase into position. I felt a rush of resentment at how easily she could multitask during my big emotional moment.

"Nothing has to make sense, McGuinn. We're young. Have you forgotten that? We're on an island and it's summer. You're a dockporter. Well, you were. I'm a fool. We have our whole lives to make sense." *Fold, pack, zip.* "I forgive you. But tomorrow I'm leaving. My contract is up. There's nothing keeping me here."

I pulled the letter from my front pocket, now crumpled. I opened it up and displayed it for her. Her face instantly lit up. She moved next to me, scanning the letter. Her jaw dropped. "They want to meet you! That's *absolutely class!*"

"It is … absolutely class. But I don't quite remember applying."

"Oh, you applied. You just didn't know it."

"So this was all you."

"I couldn't let all those wonderful photos gather dust. So, I gathered 'em up and shipped 'em off." She opened another empty suitcase on the bed and looked at me slyly. "We happen to have a family friend from Dublin who's a visiting professor there in Rhode Island. He's on the admissions board. I Fedexed your stuff to him a few weeks back. By the way, you wrote a *lovely* application essay. The theme was 'How I Found My *It*.' I couldn't have written it better myself."

I shook my head. "It's one of the best art schools in the country. I looked it up."

"Damn right, it is. So you better not miss the appointment, you vindictive asshole. That's the least you can do."

"Thank you, Erin."

She looked at me with a hint of a smile. "No. Thank *you*," she said.

"For what? I ruined everything."

"For what? Hmm." Her eyes glanced upward as if she was checking a list floating a few feet in front of her. "For chasing me down with a purple, old lady scarf. For teaching me to trust the stars. For your front porch. For your grandfather. For your father. For the basket of your bike."

She sat down on her creaky bed, deep into the task of remembering. "What else? For Anne's Tablet at night. For indoctrinating me in the cult of Schwinn. For pretending to like *Somewhere in Time*. Oh, 'the crazy dream.' Who could forget that one? There must be more."

"Please," I said, smiling. "Continue."

"For *doing something*. You did something."

"I failed at something."

"Ah, well. You failed at many things. But you fought for what you believe in, and you deserve credit for that. I saw the article and the photos, Jack. I was moved to tears."

"I did it to get you back." I studied her face, waiting for a reaction. She took her time.

"It's a good line, Jack. But I don't believe it. You had loftier ambitions. And I love that." She stood up, turned away quickly, and pulled a tissue from a box on the dresser.

"It's time for me to go," she said.

I looked around the room. "You're going to need help tomorrow evening."

"I needed help a week ago, Jack. I'll handle the bags."

"Please?"

She sighed, waving me away. "Fine. The 5:30 boat tomorrow. *No romantic gestures.*"

She stepped into the bathroom and closed the door. "Now go away," she called through the door. "I need a right proper girly *fookin'* cry."

The concept of faking joy by pouring beer over my head with a bowtie strapped to my forehead made me nauseous. I admired the ability of the boys to focus on hedonism over psychological or physical pain. Despite whatever personal issues they had, the dockporters never failed to make it to Horn's Bar at night to cleanse themselves with the beat of a bar band and the soothing communion of cold Stroh's. I remembered being the same way when the summer began. Emotionally bulletproof. I envied and mourned my former selfish self.

I'd ghosted, avoiding the boys until I heard the blaring horn of the chartered ferry as it pulled away from the dock. I sat on the grass slightly obscured by Father Marquette's statue and watched the boat round the break wall, headed to Squeegie's Bar on the nearby island of Bois Blanc, the venue for this year's ball. Locals pronounced it "Bob-lo," perhaps due to a lack of interest in learning French. Even from this distance, I could hear the music and laughter from the ferry as it ratcheted up in direct proportion to the diesel's competing roar. They were going to have the time of their lives. Antics. Perhaps even shenanigans. It was the Dockporter Ball. Probably the last one ever.

After I devoured two slices of pizza from Sarducci's and the park was shrouded in darkness, I rode back to the barn. I climbed the stairs, stripped off my jeans, and collapsed on the bed, not bothering to pull back the sheets.

Was she packed? Ready to go? A subtle but noticeable switch seemed to have flipped. Despite her "right proper girly *fookin'* cry," it was clear she was no longer … what was the right word … *intrigued* with me. Maybe it was all in my head, but something was different.

But there was still tomorrow. There was always tomorrow.

The apartment was dark now. A chilly fog—but no

rain—enclosed the island. Damp, cool air drifted in through an open window, but I was too tired to slam it shut. My eyes became heavy.

The sounds of a steam shovel and crunching concrete pierced my eardrums. Gigantic, repetitive jackhammers pummeled a paved street. I remembered those spindly machines from my childhood. When I was six, Big Jack had taken me to a construction site a few blocks from the dealership for fun. He figured I'd dig it. I didn't. I watched as a collection of massive, robotic machines demolished a row of old row houses to make room for a strip mall. It was methodic and organized. And, to me, terrifying. Something about that inhuman, never-ending pounding didn't intrigue me like I'm sure Big Jack hoped it would. Instead, it felt like the end of the civilized world.

The construction workers, all clad in reflective yellow and orange, also appeared inhuman. They never flinched at the endless *BOOMS* and *CRUNCHES*. They directed and redirected impassively as if they too were machines. I hated it, but I kept my feelings to myself, a fake smile plastered on my face as my dad pointed out the various machines' names. *That's called a steam shovel there, Jacky.* It's not particularly manly to be spooked by giant machines, but the feeling of dread was visceral.

Now, these machines were on my island. *Boom. Boom. Boom.* I sat up straight. What time was it? How long had I been sleeping? I pulled on shorts and a T-shirt, ran down the stairs, and emerged from the barn apartment to daylight.

The sight was horrifying. A line of machines had torn up the road in front of Wildcliffe. I looked right, then left. Three of the East Bluff houses—our neighbors since I was a kid—were leveled. Crushed, painted white pine piled up like broken matchsticks, along with the remnants of wicker chairs, a porch swing, and old bikes tangled and mangled in the dirty mess of debris. And the sound. The sound was deafening.

I ran to the fence that lined the bluff and leaned out, inspecting the harbor below. It was sickening. Cranes tore pilings from the yacht docks up from their roots. Lake water cascaded down, caked with brown seaweed. The boats were all gone.

Main Street, now pockmarked with construction, was half-leveled. The *beep-beep* of machines in reverse, the cacophony of *smash-smash-smash, boom-boom-boom*. Timber uprooted and dropped in piles. The ragged, smashed remnants of history.

Vomit pushed its way up, but I held it in. I ran to the closest construction worker, a huge man in orange coveralls and a hard hat. I waved my hands, trying to get his attention. I yelled to him, but no sounds came out. Struck deaf. He didn't look up and continued to direct another machine into place.

Then it was horns honking. A traffic jam? I looked up the road. Five or six cars were waiting to pass. Wait. *Cars?* No, there were more than five. It was twenty. *Fifty.* They were lined up. Waiting to pass. Honking, getting louder. Thumping. Louder. Horns. Louder. The ground was now giving way. I screamed. Again, nothing came out. A bulldozer smashed into the front porch of Wildcliffe, tearing out the supports. The roof came down in a sickening smash. *What the hell was happening?*

My eyes shot open, but I was staring at the worn ceiling boards of the barn apartment. The thumping continued. My heart? But it wasn't a machine. It was the door. *The door?* Someone was knocking. Holy shit, *it was a dream*. The knocking continued as I caught my breath. *Thump-thump-thump.*

I'd always had vivid dreams. While most kids have the "in school, wearing pajamas" dream, mine were a bit more specific and way more embarrassing. I once had a dream I was stumbling around Johnson Elementary wearing nothing but a giant Sun-Maid Raisin box to cover my swimsuit region. I wandered down the hall and into a cooking class, where every girl pointed at me, laughing hysterically. In unison. Then they threw brownie dough at me, all while singing a slow, creepy version of *Yellow Submarine*.

Thump-thump-thump. I shook off the freaky construction nightmare, stomped down the stairs, and whipped open the door. Cap Riley, in mid-knock, looked at me closely. It was an almost curious expression. He'd never seen me in a post-nightmare state. Or in my boxers. It was hard to know what startled him more.

"What's wrong with you, boy? You look terrible."

"I'm fine," I stammered. "I had a bad dream."

"Yeah? Well, that makes two of us. We got a big problem on the dock. Your knucklehead crew. They're stranded on Bob-lo. *All of 'em.* The freight boat had engine problems. We got a metric shit-ton of luggage coming in today, and you're all we got."

I stared into nowhere. "They pulled my card, Cap. You know that. I'm banned."

He rolled his eyes as if to say, *You going to hang me up on the details?*

"Just handle the loads today, kid. Nobody's going to write a goddamn complaint letter. Trust me."

The luggage piled off the boats every thirty minutes at a volume I'd never experienced. Why? Well, for one, it was the end of the summer. The last blast. Winters hit Michigan like a frozen two-by-four to lay everyone flat for five months, with nothing to do but binge-watch the Red Wings and gain pretzel weight. The Great Lakes State is a tease in that way. Endless forests and trails. Eleven-thousand pristine lakes and bays. Perfect summer temperatures. All this fun, and only three-and-a-half months to pack it in.

The panic usually sets in around late August. Everyone who has neglected to take a summer vacation decides, in unison it seems, to pack up and head north to places like Mackinac Island. And that summer, there was an added urgency. People knew the island was about to become a construction site and casino town shortly after that. This might be the last chance to experience the magic before the place became an unrecognizable row of slot machines.

My morning was about the loads. Loads of loads. I stood in the epicenter of freshly deposited luggage, frantically sorting through a garden of name tags. What began as a Mt. Whitney-sized task grew to Everest, its snowy peak obscured by my own limitations. I was one guy on one bike.

But there was also joy. It felt fantastic to be back on

the dock, and soon I entered that realm artists and athletes call "flow." It was an unconscious state where every move was right, and every big fat tip was well-earned. I chatted, charmed, loaded, and unloaded, swerving through the insane, chaotic streets with a focus and clarity I'd never before experienced.

I channeled Foster in his prime. I imagined High-Rise Jimmy Oliver, a legend I'd never met. I stole some of AJ's corny theatrics and Spengler's bookish logic. Smitty's skill for under-thinking came in handy, and Fly's engineering adjustments finally made sense. On that day, I likely could've kicked a football like Bull. Anything was possible. For that one shift, I was every dockporter, going back to the time dockporters pushed steamer trunks off cruise ships for ten cents. But still Jack McGuinn.

Hours later, patches of sweat darkened my green polo shirt. I checked my watch as I skidded back to the Arnold Line dock. Somewhere else, Erin was prepping her luggage. There was still time. Cap Riley was watching from his perch on the upper deck behind his dark shades.

"Two more and it's over, boy!" he said.

I stared at the last of the luggage doubtfully, ran my fingers through my sweat-drenched hair. I had done my duty and I had a date to keep. I called up.

"Can't do two trips! I gotta meet someone." Cap Riley frowned. "These are important. Big-shots. They paid extra for luggage service, and they already headed up to the West Bluff."

I shook my head, adamant. "I can't do it, Cap!"

"Listen," he said. "I can see you're wrecked. Time isn't an issue."

"It is for me." I studied the luggage and did some quick calculations. "Screw it. I'll ride 'em both."

I straightened the bike and began the stacking process—bag after bag. No reason to hop out of the flow once you're in it, right? The load grew as I strapped in double-sided wings with Fly's cobalt bungee cords. A cooler here, carry-ons will work there, slip in this second set of golf clubs here.

Soon, it wasn't me stacking. It was ancestral DNA from my Irish-Scot-caveman heritage. Had they been stackers? Grunting, leopard-skin wearing ... loaders of things? Had hunting techniques evolved by stacking rocks to see approaching predators? Was dockporting a *survival skill?* Part of Maslow's hierarchy, located in a secret subcategory between food and shelter? It sure as hell felt like it at that moment. I glanced to my right. Standing not five feet away was Rick. Perfectly still with an enigmatic smile.

"Hi, Rick," I said, straining to strap in another case.

"You still got three more to get in there."

I looked over. Sure enough. Three more bags. The rear wheel lifted a bit as the weight countered forward, threatening to shoot me over the basket and straight into the pavement, a brutal dump before I even pushed off. "It's too heavy. I can't ride it."

"Yeah. High-Rise was *beefy*. You don't have enough counterweight." He looked around. "Gimme a sec."

He set down his shovel and strolled into the darkness of the Arnold Line freight shack. He came out moments later with a ten-pound dumbbell in one hand and a rear bike rack in the other. A huge wrench poked out of his back pocket. With Penske pit crew efficiency, the old shit sweeper went to work rigging a small platform on my rear fender, then chained the dumbbell to the rack. It worked like a charm. The bike was now steady. Balanced. Rideable. It was ingenious.

"Now we need to get those three bags up," said Rick. He hustled over and, one by one, loaded up the final bags in the basket. The load was now enormous. A monster. The biggest by far I'd ever attempted.

"This is a great photo-op, Rick, but I can't see over it." I was struggling already.

"Shut yer pie-hole, boy, and let me finish." Rick moved to the front of the load and meticulously slid out one bag, Jenga-like, revealing a perfect window to the road ahead. He strapped the bag to the top of the load. I was dumbfounded.

Rick had just revealed the Holy grail. *A window!*

"It's so simple!" I said.

"That's how High-Rise did it back in seventy-five."

"How do you know that?"

"Jesus. At least I have an excuse for havin' shit fer brains. I toldja this in June, boy. *I loaded him.*"

Rick *had* helped construct that legendary blackjack load. He *had* told me. But he hadn't told me *how*. I looked through the tiny, perfectly-formed porthole like a tank commander. No peripheral vision. No warnings. No wingmen. And I was already exhausted. I leaned the load again, testing the balance. Heavy but rideable.

Was I going to pedal this monster through the busy streets of Mackinac Island and up the Grand Hotel hill to the West Bluff while navigating through a one-by-three-foot hole? Yup.

As I leaned the bike again, a leather luggage tag smacked me in the face. I glanced at it absently. I looked closer and saw: *Property of Gordon Whittaker.*

You gotta be kidding me.

I inspected a few more. More Whittaker tags. I reached for a golf bag handle. *Property of Bluewater LLC.* It was the developers. The casino crowd. It had to be. They let the press die down and were back on the island to get down to brass tacks. And I was hauling their shit. I was straddling it, strapped in with no possible escape. I looked up at Cap Riley.

"I'm not haulin' this!" I called up.

Cap Riley darkened, pulled off his shades.

"You gotta! They paid the ferry line extra for special luggage service. You don't haul it, it's *my* ass that gets chewed out. Not yours!"

"I don't *gotta* do anything! This Whittaker guy is …"

Cap Riley exploded. "*Jesus!* This is *business!* Forget your goddamn useless vendetta and get that shit up to the Whittakers! It's over! You and the boys fought hard … *but you lost!*" The old man was a professional ferry boat captain. He had a job to do and schedules to keep. Providing me with free trauma therapy was not on his list. I was trapped.

I looked away from him in frustration. I recoiled. Rick was less than a foot away from my face. A lit Pall Mall hung from his lower lip and he was breathing smoke like a sunburned dragon. His eyes focused on me.

I'd always thought of him as a bit beat-up from a distance; too much horse shit and too much sun. An old, worn-out man. But at that moment, he looked almost *handsome.* Intense and energized, like a ragged but fiery Paul Newman. He put his gnarled hand on my shoulder and leaned in. His voice was deep and gravelly and almost tickled my ear.

"Boy. This here is twenty-two bags." He patted one of the bags like it was an old friend. He leaned in even closer now, breathing on me, the tip of his lit smoke almost touching my chin. "This here is *blackjack*. You wanna show those assholes something they won't forget?" His eyes were now blazing.

"Then ride the load."

CHAPTER FIFTEEN

The Ride
  September 2, 1989

The rectangular portal Rick created worked perfectly, so I continued gliding like a shark, tentative but in control. Main Street came at me like some real-world arcade game that combined *Frogger* with *Pole Position*. Adding to the insanity were other issues: weight, balance, and a limited line of sight. There was also the subconscious reality that I was, once again, doing the bidding of my arch enemy. None of it mattered. I was committed. Strapped in. Loaded down.

I was riding it.

Who would have believed it would all come down to Rick? Before that summer, I'd never paid much attention to him. He was merely a presence. Like a soda machine or a fire hydrant. Always there, reliably plying his trade. A shit sweeper. Not a man I ever envisioned as my own personal Knute Rockne. But he made the call. I could almost hear his unspoken rationale echoing behind his steely gaze:

Ride the load. Casinos, business, money, fat-cats, the future. It all can go straight to hell. It might be your very last chance to do something memorable before the mainland world snares you in its web of careers, marriage, mortgages, and all that other big-boy shit. So just ride the sonofabitch!

Or, more likely, he wanted the bags off the dock so he could finish his sweeping, close out his shift, and buy a Pabst or two at the Mustang Lounge. Either version worked for me. There was no turning back.

My arms were tight as piano wire and my eyes already burned from sweat. It was a moving mountain. There were gasps as I passed by. A near-miss of a clip-clopping carriage and a hard swerve. I half-expected to hear the angry shout of a carriage tour driver or even the crack of his horsewhip on my backside. It had happened before to overloaded, out of control dock-porters who threatened to spook the horses. Instead, it was "nice load!"

What was happening? The ride was becoming a perfor-mance. What the Round Table knights would call a *deed*. I picked up velocity with a renewed confidence, weaving through traffic. Momentum was critical. Gravity was the enemy.

I heard a familiar voice call my name, cutting sharply through the din of horse hooves and murmuring tourists. A low belch followed, rattling the windowpane of Ty's Restaurant. It was unmistakable. A Smitty belch. All subwoofer, no tweeter. He appeared on my right as if by magic. Vicky, the swimmer from State, slumbered in his basket, still in her rumpled ball dress, swaddled in a wool blanket and snoring lightly.

"Good God. How many ya got?" he asked.

"Twenty-two." Eyes never leaving my porthole.

"Twenty-two? *Twenty-two?!* This is blackjack! With no crossbar! This is amazing!" Smitty called out loudly to anyone on the street who would listen. "People! This is history! He's riding a historic load!" Heads turned. Smitty surveyed the road ahead, suddenly serious. "You're gonna *die.*"

"Check the front of the load," I gasped. "You won't believe it."

Smitty pedaled hard to get ahead and looked back toward me. I could see his face peering through the opening, smiling, elated. "Oh my God! That's genius! A little window! You got … *a little window!*" He began calling out again. "He's got a little window! Check it out! A little window! That's how he can see!" More heads turned.

It was all becoming a spectacle.

"Shut up, man! This is hard enough without you screaming like a maniac."

He slowed a bit and we were again ridding side-by-side. "Sorry, brother. I'm … I dunno … just so … *proud!*"

I had to smile. Smitty's straightforward brand of enthusiasm was like a drug. Always had been. "I've been covering for you guys all day. What the hell happened?"

"Oh, it was great!" He eased effortlessly into story mode. "Last night, the freight boat blew a gasket or some shit. They couldn't get the engine started. So, we just, you know, *kept drinkin.'* The owner of Squeegie's kept the place open for us and we *threw down.* That guy can prolly retire on what we blew there last night. We literally just got back."

A hard right on Hoban Street and I prepared for the first hill, standing up on my pedals. From a side alley, AJ emerged, then Foster, Bull, and Spengler, all still dressed in formal, thoroughly thrashed ball attire. They glided into formation like a hungover squadron of Hellcats, clearing traffic with booming calls of "watch the bike!" I was already quivering from exhaustion and still had the brutal Grand Hotel hill *and* the length of the West Bluff ahead. Smitty was probably right. I *was* gonna die.

Slowly at first, Bull began chanting, low and solemn, like the die-hard Michigan Wolverine he was.

"Blackjack … blackjack … blackjack." He was dead serious, focused on the task. *You gotta love third-string kickers,* I thought. *Always ready when the chips are down.* The chant soon took hold, and the boys joined in. We made it up the first steep grade and took a hard left, then a right, passing the riding stable where rental horses willfully ignored us between snorts and mouthfuls of hay. *Nothing impresses horses,* I thought to myself.

The French Outpost lunch crowd took in the spectacle next. The perplexing, infectious chant spread: *blackjack … blackjack … blackjack.* The lunch crowd now joined in. Tourists stopped in mid-bite to watch, pulling out cameras and snapping pictures.

The collective energy was exhilarating, and a critical second wind kicked in. I noticed a parade of islanders followed me on bikes and foot. Blinded by sweat burning my eyes, I still managed glimpses of eager island faces. A gaggle of waitresses I recognized from the Pink Pony pedaled alongside me. Snake, the Horn's bartender, was there on his yellow Schwinn Continental ten-speed.

Buckshot, the bandleader in jean cut-offs and a ratty t-shirt. Wait, was that the mayor? Like, *the real mayor?* To my right, Emile Cranston, Jr, in a red cardigan, white shorts, and a fishing hat with an anchor pattern, pedaled a new mountain bike furiously as an out-of-breath photographer jogged alongside him. The kid was snapping shaky, likely out-of-focus pictures of the load.

Cranston called ahead, winded. "Spengler! I get the exclusive interview, right? I mean, you know this guy!"

Over his shoulder, Spengler called back. "Of course, Mr. Cranston. But this time, you're going to have to pay me."

"This is an unpaid internship! We discussed this when I hired you!"

"Yes, well the situation has changed. Talk to my agent!" replied Spengler, laughing as he weaved around a one-horse rental buggy.

Without missing a beat, AJ called to Cranston. "My client wants three benjies for the interview and the right to republish should the big boys come calling!"

The Hellcat crew broke out in hysterics. I could hear Cranston grumbling as he shifted gears on his bike with an uneven *click*. *"Fine.* Just get me that interview!"

"Will-do, Mr. Cranston!"

I suddenly recalled watching Greg LeMond as a kid on *Wide World of Sports* wearing a yellow jersey, pushing through the Alps, enveloped by rabid fans. Bells ringing, people screaming, barely able to maneuver through the adoring crowd.

Well, it wasn't like that, but the momentary delusion of grandeur provided another workable jolt of adrenaline.

Next up was Fly. "Ass on seat, arms strong," he

called out as he drifted close. "You're almost there." He looked up the long, steep hill. "Well, you're *almost* almost there." He noticed the dumbbell chained to the rack on the rear fender. "Why the dumbbell?"

"What did you call me?" I shot back, never taking my eyes from the hill.

"Not *you*, man. The dumbbell. Behind your seat."

"That was Rick's idea," I grunted out.

"That guy is a *genius*. Why is he shoveling shit and I'm at MIT? I would *never* think of that!" With that, he rejoined the formation. Smitty now dropped back for another moral support shift. Vicky, the swimmer from State, awoke with a start. She blinked a few times and looked around, unfazed, as if waking up in the basket of a bike was the most natural thing in the world. And maybe, on Mackinac Island in 1989, it was. It crossed my mind: *This woman could sleep anywhere.* She looked over at me.

"Hi, Jack the dockporter. That's quite a load." *Chipper as always.*

"Thanks," I said, straining harder as the grade of the hill increased.

Then she launched right into it. "Did you ever work things out with Erin? That was such a weird night. I have no memory of us having a macky make-out roll, but *boy*, was she *pissed*. I mean, I understand because she was probably hurt and felt betrayed, so I was wondering if you two ever talked things out or—"

"Vicky. Could we talk about this another time?" It was tough enough to keep my balance without reliving my lousy reality show of a life.

Smitty jumped in. "Yeah, Vick. Our man's trying to make some history here. *He's workin'!*"

She nodded, not the least bit insulted. "Of course! Yes! Good luck!" She instinctively joined the chant. *"Blackjack ... blackjack ... blackjack ..."*

I grinned. *Summer girl.*

I stood on my pedals. Foster, AJ, Spengler, Fly, and Bull rode directly in front, clearing the path of every living horse, bike, and fudge-gorged tourist. Brothers of the Bag! The Legion of Luggage! Cowboys of Cargo! On steel Schwinns, we ride! I may have been hallucinating because these preposterous *noms de guerre* raced through my head without a trace of irony.

Another rush of strength surged.

We pushed up the final thirty yards of the Grand hill. The road leveled a bit, and I could finally sit my ass back on the seat and follow my advanced wingmen's lead. Gassed, but still moving. The porch clientele rushed to the railing to watch the rowdy caravan pass. For no other reason than that it looked like fun, they spontaneously joined the chant: *blackjack ... blackjack ... blackjack!* I mean, really, who doesn't enjoy a good chant now and then? It's just not done enough.

———

But now my ears were starting to ring, drowning out the chants. My legs were screaming with burning fatigue that stretched from my hips to my ankles. I suddenly wanted desperately to bail on the ride in front of the hotel crowd. Maybe a little tuck and roll while the bike and load continued on its own for ten yards or so before imploding.

Hell, I thought, I made it up the Grand hill, people! *Isn't that good enough?* Does the blackjack-riding dockporter have to *deliver* the luggage or just ride it? It must be written somewhere. *Can I see the rules?* I banished the thought. I couldn't risk slowing down now, or the load would topple. I took another greedy gulp like an incompetent marathoner.

Smitty looked over. "You're gonna make it, friend. You just need to get to the end of the road and you're golden. Two hundred yards." He continued. "One hundred ten percent! Stay strong. Focus. *Ummm...*" He trailed off and went silent, out of motivational gas. I stole a glance toward him.

He looked to be deep in the recesses of some private memory, but then snapped out of it. "Hey, remember that time we hung your sister's pink bra from the flagpole of the Boy Scout barracks? We were about ten, I think." I was unable to speak, so I waited for the follow-up. There wasn't one. "That was *hilarious*," he said.

I struggled to get a few words out, my breath heaving. "Is my sister's bra ... supposed to ... somehow help me ... *focus?*"

"Not really. It just popped into my mind. Keep it up, Jack. You got this!" It was another classic Smitty non-sequitur. Technically, it was time I'd never get back. But I was also another thirty-five yards closer to my goal. That was Smitty. A natural mystic, cleverly disguised as a luggage-lugging knucklehead.

The road's final stretch was lined with the stately Victorian cottages of the West Bluff, with sprawling verandas and insane views. The term *cottage* was a misnomer. These were not cottages in the traditional sense. No ramshackle, rustic cabins on a lake, loaded up with old fishing poles and inner tubes for the cousins to bounce around on while being towed behind the

Bayliner. No, these cottages were *mansions*. Sprawling verandas, immaculately maintained. They put Wildcliffe to shame, although their bashes didn't come close and never would.

I exhaled, finally feeling I might just survive. The ringing in my ears was subsiding, and I could hear the chant echoing again. *Tip man,* my ass. *I was a load man.* A Samsonite astronaut on his way to the moon. It was my own personal Apollo mission, and failure was not an option.

The front tire exploded about three houses away from the Whittaker cottage. It was an ear-piercing *pop*. I flinched, veered hard to the right, then left, the load nearly toppling, now feeling ten times heavier and nearly impossible to control. A two-wheeled bucking bronco. I could hear the awful *phlefl-phlefl-phlefl* of the tire shredding. Now I was riding on a pure steel rim. Thank God for Fly's overpriced bungees or the entire creation would have gone down instantly. The load fought me but I wrangled it back into line. My leg napping muscles awoke like two newborn babies and began wailing in unison.

Houston, we are fucked.

After a gasp from the crowd and a few shrieks, the chants dutifully resumed as I righted the Schwinn. In my hazy memory, the chants lined up perfectly with each pedal stroke. James the bike was now slowing, emitting a wheezy scrape as the rim of the wheel ground into the pavement. Rhythmic nails on a chalkboard. I focused on the chant.

"*Blackjack McGuinn [scrape] … Blackjack McGuinn [scrape] …*

I peered through the luggage porthole. It was in my

sights: the magnificent Whittaker front porch, packed with guests, all observing our rolling cacophony like nervous VIPs at the Kentucky Derby. Gordon was standing at the top of the stairs, shielding his eyes against the sun under the front porch sign. Their place was called *Lilac Grove*.

I'm not making that up. *Lilac Grove*.

The load shifted again. The front rim was bending. I heard a few spokes *pop-pop-pop* from the wheel. I could feel a new, more deadly shift. *Please not now*, I thought. *Not in front of this khaki royal family and their pink Polo courtiers. Just give me that.*

Ten more feet. I tried to focus on the road ahead, but my eyes drifted back to Gordon. My left arm was now numb. *Was I having a heart attack?* The bike bobbed and wobbled like a spinning top in its desperate, final moments.

But the chant. *The chant!*

"*Blackjack McGuinn [scrape] ... Blackjack McGuinn [scrape] ... Blackjack McGuinn [scrape] ...*"

Then ... I was there. There was a weird, silent lull, like the quiet moment after a jetliner finally settles to a stop after a particularly horrifying bad-weather landing. Then, a mad cheer erupted from my entourage.

Gordon approached slowly, his wallet in his hand. I'm not sure what I expected; perhaps a dismissive Ivy League smirk. I was clearly in smirk-worthy condition, gasping for air, beet-red and sweat-soaked, my hair in unruly clumps. The bike was even worse, sagging from the burden and deformed from the journey.

Gordon smiled. I remembered that smile. It had been ten years. Maybe more. It was the toothy, open grin of an unburdened ten-year-old kid with a stack of autographed Gordie Howe pucks. He poked and prodded the load like a curious farmer at a pig sale. He peeked through Rick's custom porthole.

"That's *genius,*" he said, almost to himself. Finally, he spoke to me. "Still a buck a bag?"

I was heaving from lack of oxygen. "A buck a bag. But whatever you think … is appropriate. We work … *for tips.*" I dropped my head. Gordon silently counted the suitcases in my basket, his finger moving across the stack as I recovered. He pulled out a twenty, followed by a single dollar bill.

"Looks like you won't have to wear kelly green pants next summer," he said. "You did it."

I leaned against my handlebars for a minute until I was able to speak without gasping. "Gordo. I would have been terrible at that job. Truth is, I don't even know what kelly green is."

He just smiled. "Yeah. I figured. It's just green. For rich people." He stepped back and gave the ride another long look as I began to unload along the curb.

"By the way. Count it again," I said. "It's twenty-two." His brow furrowed and he recounted. He nodded, satisfied, and removed another bill, folded the money carefully, and handed me the tip.

"Twenty-two it is. Buck a bag."

He glanced curiously at the boisterous crowd across the road, still jacked up from the weird civic pride of the accomplishment. He stole a glance at his own front porch scene, which looked like it could've been clipped from *Town and Country* magazine. His expression turned speculative. They murmured politely holding glasses full of summer drinks. Not a beer in sight. Carter Eagan, the man in black, watched us from the porch.

I unloaded another large suitcase and reached to unhook a bungee cord when I felt something snap around my midsection. I grabbed my sweat-drenched shorts an instant before they dropped. *Wonderful.* My cheap souvenir Mackinac Island beaded belt was a goner. In a quick move, I yanked the useless strip of pleather out of my belt loops and wrapped it around the handlebars with one hand, holding my shorts up with the other. Nothing was easy today.

Gordon noticed the colorful belt and brightened. Half the beads had popped long ago. It looked like a movie theater marquee in some fading small town. Aged, with letters missing, barely spelling *MA KINAC I LAND.*

"Still wear the belt?"

"Of course. It's tradition," I said as I rolled my shorts down and tucked in my sweat-soaked golf shirt. "Although I snap four of these things a summer. If I had any brains, I'd buy them by the crate."

"Yeah. That's what I do." As if to prove his point, Gordon raised his crisp white button-down and revealed a Mackinac Island beaded belt of his own. I was shocked.

"See? I'm not totally hopeless," he said. He unbuckled his belt, yanked it off, and handed it to me. "Take mine. I have a box of them in the attic." He patted his stomach. "Plus, I don't need a belt this summer. I think I need Weight Watchers."

I took the belt. A wave of sadness washed over me as I slid it through my belt loops. A week earlier, I would have gleefully wiped my ass with a peace offering from Gordon Whittaker. Developer. Destroyer. *Douchebag.* Maybe it was the delirium from the ride. I was too exhausted for simmering resentment. Perhaps it was the recent domino-like series of disasters that had befallen me. Or maybe I just wanted to connect with an old pal. So I started talking.

"I know you never really had a choice," I said, focusing on adjusting the belt. "Your old man dragged you into the family business, and it turned out you were damn good at it. And I get it. My dad wanted the same for me, and not a moment goes by when I don't regret not pitching in. I could have saved Wildcliffe."

"Just stop," said Gordon quietly, shaking his head.

I paused, but then plowed ahead as I pulled more bags off the bike. "Remember when we were kids? The three of us. *Just riding around.* Who gets to do that? Remember that time we hung Beth's pink bra from the Boy Scout Barracks? There's nothing like it in the world. I mean—"

"Stop talking," Gordon said, more forcefully this time.

I ignored him. "And yes, there's money to be made for your family, probably millions, but—"

"—It's not happening."

"—You can find another island to—"

"Jack!"

I stopped talking.

"It's not happening!"

My screed came to a sudden halt. I was holding a set of golf clubs, which I leaned carefully against a suitcase on the curb, my eyes never leaving his.

"What do you mean, *not happening?*"

Gordon took a deep breath. "It's not happening. The casino. The development." He looked at me straight in the eyes. "It's not happening."

I blinked stupidly, processing. "When did you decide this?"

Gordon's eyes drifted to the boys across the street, who were mingling with the island crowd, adding the arcane details—some fabricated, some not—that would transform the last twenty minutes into something akin to island legend. It was no longer a ride; it was *The Ride*.

Gordon spoke slowly as if he didn't want me to miss a word.

"Just now," he said. "I decided … *just now.*"

We were silent, absorbing the moment. A light gust blew through the pines behind the bluff. Steady Lake Huron waves crashed on the beach a few hundred feet below. I was terrified to break the spell, but I had to know. "What happens next?" I asked.

Gordon let out a heavy sigh and glanced furtively toward the front porch, thinking it through.

"What happens next? What happens next is I drop a huge bag of shit on the front porch during cocktail hour. Then what happens is my dad berates me for the rest of my life for blowing the biggest real-estate deal in Michigan history. Then what happens is he asks me why the hell I did it. Then I mumble some gibberish about *blackjack* and *beaded belts* and *Gordie Howe signed pucks.* Then, what happens next—"

He stopped short and shook off a quick, cold shiver. "Here's some advice: Stop asking me stupid fucking questions before I come to my senses and change my mind."

I smiled and nodded, reaching out my hand. He took it. A quick *Happy Days* meets *Good Times* handshake. He turned and walked toward cocktail hour without looking back.

Once the luggage was lined up on the Whittaker porch, I checked my watch. My heart sank. *Shit.* Was it too late to catch her? Had Cap Riley held the 5:30 boat? Hell, he was the reason I was even in this situation. In the rush of loading up, I didn't have time to explain it to him. I looked back toward my bike. Ol' James was leaning on the Whittaker's retaining wall. Unrideable. Out of commission.

I looked across the street. "Smitty, let me borrow your bike! I need to get back to the dock. Erin's taking the—" But there it was. The tell-tale sound of the *Straits of Mackinac II,* a steady horn blast that went on for three seconds, and then leaped upward a few octaves at the very end.

Baaaaaah-WAP!

The sound echoed across the limestone bluff and bounced off trees. I knew Cap Riley. The horn was the horn. I saw the ferry churning out of the harbor, cutting across the calm waters of the bay. Was she scanning the island from the upper deck, barely wondering why I let her down yet again? Or, more likely, she expected it all along.

I walked across the road and steadied myself on the wood fence that lined the edge of the bluff. What I wouldn't have given to look through my telescope at that moment. To frame up and focus on her. To catch one last look. But the telescope was gone, packed tight in some cardboard box downstate with the game of *Clue.*

AJ, pumped from the ride, bounded over with Candace on his arm, bringing me back to the moment. "Why the long face, Mr. Ed?" He turned to Candace.

"Mr. Ed is a horse from an old TV show, and horses have these long faces so—"

"—I get the joke, AJ." She turned to me. "So Jack! You're a legend! *Blackjack* McGuinn. The only modern-day porter to ride twenty-one bags since…" She trailed off. "Some crazy-ass, convoluted story. Something about *crossbars* maybe? I forgot the rest. But I do remember that it's supposedly a huge deal."

"That's it, baby! You got it right!" AJ pretended to gobble her ear. She giggled and pulled away. I waited for their irritating lover's moment to pass.

AJ turned back to me. "But seriously, Jack. What's wrong?"

I kept it simple. "I missed the boat."

"I see," said AJ. But he didn't. Both he and Candace dutifully followed my gaze toward the departing ferry. After a long, respectful moment, Candace spoke up. "Are we supposed to be sad right now?"

"Yeah, Jack. Just let us know when this weird moment is over," added AJ. "Because I have a little speech."

I broke away from watching the ferry as it rounded the break wall and nodded. "Let's hear it."

"Wonderful." AJ then shouted out to the crowd. "I'm going to keep this real simple! Let's hear it for *Blackjack* McGuinn! With no crossbar and a shredded front wheel, he's the first dockporter to ride twenty-one bags in *fourteen years!*"

The group exploded with a wild whoop. The guys swarmed, raising me on their shoulders, slapping my back, mussing my sweaty hair. It was a glorious dock-porter-caliber ambush. Soon the rest of the island crowd joined in, and the chant began again. *"Blackjack McGuinn! … Blackjack McGuinn! … Blackjack McGuinn!"*

I won't lie. I enjoyed being a hero, even if it was just for a moment, even if it was big fish/small pond stuff. As the gang hauled me away, I stole a quick look back toward the Whittaker porch. Gordon was watching us with a slight huckleberry grin on his face. As I was swept away by my crew, he prepared himself to be swept away by his.

Later that night, AJ and I pedaled through the light of a sunset washed with violet and indigo, sipping the beers we had strapped into our baskets. I had a spanking new front wheel, but my thoughts were on the recent past. I glanced over.

"I always wondered. How come you never took that acting job. The soap opera thing?"

"Eh. Who wants to be on some cheeseball soap anyway, right?" He transformed into an over-the-top doctor character. "Hello, Nurse Roxie," he intoned in a lustful voice. "What seems to be the problem? How can I … *help."*

I managed a chuckle. "I know. It's cheese. But it just seemed like one of those once-in-a-lifetime chances, right?"

"Please. I'll get other chances." He spoke to me as if I were a naïve newbie, green to the Hollywood scene's inner workings. "Jacky, see, when you're as loaded with talent and charisma as I am, you don't need to sweat it. Opportunities just never end." He was grinning broadly but was uncharacteristically quiet. He was somewhere

else. Was it on some Hollywood soundstage wearing scrubs, awaiting his close-up?

I thought about that perfectly designed letter from the Rhode Island School of Design. The thick bond paper and the raised lettering. High-quality stuff. I thought about opportunities grabbed and opportunities missed. After a few moments, AJ broke the silence.

"Whaddya say we do some carving, Blackjack?"

"That's the best idea I've heard all day. And I know just the guy to do it."

The Straits were calm, the sky dark. Fly closed his Swiss Army knife with a click and stood up to examine his work. He'd carved a new name into the side of the freight shack. It stood out starkly against the list of old-timers. The most recent carving, the enigmatic High-Rise Jimmy Oliver, had been there fourteen years and was just as faded as the legends who worked the docks before the Great War.

Fly's carving style was perfectly legible. An engineer's hand. We all stepped away to get a better look. Fly nodded at his work, satisfied. "Inclined gothic. Vertical strokes at 75 degrees."

It would surely stand the test of time:

(Black) Jack McGuinn. 1989.

I tried to imagine the island in ten years. Thirty years. Even a hundred. Maybe here, in this one place, bikes and horses would continue to rule. Silly rituals and small-time legends would survive. Sweaty young scoundrels would prowl the same docks, hungry for experience, big loads of luggage, and pockets full of sweet, hard-earned cash. The scene would live on.

My bags were packed, stacked carefully on a cart near the loading ramp. I was waiting for the first boat. A cool breeze blew across the dock. The temperatures were dropping daily now. For the fiftieth time in the last week, I pulled out the crumpled RISD letter and scanned it. The words hadn't changed. I hadn't been dreaming. It wasn't disappearing ink. I slid it back into the pocket of my nylon windbreaker and headed to my bike. I wrapped my hand around one of the handlebar grips, then did the same with the other. I rolled it to the very end of the dock. It took a few minutes. It was a long dock. I stopped at the edge and looked down at the water. The morning sun reflected off my face in odd, unpredictable patterns.

I patted the seat.

"Adios, James. You were a good ride."

In one motion, I picked the bike up by its frame and hurled it into the lake. It hit the water with a deep, resounding splash. I peered over the edge of the dock. It rotated lazily downward until the bent Wald wire basket was all I could see, illuminated for a flash, and then it too faded from sight into the deep water, settling into the silt. I looked down until the water became calm again, and there was no trace of the bike. To this day, I'm not sure why I tossed my dockporter bike into the lake.

But at least I'd know just where to find it.

CHAPTER SIXTEEN

Reunion
August 29, 1999

The storm had finally passed through the straits, and the whitecaps were fading into intermittent, random specks along the horizon. Jack turned his face into a lingering gust, feeling the last of the spray on his face.

He took a deep breath of the fresh air and turned back to the biker. "And that was pretty much the end of Jack McGuinn on Mackinac Island. I left on the next ferry and haven't been back since. I went to Rhode Island. Later that fall, my dad sent me an article clipped from the *Free Press*. Said the Whittaker family scrapped the casino plan. I think they called it a 'legal mix-up in the land deal.' But that was just to save face. I knew better. It was Gordon's call." Jack paused a moment. "Big Jack didn't say it, but I knew he was proud of me."

The biker nodded, hands on his hips. "Hell yeah, man. He shoulda been. I mean, you did it. You kept the family name alive. Stopped the bad guys. That's good shit." He regarded Jack with the face of a juror, considering various details that had passed during the story. "I think it was them fuckin' belts you dudes wore. With the beads. And the big blackjack load. You shook the guy up. Made him remember what matters. The simple things in life. Bikes and fudge. Friendship."

Jack smiled. The big guy had obviously been paying attention. He took the photo album from the bench and slid it back into his faded Jansport backpack. "I guess I saved the island but lost the girl." He zipped up the pack.

The biker pulled a last drag from his cigarette. The ferry's engine reversed, slowing it to a crawl as it eased closer to the dock. "Never saw her again?"

"Nope. But I never promised a happy ending."

The biker dropped his spent cigarette and stepped on it.

"But who knows. Maybe I'll run into her this weekend," Jack added.

"Why? She gettin' hitched?"

"How do you always know this shit?" Jack asked, genuinely curious.

The biker shrugged. "I dunno, man. Bob Dylan said it best. *It don't take no weatherman to know which way the wind blows.* Figure you ain't been back in ten years, and you pick this weekend. Must be something big. Can't just be a party."

He leaned in with a curious smile. "So you planning a Dustin Hoffman maneuver, like in that movie from the '60s? *The Graduate?*" He pretended to pound on a church door and yelled out "Elaine! Elaine!" A cackle devolved into a hacking cough. "You know what? It don't matter. Go make a fool of yourself, man. I say you earned it. I'm talkin' to a real legend. *Blackjack McGuinn.*"

Jack shook his head. "Maybe if I stayed, but I didn't. On Mackinac Island, you gotta stick around if you wanna be remembered. Put in the hours. Like anything, I guess."

The biker nodded. "Maybe. Maybe not. I mean, sure, you gotta keep your shit *active* if you wanna wear the patch." He showed a cloth shield on his faded jean vest, which read *The Blazing Monarchs* in an intricate blend of skulls, fire, and Harley spokes. "But it's your name carved up there. You rode the load. And I never hearda no Wildcliffe Casino on Mackinac Island. And I'd know. I've hit 'em all. Nobody can take that shit away from ya."

He glanced toward the dock as the ferry bumped against the pilings.

"Welp. Time to buy me a pound of pistachio fudge and drink some beer. That was a helluva tale, brother." He adjusted his vest and smoothed back his unruly long, grey hair. "Don't worry, man. The wind'll blow your way."

The biker lumbered toward the stairs, his heavy boots echoing off the steel deck.

Jack realized he never got the big guy's name.

Still a little queasy from the trip over, Jack slung his backpack over his shoulder and strolled down the dock to claim his bags. The rolling waves combined with his long trip down memory lane had him disorientated. Sunlight burned through the clouds above Fort Mackinac, revealing patches of a brilliant blue sky. Ten years now, and thankfully, he still felt it. *Island butterflies.*

As he looked toward the cottages lining the East Bluff, Jack thought back on a story his mom loved to tell. It was about the enchanted Scottish village of Brigadoon. Unseen by the outside world, it appeared to the "real world" only one day every one hundred years out of the mist of the Scottish Highlands. If you stumbled upon the village on that day and spent the night, another one hundred years would have passed by morning. *Brigadoon* was made into a movie starring Gene Kelly, and the soundtrack album was never far from the turntable at Wildcliffe.

During the end-of-the-summer ferry ride back to the mainland, when Jack was at his lowest—sometimes close to tears—his mom cheered him up. "Don't be sad, Jacky-boy. We'll be back. This is *our* Brigadoon. Mackinac Island. Wildcliffe. All of it. Next summer, it'll reappear out of the mist, just for us."

And she was right. The next summer, out of the mist, it did.

For a time, anyway.

Before he set foot on the island, he needed to make sense of the Gordon and Erin wedding. A plan. Should he bring the happy couple a toaster? Sign the guestbook? He wasn't even invited. Was the biker right? Should he bust in right before "I do"? Maybe he should jump in the lake with an old lady handkerchief.

That worked once. Sorta.

Shake it off, boy. He rolled his shoulders like a boxer. He looked down the dock and couldn't help but smile. A new crew of dockporters, strapped with talkies, hotel-issue polos, and cargo shorts, sorted the bags. The updated models of his famed crew from ten years back. He stopped to watch them work. He could almost match them one-to-one. Compact, sleek sunglasses guy? That's the new Foster. Guy examining his bungees for flaws? The new Fly. Only white. The precise guy with glasses and interlocking fingers is the new Spengler. That reassuring grin with the sexy tennis mom? *Absolutely* the new AJ. That guy over there, blithely mumbling to himself is the new Smitty. And that guy sorta looks like Bull. Older and stronger, but if you squint, still Bull.

What a minute, Jack thought. His jaw dropped and he wandered closer.

"Where the hell is a goddamn dockporter when you need one!?" The older porter looked up and flashed a sharp, unsmiling look toward Jack. He squinted. Then he dropped the garment bag he was holding and sprinted over, nearly tackling Jack, picking him off his feet. "Blackjack McGuinn! The prodigal son returns!"

"Bull-dog!" Jack responded, his voice muffled by Bull's embrace. They broke apart, and Jack looked him over. Strong. Confident. In his element. "You lucky young fool. You stayed!"

"When you're trained by the best, you might as well make it last. Besides, after Foster retired, we needed a new lifer." He gestured to himself with both thumbs and a grin. "May as well be me."

"Best job I ever had," Jack said.

"No. The best job would be the Detroit Lions kicker.

Since they can't score a touchdown, you'd always be busy."

Bull looked toward the water for a moment, sheepish. "You know Jack, that reminds me. I never apologized for smashing you in the face with the football. I honestly didn't think I'd have that much accuracy, what with the crosswind. But the wind just stopped." Bull looked off with just a touch of melancholy. "Ya know, I could never quite duplicate the accuracy of that kick. Michigan cut me the next season."

He snapped out of it and hit a goofy Arnold Schwarzenegger pose. "But look at me now! Grrr! Strong like ... well, like a Bull!" He put a friendly arm around Jack's shoulder. "So, you're here for the reunion?"

"I am. That and a few other things."

"Wouldn't happen to be a wedding, would it?" Bull tossed the comment out casually and betrayed nothing. Seems the island telegraph was still in full service, even after all these years.

"Let me take these bags for you. No charge." Bull pulled Jack's bags aside. "There's still a few of us around from the old days." Bull pointed down the dock. "You might remember that old coot."

Jack looked over and blinked away bright sun. He heard him before he saw him. The *sweep, sweep, scoop, plop.* Rick the shit sweeper. Stooped and grey but still at it. He looked up as if Jack had never left, never breaking his shoveling cadence.

"I thought ya up and died," Rick said.

"I went to art school."

Rick emitted something like a scoff. *"Mmf.* Same thing."

"Then I moved to LA."

"*Mmf.*" Same reaction. "Landa fruits and nuts."

Jack, eager to change the subject, approached Rick. "How you been?"

"Oh, you know. My usual answer. *Shitty. Ha-ha-ha.*" He delivered his *ha-ha-ha* with deadpan timing.

Jack approached Rick. "Listen, I never thanked you for the load-up back in '89. I left the island the next day, and this is literally the first time I've …" Jack trailed off. Rick clearly wasn't listening to a word he was saying. He had stopped scooping and was staring slack-jawed over Jack's shoulder.

"Well, I'll be dipped in chocolate-covered, pecan-sprinkled road apples. *High-Rise Jimmy Oliver?*"

Jack swung around to look.

The biker gazed at Rick with a big grin. "Rick the shit sweeper? Jesus, you must be a hundred and five! How the fuck are ya, brother!"

"Like I just said to Jack here, *shitty. Ha-ha-ha.*" Rick looked Jimmy over. "You got big, Jimmy."

"Yup," he said proudly, patting his belly. "Beer weight. And Sara Lee Nutty Bars. I eat 'em like popcorn. Or is it Little Debbie that makes 'em? I get them two chicks confused."

Jack stood between them. *High-Rise Jimmy Oliver!?* He stammered. "You're … High … High-Rise Jimmy Oliver?"

"Yessir. I'm Mister High-Rise Jimmy Oliver. Here for the reunion party. Just like you."

"Why didn't you say something?" Jack asked. "I must have mentioned your name *twenty times* in that story. You're practically the main character."

"Fair question. I thought about it. But then I didn't

want ya to get all discombobulated and shit knowing you were blabbin' to a small-time celebrity. Plus, I kinda wanted to see how the yarn ended. Didn't wanna, like, *break yer flow.*"

High-Rise turned to Rick and gestured to Jack. "This here motherfucker's *a talker.*" Rick nodded in silent agreement and went back to shoveling. High-Rise waved and headed off. No luggage, just a lit smoke and a leather fanny pack. He paused and shot a quick glance toward the list on the wall of the freight shack and nodded, satisfied.

"Still there. *Sweet.*" He called back. "See ya 'round, Rick! See ya 'round, Blackjack! Tonight we're gonna party like it's 1999. You know why? Because it *is* 1999! Makes it real easy!"

"Yeah," Jack responded weakly. "See ya 'round … *High-Rise.*" Jack whispered to Bull, "I named my *bike* after that guy."

"*Respect,*" said Bull. "So. Where are you staying?"

Jack snapped out of it. "Foster's place. But I have no idea what that even means. He just told me to ask when I got here." He paused. "Foster has a *place?*"

Jack caught a hint of a smile from Bull, but it passed quickly. "You'll be happy to hear the reunion party's at your old party pad on the East Bluff. I guess someone had a connection. Head on up. I'll handle the bags."

———

A line of over-ridden, semi-rusty dockporter bikes decorated the curb in front of Wildcliffe. Jack, who was carrying a cold case of Stroh's, heard laughter mixed with The Clash's *Train in Vain* drifting from the porch.

He stopped short at the curb. The old place never looked better, with a fresh coat of paint, a new sign, and spotless, untracked windows. A few workers pounded in the spikes of a beer tent. Assorted guitars, speakers, and a drum set were standing by on a makeshift stage.

Jack could make out figures on the porch and hear snatches of familiar stories punctuated with machine-gun bursts of laughter. The years instantly dropped away. *The crew.* Jack took it in from a distance. A few hauled some extra Michigan hibernation weight, but overall they looked solid. Fly, in mid-story, saw Jack in the corner of his eye.

"Aw mah gawd! Blackjack McGuinn is back!" Heads turned. Hoots and fake screams cut the chit-chat short like an axe through dry wood. Jack took a deep breath and bounded up the familiar steps of Wildcliffe. He was quickly swallowed up in a collective embrace like it was last call at Horn's. The nagging sting of apprehension about weddings and the missed island years vanished. Spengler, still bookish but now New York City nerd-chic bookish, delivered an ice-cold can of beer to Jack. "My liege." Spengler smiled. Jack accepted the beer and quickly cracked it open.

"Spengler Woodstein!"

The boys backed off, giving Jack space but watching him as he inspected the details of his old family home in astonishment. Everything was repainted and refurbished. He turned to Spengler. "I'm confused. Who owns the place now?" he asked.

"Foster has a connection," Spengler responded cryptically, sipping his beer. The *Wildcliffe Cottage* sign was back, hanging above the scene like a beacon, the hand-painted lettering precisely as it had always been. He looked over toward the hanging flower planters that lined the far end of the porch. Red geraniums, just like his mom preferred. It was a pleasant version of the dream from that night in the barn apartment, when everything was destroyed by machines, and honking cars clogged the East Bluff road.

After Jack had left the island, he never looked back. His time there was in the rearview mirror, and it was best to leave it that way. Clean break. He'd done his part and punched his card. And the idea of returning to the island like an ordinary tourist had always made him feel vaguely nauseous. *How would that even work?* Rent a bike? Stay at a hotel? Take a carriage tour? So he stayed away. Like Gordon Gekko said in *Wall Street*, "If you're not inside, you're outside." And without a place to call home, Jack was most definitely *outside.*

Foster burst through the creaky screen door carrying a replacement bucket of ice, followed by a stunning raven-haired woman with long braided hair and two small boys dressed in matching outfits behind them. He walked straight up to Jack with a broad smile.

"Who owns Wildcliffe, I heard you ask?" He stepped back and posed. *"You're looking at him!"*

Foster enveloped Jack in a monster hug.

"It didn't seem like the rock without the McGuinn cottage. So, having come into an obscene amount of money, I bought it."

He gestured with open arms. "But of course, not before marrying the lovely Isabella." Isabella, the legendary deported Mexican maid from Vera Cruz, stepped up and gave Jack her hand.

"It's lovely to meet you, Jack," she said with a strong

accent. "Foster tells me many stories about the old days and the fun you all had."

Smitty called over. "But I betcha he doesn't tell ya all of 'em!"

Foster grinned and made a "zip it" gesture to Smitty. He turned to Isabella and pulled her close. "Don't you worry about the past, honey. What did I tell you? If it were a movie, what would it be rated?" She made a silly face, pretending to ponder the correct answer.

"Hmm. *Oh! I remember!* PG-13." With her accent, it came out as an unabashedly adorable "*pee-gee tour-teen.*"

Foster was reading Jack's mind and pulled him away for some privacy. "I'm guessing it feels a little weird to be standing on your old porch after so long. Folks gone. Memories packed up. But you *always* have a bed and a cold beer waiting for you at Wildcliffe. It sounds a little *woo-woo*, but your family spirits remain." He patted Jack on the cheek tenderly. He pointed toward the harbor. "And it's your name carved on that dock."

Jack was overcome with a rush of gratitude. Maybe there could be new memories created on the island after all. In a different form, sure, but still new.

"I'm sorry I disappeared for so long."

"You're sorry you disappeared for so long ... ?" Foster leaned in and arched his brow, as if waiting for something.

Jack smiled sheepishly. "I'm sorry I disappeared for so long ... *master.*"

"There's still hope for you yet, McGuinn."

"Hey! What about me?" AJ's voice boomed from across the porch. "Do I always have a bed and a cold beer ... and a whatever the hell you just promised this wayward vagrant?"

"Nope!"

Jack wheeled around as AJ strutted in. Other than a few extra pounds around the middle, he looked very much the same, his devilish gleam undiminished.

"I mean, really," AJ said, "I keep coming back every summer like the bad penny in *Somewhere in Time*, but somehow I'm sleeping in a Star Wars-themed pup tent out back with Foster's rugrats." He gestured to Jack with his beer. "This piece of shit vanishes for *ten years* and gets the *Rain Man* suite? It's not fair!" AJ hugged Jack as Foster slipped away to tend to other hosting duties.

Jack was excited to see his old friend. "Hey, I heard a rumor you went with Candace to Hollywood after that summer in '89."

"I did. And she dumped me three weeks later for the key grip on some TV show. See, the key grip is the guy who knows how to, like, do things. I mean, how could I compete with *that?*"

"Yeah. That's tough," said Jack. "I know what a key grip is. Hard to beat a handyman."

"That's right! I forgot. You're a big-shot photographer now!"

"Toss in a few filters, make sure it's in focus, and you're good to go. *Ka-ching.*"

"Anyway. It was all good," said AJ. "We still keep in touch. She married the guy. I've been living in South Lyon, downstate, selling life insurance for years."

"Life insurance?" Jack was surprised. "You enjoy it?"

"Weirdly," AJ said, now serious, "I love it. All day long, I act …" He paused dramatically, "… *like I give a shit!*" He leaned in, as if spilling a precious trade secret. "And those quote-unquote *real* actors? They spend all day in trailers waiting for someone to tell 'em what to do. I said, screw that. I *grew up* in a trailer waiting for someone to tell me what to do. *Insurance.* That's my act now."

"Hey, Jack," Smitty broke in, like zero time had passed. He had a tan, pretty, dark-haired woman on his arm. She looked vaguely familiar. Smitty stared at Jack for a moment, then at the woman on his arm. Then back to Jack. The woman held a weird, expectant smile. There was a long silence.

Then it clicked. "Vicky! The swimmer from State!"

"Jack the dockporter!" She broke away and gave Jack a friendly hug. "And I didn't even need a name tag!"

Jack stepped back to look at the couple. "You guys must've had a helluva time at the Dockporter Ball."

As if rehearsed, they held up their left hands in unison and wiggled their wedding rings.

"Best night of my life," said Smitty. "One day I'm ridin' Vicky around in my basket, next thing ya know? A daughter, two jet skis, and a dog named Steve!" Smitty pointed at AJ. "AND a life insurance policy from this hambone. So far, so good." He furrowed his brow. "Although, I haven't died yet, so who knows?"

Vicky smacked him playfully. "I'll make that happen if you keep farting under the covers."

"Gotta admit, keeps the heating bills low," said Smitty, while Vicky held her nose and giggled. Smitty turned to Jack. "I got something for you! Shit. What was it?" Vicky leaned over and whispered to him. "Oh, right!" He headed for the steps. "Stay right here!"

Jack watched as Smitty raced down the porch steps and disappeared around the side of the house. Moments later, he reemerged, proudly wheeling out James the bike.

Jack walked down the porch steps, stunned. He took in the rusted bike like an old friend. AJ called down. "Smitty fished it out of the drink after you left. Guess someone saw you toss it in. We figured you'd be back eventually."

"Yeah but we didn't think it'd be *ten years*," Smitty said, guiding the bike to Jack and handing it off.

"I replaced the crank. And the back tire. Brakes work fine. Few other tweaks. You're gonna wanna oil the chain. Other than that, not too bad, huh?"

As Jack inspected the bike, AJ launched into the song *Reunited*. Soon everyone joined in. It was off-key and clearly nobody knew the correct lyrics.

> *We all are super excited … when we're reunited,*
> *yeah-yeah!*

As the porch crowd gleefully butchered the sing-a-long, Jack straddled the bike and turned his head away from the crowd, fearing for a passing moment that he might break down and start bawling like a little baby.

The revelry continued as the reunion crowd swelled and the sun dropped behind the distant Mackinac Bridge. Dockporters from years past, some with families, some alone, joined the party. Jack found himself plopped down on the newly painted wicker swing, exactly where Gramps loved to sit. Sitting next to him was Fly, talking a mile a minute, in the midst of a story.

"You remember my bungee cords? Well, after graduation, I hooked up with an engineering firm out of Tewksbury, Massachusetts. They specialize in patents, shit like that. Brother, what a joke. I spent years trying to get this thing through the pipeline. *Proof of concept?* Shit, man. I got the proof of concept. It's called Mackinac Island!"

Spengler nodded. "It's called fifty thousand pounds of luggage on your bike."

"Exactly!" said Fly. "With *nary a snap!* One day last summer, I'm at my lowest, feeling I wasted my life. Wiping my ass with my MIT degree. I get a random call from a guy at some investment firm who says they're interested in my bungee cords. Guy's got a weird English accent. Says he heard they're the best in the world. So now I'm starting to get intrigued." The group grew larger as the story ramped up.

"Understand, I've been chasing this dream down for years by now. Then the guy says 'well, Mr. Fly'—he calls me *Mr. Fly,* which should have been a dead giveaway …"

Fly shifted into a lousy English accent. "We heard from reliable sources that you could … what was it … *jump off the Mackinac Bridge with this stretchy little bitch and bounce back grinning.* In-*tact!*"

The porch crowd erupted in laughter, totally engrossed in the story. "I say, 'Who is this?' The voice says: '*I* … am your father.' I'm like, *what the hell?*"

Fly suddenly hopped off the swing and began jumping around, laughing hysterically and pointing at Foster, who was nonchalantly approaching with a case of fresh beer. "It was *that* maniac! That's my investor!"

Foster nodded and pointed at Fly. "And what was the only condition of my modest investment?"

"Well, interesting you'd ask," said Fly. "I just happen to have the prototype right here in my backpack." He reached into a leather backpack hanging on a wicker chair and pulled out a clear plastic package. Inside, Fly's trademark bungee cord was coiled neatly. "What does the label say?" He handed it to Jack. "Read it to the class."

Jack looked at the package. His jaw dropped. "Blackjack Bungees," he said.

"Boom!" said Fly. The porch crowd gathered around to inspect the newest product poised to take the luggage-hauling world by storm. But Jack found himself drifting toward other stories unfinished, mentally flipping through a slideshow of island church options as he absently watched the band set up. From the looks of it, it was going to be the Buckshot Band tonight. Foster was pulling out all the stops, local noise ordinances be damned.

... Would it be Ste. Anne's Church? Erin must be Irish Catholic, after all. I mean, right? But maybe not. There was also the Little Stone Church near the Grand ... Jack snapped out of it. "What the hell am I doing?" He glanced around, praying nobody heard him.

Foster was now standing on the stage holding a microphone. With his white pressed cotton shirt, suntanned face, and khakis, the old dog looked healthy and happy. His smile was infectious. "Ladies and gentlemen, welcome to the first annual dockporter reunion party. But surely not the last!" A joyful cheer echoed through the trees. Jack spotted High-Rise near the front of the stage, yelling and making heavy metal devil horns and "woo-hooing."

"We've got folks from all over the country here tonight to celebrate and remember the good times we had when all that mattered was a basket full of luggage, a pocket full of cash, and good friends to load you up. A simpler time for all of us. So, as we used to say back in the eighties: *Tonight we drink, tomorrow we ride!*"

Jack grinned, instantly taken back to those nights at Horn's, sweating magnificent buckets to the beat, wondering when the dance floor might cave in from the sheer weight of unrestricted joy. *It had to be St. Anne's. Gordon was Catholic, right? Didn't he used to go to mass with his family every Sunday?*

Jack caught himself again. "Stop it!" Again, he said it out loud and looked around. Again, nobody noticed.

Foster looked up toward the porch and locked eyes with Jack. "We have a very special guest to jam with the band tonight, the sexiest damn fiddle player ever to grace Horn's Bar." Jack froze. "Miss Erin O'Malley, here for one night only. Let's give her a big round of applause!"

Jack's plastic drink cup, lined with condensation, slipped through his fingers to the floor, splashing beer on his legs. He looked around and noticed Smitty standing next to him. Nonchalantly, he pointed at the stage. "Hey. It's what's her name. Erin."

Then he murmured, almost to himself: "Well whaddya know about *that.*"

The band's set was electric, eclectic, and magical. A blend of all the best bar-band standards mixed with the perfect selection of raucous Irish folk tunes. It was, in many ways, the spiritual encore to the Horn's gig from long ago. Erin, dressed in a loose red flowered dress and scuffed Keds, was stunning. She played, if possible, even more beautifully than she had ten years before.

As the last song of the set wrapped up, Jack pushed past the crowd toward the tiny makeshift stage. He locked eyes for an instant with her. She was playing hard as the last drumbeat of the song came fast. *Boom!*

Buckshot leaned into the mic. "We'll be back in thirty minutes! That's if the cops don't shut us down, in which case we'll move it inside."

Isabella's slightly worried, slightly buzzed voice called out from the crowd. "But you must take off your *shoooes!* We just waxed!" The crowd laughed appreciatively as the band took a Beatles-esque bow in unison and wandered off the stage.

Jack watched Erin as she approached, holding her fiddle. She was radiant. "Jack McGuinn! I heard rumors you might make it up." She hopped off the stage and hugged him. "What's the craic?"

"The crack?"

"Sorry. More Dublin slang. Can't shake it. How about this one: How the *fook* are ya?"

Jack smiled, basking in the accent he'd been dreaming about for ten years. "A little overwhelmed but good."

"Overwhelmed? What, you never heard *Wild Thing* done with a fiddle? Or was it the extended version of *American Pie* that caught you off guard?"

"It's you. I didn't know you were coming." He

recognized that he sounded flustered. "I mean, not that that's a bad thing. I mean … it's great to see you, Erin."

"Aye, well, your old pal Foster tracked me down and offered me a *boatload* of cash, so how could I miss it?"

Jack thought to himself: *Don't be weird. Congratulate her. It's the right thing to do.* He squared his shoulders and extended his hand.

"Congrats. He's a good man." It was a sloppy, ham-handed segue. "I know I said a lot of bad things about him a long time ago, but I respect what he did. He was the one that stopped the casino plan, not me. I just rode a big load of luggage."

Erin looked at him blankly, waiting for more. Finally, she spoke. "What the hell are you going on about, Jack?"

"You and Gordon? The wedding?" Foster and Smitty appeared on either side of Jack. They said nothing. Erin furrowed her brow.

"I'm not getting married to Gordon, Jack. I'm here to play fiddle and see some old friends."

Jack opened his mouth. Nothing came out. He turned to Foster. "You wrote me a letter!" He turned back to Erin, pointing an accusatory finger at Foster. "He wrote me a letter!"

Foster pursed his lips, straining to recall. "Oh, that? I made that all up." Jack's eyes widened. "Yeah. Sorry. I figured you'd never show up otherwise. So … I lied."

Jack looked at Smitty. "Did you know about this?"

"Nobody tells me nothing." But the gleam in his eye said otherwise.

Foster and Smitty shared a look, quickly linked arms, and headed off, literally skipping in time like elves. Jack and Erin watched them disappear into the fray of the party, then turned back to each other.

Jack scratched the back of his neck. "So. To be clear. You're not getting married this weekend?"

With the tiniest of smiles, she sat down on the edge of the stage and placed her fiddle next to her. "Jack. After that exchange, you're still unclear? No. I'm not getting married." She covered her mouth to keep from laughing. "I'm sorry. This is a ridiculous moment." She glanced in the direction of Smitty and Foster. "I think you were played."

Jack sat down next to her tentatively. "I think we were both played."

She absently plucked a few strings on the fiddle and shook her head in wonder. "Crazy lads played us both."

"Erin, would you like to go for a ride?"

She looked up. "No overly romantic gestures?"

"No promises."

Hours later, they were talked out.

It was 3 a.m., and Erin was settled into the basket of Jack's bike as they cruised down a deserted Main Street. A fog had rolled in, creating rainbow halos around the streetlamps. Ahead they could just make out a lumbering figure weaving his way down the street, singing songs from the band's last set. The bellowing, joyful sing-song voice echoed off the clapboard stores and into the night.

"*Louie, Louie … oh baby … me gotta go!*" They rode up and Jack looked over at the happy drunk.

"High-Rise Jimmy Oliver. You gonna be okay, buddy?"

High-Rise looked to his left. "Blackjack McGuinn! What a party! *What ... a ... party!*" He looked at Erin and smiled broadly, drunk and happy. "And this must be the lovely and talented Erin, the fiddle player. At least I'm hopin' so, otherwise, I just made a big, fat fuckin' fool of myself."

She smiled. "I've heard the legend. Nice to finally meet the man." High-Rise kept walking and weaving, weaving and walking. "Hey, Blackjack. It looks like your boat yarn might just have a happy ending after all."

"We shall see," Jack said, not wanting to get too tied up in hypotheticals with a high-flying High-Rise.

Jack eased ahead on the bike. "You be safe, High-Rise!"

"You be too," High-Rise called. *"Do-be-do!* She's special. Treat her right. She'll crack ya one with a fiddle bow if you screw up!"

Erin craned her neck and shot a puzzled look at Jack. He shrugged. "What can I say. It was a long boat ride." She smiled and settled back in, seemingly satisfied with the answer. After a few pedal strokes she said: "You deserved it."

As they rode away, they could hear High-Rise call out from behind them. *"On it goes!* I mean, seriously, brother. *On ... it ... goes!"*

They kept riding, past where the Main Street shops gave way to the boardwalk. They heard the rhythmic lapping of the lake. The Mackinac Bridge was not visible tonight; its lights shrouded in a deep, mysterious fog. But it was comforting to know it was out there somewhere. Erin leaned back, closer now. She settled her head on his shoulder and took in the foggy night air, her feet hanging off the front of the basket.

For a moment, Jack felt that all-too-familiar twang of anxiety, as if he were dreaming and Erin would disappear again. Her long black hair caught a current of night breeze and it blew across his eyes. For a moment, he couldn't see. Riding blind. And just like that, the anxiety vanished. Jack chuckled to himself.

"What's funny?" she asked.

"Nah. It's dumb. I was just thinking about an idea for a Main Street shop."

"Do share."

"Photos and … cello lessons? Nevermind. I told you it was dumb."

She was quiet. "I don't know. I quite like it. You could also sell Mickey's Malt Liquor."

"And Fly's bungee cords," Jack added.

"And fudge. Irish fudge," added Erin.

"Never heard of Irish fudge. But okay. And beaded belts."

Erin leaned back. *"Brilliant.* So it's a photo shop that offers cello lessons, but also sells Mickey's Malt liquor, bungee cords, Irish fudge, and beaded belts. Bloody hell, Jack. Sounds *fantastic.* What should we call it?"

"We? It's my shop. Jack's … Place."

"Jack's Place? *Boring.* Erin's Place. Much better." Jack pondered it. "To be continued," he said. The word hung in the air between them like the scent of pines. They both privately breathed it in.

Continued.

They grew quiet, each deep in their own rippling reflections. The bike was rusty and made a rhythmic clicking sound with each pedal stroke. The chain needed oil. The seat would need to be raised up a few inches. Someone had probably been riding it. The twisted basket might have to be completely replaced. It never fully recovered from the blackjack load and it sagged like an old porch. Yeah. The bike needed work. But all the deeper questions that needed to be answered, as well as bikes rebuilt, fates pondered, gift shops named, and connections rediscovered could wait until tomorrow.

Because tonight, they would ride.

THE END

JOIN US

This is the first book in the
Mackinac Island Series.
Look for the next title coming soon:

SOMEWHERE IN CRIME

If you enjoyed *The Dockporter*, please leave a review on
Amazon. It makes a big impact.

JOIN THE MAILING LIST AT:
TheDockporter.com

Our Facebook Group is also a blast.
facebook.com/groups/mackinacdockporter

ACKNOWLEDGEMENTS

*A quick note of gratitude to
all the people who touched this project.*

From Dave: To my wife Mardy and daughter Kelly who are always the first ones to believe in taking risks. To my brother Scott, my creative partner in crime back when *The Dockporter* was a film project. To Chris Swain, Ben Parrillo, Scott Kennedy, Keith Mitchell, Dennis and Fred Brodeur, Meta Valentic, Mike Mitri, Glen Allen, Graham Taylor and many others who helped with ideas and passion. To sister Amy, brothers Greg and Scott, who have always encouraged me to keep this tale alive. To Jessica Klimesh and Dan Riney for fantastic copy editing working with a couple of seriously backasswards first-time novelists. To Stephanie Tam and Janssen Vercides, who created a beautiful, eye-catching cover designs and branding. To Jim Bolone, friend, inspiration, and co-author. To dad and mom, for conjuring up Brigadoon every summer, a legendary gathering place shared by generations. And to the real dockporters of

Mackinac Island, past, present and future: here's to you. The bonds and experiences we shared on the docks made us all better men.

From Jim: To my wife, Lori, and the summer of 1989, when it all started on Mackinac. To my kids, Anna, Charlie, and Grace—how lucky can a dad be? To my siblings, Tom, Cynthia, Robert, Irene, Larry, and especially Terry, whose light glows brighter than ever. The little things, yes? To Mackinac Island. Thank you for the memories and the friendships and the inspiration. After all, it's where two English majors met on the docks, and some three decades later made this!

Special Thanks: To all the legendary characters that made a certain era on Mackinac Island magic. The list is endless, but the main stagers include: Ada Chambers, Tut Louisignau, Bud Bowen, Beans, Frank Nephew, Harry Ryba, The Bensers, Dan Seeley, The Huthwaites, George Stella, Steve Kosar, Victor Countryman, Pat Pulte (and his birthday), Joe "Mama" Matyskella, The Brown Family, Shawn Riley, The Mussers, George Arnold, Phil Porter, Dan Dewey, Angelyne Reywald, George Staffan, The Sheplers, Roger Priebe, Louie "The Thief" Deroshia, Biff Condor, Nathan Shayne, Jerry Horn, The Callewaerts, The Brodeurs, Otto Wandry, Don "Duck" Andress, Kitty Bond, and many, many, many more. *On it goes.*

ABOUT THE AUTHORS

Dave McVeigh is an award-winning creative director living in Cebu, Philippines with his wife Mardy and daughter Kelly. He's collaborated on video campaigns for Disney Channel, HBO, Warner Bros, and Nike. Michigan-born and raised, he spent 23 summers on Mackinac Island, where he specialized in stone-skipping, dish-shlepping, bike-riding, and fudge consumption. He also spent years hauling luggage in the basket of his bike, where he formed friendships that grow stronger every year.

Jim Bolone grew up in Detroit, Michigan and graduated from Wayne State University. He has been a bartender, waiter, historical interpreter, drummer, and for the last few decades, a junior high creative writing teacher in Ohio. Jim worked on Mackinac Island, where his job as a dockporter led him to lifelong friendships, and where he met his wife Lori. Together they share their home with three great kids, a dog, a cat, and lots of books.

The Dockporter is the first novel in the **Mackinac Island Series.**